OWEN SLOT

The Proposal

D1426206

HODDER

Grateful acknowledgement is made for permission to
reprint from the following copyrighted material:
Theme from 'New York, New York', words by Fred Ebb, music by John Kander
© Unart Music Corporation and EMI United Partnership Ltd, USA. Worldwide
print right controlled by Warner Bros. Publication Inc/IMP Ltd, USA. Reproduced
by permission of International Music Publications Ltd. All rights reserved.

Lyrics from 'Leaving on a Jet Plane' © Cherry Lane Music Inc.
Administered in the UK and Eire by Harmony Music Limited.

First published in Great Britain in 2005 by Hodder and Stoughton
A division of Hodder Headline

The right of Owen Slot to be identified as the Author
of the Work has been asserted by him in accordance with the
Copyright, Designs and Patents Act 1988

A Hodder paperback

1

A CIP catalogue record for this title is available from the British Library

ISBN 0 340 82465 4

Typeset in Monotype Sabon by Palimpsest Book Production Limited,
Polmont, Stirlingshire

Printed and bound by
Clays Ltd, St Ives plc

Hodder Headline's policy is to use papers that are natural,
renewable and recyclable products and made from wood grown in
sustainable forests. The logging and manufacturing processes are expected
to conform to the environmental regulations of the country of origin.

Hodder and Stoughton Ltd
A division of Hodder Headline
338 Euston Road
London NW1 3BH

For Ivo, Madeleine and Oliver, three major little distractions, and Juliet, the greatest distraction of all

ACKNOWLEDGEMENTS

Many thanks to Sara Kinsella, my brilliant new editor, Ant Harwood, my agent, who's not bad either, and Emma Longhurst, who is great to work with. Also to Stuart Southgate, Will Oatley, Stephen Quallington, Tim Delaney, Lucy Meredith, Gerald Tremlett, Val Hepplewhite and my family for your particularly intoxicated input.

1

The following marriage proposal, I know, is a little unusual. It contravenes most of the rules. I'm not sure what all the rules are, but if anyone had ever written them down and I had a copy in front of me, I'd be surprised if I didn't discover it breaking every single one.

I guess the number-one essential ingredient for a marriage proposal is to have both parties in attendance. It would help, wouldn't it? Yet already we appear to have come up one party short.

I am sitting alone on a bench at the top of Greenwich Hill alongside the Royal Greenwich Observatory and, aside from a smattering of tourists, most of them Japanese, some children playing and the occasional dog-walker, there is no one here for me to proposee to. I, Dominic Lord, do hereby aspire to be married, but not to a Japanese tourist, or to the occasional dog-walker, or even the dog.

Another helpful hint for a successful proposal: ensure that you are in some sort of on-going romantic liaison with your proposee. Again, I fail. Lucy and I have had our moment, our time, and, oh, yes, it was special, albeit sixteen years ago. I'm pretty sure – though it's possible that an assessment of the facts might veer from the path of accuracy over all that time – that, when it happened, the earth did *not* move for us, though I might be wrong because I recall reading in a Sunday news-paper the following weekend that a minor tremor was recorded overnight in Dorking. At exactly the same time in exactly the same neighbourhood, a number of the sleeping denizens of Dorking awoke to find that their glass of water had slipped

off their bedside table. Clock radios and bedside lamps were grounded too. It was carnage. Maybe Lucy and I caused all the trouble.

But the way I remember it, the earth didn't move. Quite the opposite: all natural forces ceased to operate and the earth stopped spinning on its axis. At around the time that disorder was unleashed on Dorking, the only natural forces in operation were those between Lucy and me, an inescapable magnetism, a racing of hearts, that wonderful mutual whiff of hedonistic adventure, and all those splendid late-teenage hormones crying in a heavenly chorus, 'Hallelujah! The moment is nigh!' We were edging gradually closer to each other, faces, eyes, lips converging towards a delicious collision. She was holding in place the hat she always wore so it didn't tumble into my mouth, and I was sitting so awkwardly with my left leg tucked under me on the edge of a piece of cheap green furniture that I had to force myself to ignore the ache from my blood-circulation crisis. Neither of us spoke, our silence acknowledging what was about to take place as the outside world dissolved into a blur, the music faded, the dancers around us tapering out into such slow-motion that they barely moved. That was when it seemed as though the earth had stopped spinning, causing all that spillage by the bedside tables of Dorking.

So, sixteen years later does seem a little tardy to execute the follow-up.

If I was the one writing the rules for a successful marriage proposal, they would also, in no particular order, include:

(1) Asking the proposee's father for her hand in marriage. Old-fashioned, I know, but it can get the important people on your side. Lucy's father remains uncontacted.

(2) Turning up for your proposal behind the wheel of a silver open-top Cadillac (I've arrived today on the tube), looking smooth in a new cream linen suit (I'm in a black overcoat, grey woolly sweater and jeans), brandishing a whole shop's

worth of red roses (not many flower-sellers open for business round here today).

(3) Ensuring that the proposee isn't already married — I have at least done this right.

(4) Being unmarried yourself.

Point number four is another on which I have failed. Nadia, my wife, is on the other side of the Atlantic. Indeed, the only reason that I can furnish potential proposers with the above advice is because it worked for me when I persuaded Nadia to say yes. I did ask her father, I did do the Cadillac-linen-suit-red-roses routine, she was unmarried and so was I. Indeed, other than that she was pregnant, it all seemed so simple. Would that had been the case with Lucy.

Lucy. The last night we spent together at Durham University was the most memorable. At least, it was for me. So memorable that it drove me here today. It was crammed with excitement and trepidation. And alcohol. And Lucy said she would marry me.

The following day student life would finish, an end to three years' untrammelled breeze through Arcadia. And because no one wanted to let it go, we stayed with it. We saw out the last day, then saw in the next morning. And after we'd danced and drunk, then danced and drunk some more, the three of us confessed our mutual fear of the end and of the new beginning. We slouched in the dilapidated sofas in the miner's cottage that I shared with Tim and gradually slumped in them until, by sunrise, we were all almost horizontal.

Tim, being Tim, held centre stage, but for once his voice ran dry. Tim could really sing. His party piece was that song about separation, 'Leaving On A Jetplane' by John Denver, but he could also do wonderful chunks of Sinatra. But on this occasion he only managed a couple of numbers before the words eluded him. Emotional, drunk, unusually quiet.

Lucy caressed his handsome face and told him not to worry.

'We've all got to find new tricks now,' she said. Which was meant lightheartedly, but sounded terrifying and rang out in a long, pensive silence.

She was wonderful that night. 'How come you're so bloody full of life and so thoroughly unjaded?' I asked her, at around half past five. Tim was struggling to stay awake and my eyes felt heavy, but Lucy looked so fresh, with so much energy in her face. I remember her long eyelashes, black with mascara, curling away from her amazing brown eyes. It was as if she'd only just got ready to go out.

Some thought her beautiful but I wasn't sure: her face just stood out, I thought, boyish and distinctive. But that hadn't been what drew me to her. Nor was it her eyes, so expressive they seemed to hold conversations on their own. It was that Lucy made you talk: whether intentionally or not, she threw light on herself in a way that encouraged a similar response. I hadn't met anyone like her before.

'C'mon on, boyo,' she said, poking Tim in the ribs to keep him awake. 'I don't think there's anything wrong with admitting you're scared of what happens next. I am.'

'What have you got to be scared of?' he said, half opening his right eye.

'Heights,' she replied immediately. 'The steady deterioration of British society. Ingrowing toenails. And what my parents will think when I'm floundering like a fish on the job market and failing to fulfil their expectations.'

Thus she led us to confessional. Tim, being Tim, said that everything would be fine and that all that really worried him was breaking his fingers playing cricket.

I, being the way I am, took her far more seriously. I said I was scared that we would all go our separate ways and that old friendships would die, that I wouldn't be able to sustain relationships, and that I'd never get married.

'You? Never marry?' Lucy sat up.

'Might not.'

'How ridiculous! Nonsensical bollocks-talking best bloody catch in the year, you are.'

'I mean it.'

'I mean it too.'

'Hang on!' Tim surfaced from his haze. 'What about me?'

'Sorry, my love. You finish a close second.'

'Bollocks!' I replied.

'OK. I'll marry you then,' she responded instantly.

'I'm not that desperate.'

'Thanks! Glad I offered.'

'You weren't serious?'

'I was.'

'Promise?'

'Promise.'

'Why'd you want to marry me, for God's sake?'

'Who knows? You might make me happy.'

'Lula!' That was my name for her. No one else called her Lula, not even Tim.

'Right. If we're both single when we're thirty-five, I'll marry you.'

'No, you won't!'

'I will. If you'll have me, of course.'

'I'll have to think about it.'

'Fine, call me your last resort.'

'Or my safety blanket.'

''Er indoors. Your better half.'

'I think I prefer last resort.'

'Feel free to check in when your other options have run out.'

After a theatrical pause, I sat up too. 'OK. I've thought about it. When we're thirty-five, it'll be the year 2000. Right? If you still want to marry me, and you're still single and I'm still single, I'll meet you on New Year's Day, the first day of the new millennium, at midday at the Royal Greenwich Observatory. If you're there and I'm there, we'll get hitched.'

'What's the bloody Greenwich Observatory got to do with it?'

'That's where time is measured from. Or something like that. That's where the new millennium will officially begin. I think. I'll check. If you're going to be my wife, God fucking forbid, then the start of the new millennium would seem the right place to kick off together.'

'It's a deal.'

'Great. See you there.'

'Jesus,' shouted Tim, who had appeared to doze off again. 'You two are totally fucking mad.'

New Year's Day, the first day of the new millennium. I guess we're supposed to have woken up this morning feeling different – more modern, more hung-over. I don't know. It's not even midday so many won't have woken yet at all, but when they do they'll probably feel that the new millennium is rather similar to the old one. No one walking through Greenwich Park looks as if the turn of the century has changed their life. And no one happens to be Lucy.

But if Lucy did wend her way up the steep incline of the hill, then that *would* be different. That really would be a case of the turn of the century changing someone's life. Her life. My life. Maybe. She might walk through the park from the other direction, I suppose, and take me by surprise, but whenever I've imagined this day – and I've imagined it quite a lot – she's always been climbing the hill, winding her way up the Tarmac path that curls below the Observatory and finishes at the top of the hill, next to the modest little palace with its long view of the broad, meandering Thames.

It is eleven fifty. Ten minutes to go. And there's no disputing the time. The whole world measures time from where I'm sitting, as my addled brain had correctly recalled on that memorable last night in Durham. Nine and a half minutes until midday.

I stand up from my bench, which is perched under an imposing statue of General Wolfe. General Wolfe was born in Greenwich and buried here; he won countless battles against the French in

between. The only real battle in my life has been to save my marriage. I lost. I put up a hopeless fight and by the time I'd run up the white flag I was rather pleased I had no marriage any more. But here I am, with the general, in search of another.

I wander to the top of the Tarmac path, back up to General Wolfe, then return to my bench. This is definitely the place to await her.

Will she come? Initially it seemed that she might. In those first years after university, she referred to me as her 'safety husband' and I to her as my 'safety wife'. Even when I'd moved to New York and married Nadia, she still insisted she'd be waiting for me on the time line of the globe on the first day of the new millennium. She knew me too well to believe that Nadia and I would see in the new century together. And sure enough, six months ago, in a charming old bits-and-bobs store in Greenwich Village, Manhattan, I stumbled upon a postcard of the Royal Greenwich Observatory. Nice Greenwich connection, I thought, but I decided not to make too much of it and focused instead on the other dominating storyline in my life. 'It's been a long time coming,' I wrote on the card to her, 'but it's now finally over for me and Nadia. Don't feel sorry for me. I told you this would happen and it's a blessed relief. PS Hope you like the card.'

And that was all. We exchanged Christmas cards and the occasional email. I told her I was putting more space between myself and Nadia and moving back to London. She told me she was thinking of moving out of London.

But she might come via Greenwich Hill. Five minutes until midday. I'll give her half an hour's grace. She's probably hungover. A lot of people won't have slept last night. I didn't sleep either, but that was because my mind was on other things. I've come to the last resort. Will she join me? I've been looking forward to discovering the answer for years.

2

Lucy.

When we first met her, Tim didn't realise that we'd stumbled on someone so special.

We'd been looking for a new girl for three nights and our search had been fruitless. We'd advertised, we'd put up flyers and found no one. It wasn't for lack of response, plenty of girls came, but none was right.

Back then I wore a thin cloak of self-confidence, which was only possible because of my naïvety, and this led me to believe I could direct a student play. Tim, conversely, had a deep-seated self-assurance: he was tall, dark, athletic, strikingly good-looking, talented, socially adept and successful with women. It was this that led him to believe that he should be the star of my play, and when he informed me that he could do this sort of thing, he was so convincing that I cast him in the lead role without so much as an audition.

Two terms into university life, I still hadn't fathomed why Tim and I were friends. It had been in the first week of Term One that he had clapped an arm round my shoulders and told me I should go to the pub with him. We went to the Shakespeare. I was new to consumption of beer at the level Tim advocated, I didn't know any of the songs he sang and I hung back in his shadow when it came to making conversation with students of the opposite sex. I remember the night because it ended with me vomiting in an alleyway next to the pub. Tim barely noticed because while I was busy familiarising myself with the pavement, he was busy securing an invitation to the digs of one of those students of the opposite sex.

It was to my considerable surprise in the second week that Tim suggested I should go drinking with him again. I was sick that time, too, and found myself wondering why on earth he didn't drop me there and then, yet somehow I remained his friend of choice. As a well-financed, already-shagging (quite a lot, it seemed) fully-fledged former public-schoolboy, nothing seemed hard for Tim. As a shy, light-walleted alumnus of a Kent grammar school that most hadn't heard of and still a virgin, I struggled to keep up.

I followed Tim's lead and only attempted to step out of his shadow when occasion allowed and sufficient valour consumed me. I wouldn't go far, of course, but gradually I learned to dovetail with him. He taught me about life. To be more precise, he taught me about *his* life. And the more I learned, the better I dovetailed. I learned that Tim's brand of hair gel was in and that my Brylcream was out, that boxer shorts, not small white briefs, were the underwear of preference, that my thin black-leather tie worn at half-mast had to go, and my parka was exchanged for a denim jacket.

On wining and dining, I learned that I must never order shandy or chicken korma, and that if I bought a kebab on the way home after a big night out, I would win peer approval if I left evidence of it outside my bedroom door. On the music front, my roots as a New Romantic had to be covered up, and the inability to remember the first single I'd bought was a sin that made chicken korma almost acceptable. Your first single had to have some sort of embarrassment value, or make everyone laugh and say, 'I wonder whatever happened to old so-and-so.' My first record was a Cat Stevens *Greatest Hits* LP and it neither substituted as a single nor said the right things about my youth.

Tim, of course, knew what his first single had been and it fulfilled all the necessary criteria. It was the signature tune of the soundtrack to *Fame*. His first LP? *John Denver and the Muppets*. And I soon learned to trace his voyage of musical discovery from there through the Denver discography, past

'Country Road' and some schmaltzy Christmas LPs, to finish up on the steps of the 'Jetplane'.

It was an education from which I benefited. I learned to be Tim's wing-man; I found I could tee him up for the punchlines to his jokes and I soon knew the words to 'Jetplane'. When I was drunk, I could do 'Jetplane' too – we could even do it in harmony together, and those students of the opposite sex thought us a fine double-act. Lucy would put down her hat on the pavement in front of us when we were singing – and we got so good we were once even moved on by the police.

My idea for the play had been a theatrical version of the small-town romantic comedy *Gregory's Girl*. We had a script that had been adapted for the stage from the film, and we had Tim to play Gregory. He hadn't seen the film so I explained to him how John Gordon Sinclair performed the role: the naïve, testosterone-driven teenager from an ugly Scottish town who pursues the luscious, comparatively sophisticated football-crazy Dorothy but ends up smitten instead by the less obviously attractive Other Woman, Susan.

'So Gregory's a loser, then?' said Tim, smiling.

'No, he's our hero. He stumbles on the difference between inner beauty and physical beauty,' I said, trying not to sound ridiculous. 'He makes this amazing discovery about the meaning of love.'

'Bollocks, Dom! What you're telling me is that he's saying it's all right to fancy ugly girls.'

'You idiot!'

But Tim liked the irony of playing the guy who couldn't get the girl.

He liked our Dorothy, too. Sophie Chamberlain played the girl for whom Gregory sets off in hopeless pursuit. She was mature-looking, had obvious sex appeal and much talked-about breasts, which was all that was required of Dorothy, apart from the ability to play football. Sophie couldn't, but we'd get round that.

What we lacked was the Other Woman, Susan, played by Claire Grogan in the film. We needed someone distinctive-looking, a girl with subtle good looks who would flower as the play progressed. Tim liked this idea and suggested that he assisted with the auditions. Thus we spent three consecutive evenings in a classroom in the English schools, watching our fellow students, waiting patiently for the Other Woman to walk into the room.

It was as we were about to pack up on night three that a girl poked her head round the door self-consciously. 'Oh, excuse me,' she said, a hint of Scottish in her voice, 'it looks like I've come to the wrong place.'

'If it's the *Gregory's Girl* auditions,' I countered, 'you're spot on.' Next to me, Tim groaned.

'I'm not too late?'

'No.'

'So I can have a shot at it?'

'Absolutely.'

It would be a lie to say that this was one of those unforgettable, lightning-strike moments of revelation when the mysteries of the world suddenly unveil themselves.

The girl told us that her name was Lucy Etheridge. She wore a corduroy peaked cap and a denim jacket that she kept buttoned up, as if she had no intention of staying. As she studied the short passage of the play she would have to read, Tim and I raised our eyebrows at each other: this was another audition that would come to nothing.

Then Lucy took off her cap to reveal jet-black hair that was cropped unusually short. It was this that first interested me. After the ten-minute audition, I had come to the conclusion that her distinctive, boyishly-attractive face worked exactly as we wanted, that its beauty would become gradually apparent as our play wore on. And it helped that she read well. She wasn't particularly loud or expressive, but she had impact. A quiet strength. Almost every other auditioner had finished with a flourish, by

dropping or raising their voice or by rushing the last sentence. Lucy had maintained her pitch so that there was no full-stop at the end of the final sentence. I wanted her to go on.

'Do you fancy joining us for a drink?' I asked. Tim snorted.

'Does that mean I'm in with a chance, or is this your way of letting people down gently?' she asked.

Tim frowned at me. He'd missed her joke.

'It means you're in with a chance,' I said. But I was already convinced.

We weren't a bad troupe. At least, I didn't think so, although I didn't have a clue what I was doing. Tim seemed happy, and since he was the heartbeat of the team, the rest of the cast were cheerful enough too.

I suspected, though, that the prime justification for Tim's happiness was Sophie.

'She's got teeth,' was Tim's – Gregory's – favourite line, not the wittiest, perhaps, but the one he transformed into a flash of unsuspected comedy, 'lovely teeth, lovely white, white teeth'. The teeth were Sophie's – Dorothy's – and Tim eulogised them dreamily, completely the clown, emphasising the vowels to brilliant effect. And Sophie, offstage at the time, would invariably laugh louder and longer than the rest of us.

This was legalised flirting and she found it impossible not to respond. I was delighted, partly because I thought they fitted together – they were a glamourous couple and looked right together – partly because they had the sort of chemistry that would boost my production, and partly, too, because I wasn't interested in Sophie. At least, not like that.

My main problem with *Gregory's Girl* was the accents. The easy option was to drop the Scottish accent altogether. We plumped for the hard option and Lucy eventually revealed how hopeless she thought we were over the drink in the Shakespeare that the pair of us had taken to sharing after practice together.

'C'mon on, Mr Director,' she said to me. 'The accents are shite!'

'What's the problem?'

'Grey-grey! No one can even say Gregory, for a start. It's somehow become a sort of glottal 'Grey-grey' with a token rolled R thrown in for Celtic good measure. Sophie's the worst.'

'Did you know that she and Tim have gone back to Tim's room together?' I asked.

'To practise their accents?'

'No. To go over their lines.'

'So that's what they call it, these days, is it?'

'Apparently.'

'God, why don't they just get on with it?'

'Tim says there's nothing in it.'

'And you believe him?'

'Do I hell!' And I mimicked Sophie: 'Ooh, Grey-grey. Och, you're soo teh-rribly funny and soo teh-rribly hunsome.'

'Brilliant! Dom, you should get on the stage yourself.'

'Bollocks!'

'You should.' She laid her hand on mine. 'But what'd we bloody do without you to bloody direct us?' She left the question hanging. She left her hand where it was too. And I liked that.

Friday afternoon, five days before our opening night. That was the afternoon when I called Tim a 'bastard' and flounced off in an uncharacteristically brave artistic sulk.

My problem with Tim was that he was too damned good at his part. He made Gregory too naïve, too funny; he indulged himself to excess in all that 'lovely white, white teeth' stuff. I wanted Gregory to suffer, to be tormented, to have a vague understanding of his inability to pull Dorothy, or even to get within touching distance of her. He had to feel some sort of pain. Tim, however, liked to be the lead character in life as well as on stage so he was hard to direct. Or maybe I was too timid to direct him. I found myself having to nudge him gently in the direction I favoured and that afternoon the nudging lost its gentleness.

It all began when I had again requested – politely, of course – a less comical delivery.

'You must be fucking joking!' he replied, sitting down on the front of the stage and slapping his hand on it.

'I mean it,' I told him. And I did. I was frightfully earnest. I couldn't accept that the love thing was less than serious.

'But Gregory's a ridiculous character.' His voice was loud and challenging. 'He's so hopeless that he's got to be played for laughs.'

'He's only ridiculous to you, Tim,' my voice was loud too. I was surprised by his tone, 'because you can't relate to what he's going through. You don't know what it's like to be Gregory and set off in pursuit of women when you've absolutely no chance of catching them.'

'No need to get personal, Dom.'

'I'm not. But what is so great about this play is that almost everyone who comes to it will know what it's like to feel awkward with the opposite sex. They'll know how it feels to be rejected. That's why we can make this play so good, because we – or, rather, most of us – recognise the emotions involved. Rejection goes on every night at this bloody university. This play is about people like us.'

Tim rolled on to his back and put his hands over his ears. 'God, you talk such shit!'

Then that light Scottish accent piped up: 'Tim, it's not shit.'

This was a pivotal moment that might, perhaps, have swung the dispute my way. I should have savoured it. But I missed its significance and blasted straight on: 'Thank you, Lucy,' I said, triumph ringing in my voice.

'Lucy, it's shit!' he shrieked.

'It's not.' She was firm and assertive, but not loud like me, certainly not the type to be ruffled by a raised voice. 'He's right. I feel comfortable doing this play because it's about stuff I can relate to.'

'Exactly!' I chimed in. 'I feel like Gregory. I *am* Gregory!'

'Ah! So that's what this is about,' said Tim, menacingly. 'It's all about you and the fact that you can't get laid.'

And that was it. I flounced off. I didn't say anything, just took my coat and left.

An hour and a half later, it was Lucy who found me. I was in my room – not an imaginative location for an artistic flounce – sitting on my bed with my back against the wall, listening to Lloyd Cole and the Commotions and licking my wounds.

She explained that after I'd gone the cast had sat in the theatre for a long time, waiting for me to come back. Eventually, under pressure, Tim had relented and agreed on my interpretation of Gregory. He'd also been full of self-rebuke for 'the other thing'.

'Oh, I'm not bothered about that,' I lied. Lucy sat down next to me and laid her left hand on my knee. I fumbled for a change of subject: there's only so long that you want the fact that you're a nineteen-year-old virgin to be floating in the air.

'Do you really think I'm right?' I asked.

'Of course. And especially about the rejection thing. God, Dominic, you're so right about that.'

'Really?'

'Yes!' She pushed my knee playfully. 'Everyone seems to think that student life is all about notching up successes and conquests. It's as if it's not the done thing to fail.' She rested her chin on my knee and we shared an easy silence.

'And do you really think you're Gregory?' she asked.

'Yes.' I laughed nervously. 'Sort of.'

'God.' She fixed me with her dark brown eyes. 'You're pretty good at honesty, aren't you?'

'Not with everyone.'

'Save it for me, Grey-grey.'

Tim and I did the sensible, mature thing that night: we went out and got drunk.

'It was very exciting, that funny storming-off thing you did this afternoon,' he said.

'It wasn't a "funny storming-off thing", it was a production-threatening bust-up.'

'Well, you mustn't do it again.' He knew he was winning me round. 'It was upsetting for all of us. I insist you apologise.'

'Fuck off!' I said, with laughter in my voice. 'It's me who deserves an apology.'

'You think I owe you an apology?'

'Yup.'

'OK.' He spread his arms theatrically. 'I'm sorry.'

'Good.'

'And may I mark my apology with the purchase of a pint of beer?'

'You may indeed.'

'And then will you apologise to me?'

'You've got to be joking.'

'Oh, OK. Be like that.'

Tim sustained his apology with the purchase of the next two rounds, and by the time we had got to the end of them I couldn't have dredged up any antipathy towards him, even if I'd wanted to.

But I, as the weaker character, knew that it wasn't in my interest to fall out with him. And he had a point: I did have a problem getting laid. I just didn't want it highlighted when I was allowing myself to wonder if it was about to be solved.

The funniest moment in *Gregory's Girl* didn't involve Gregory. I thought that Tim's ego would be dented by this, but I had underestimated him.

If you are comparing all the losers in the play, Gregory is by no means the biggest of them all. He is the loser who comes good in the end, the comic hero; it's his two mates, Andy and Charlie, who don't and the play leaves you in no doubt that they never will.

When their attempts to pursue their female classmates are at their most abject, Andy and Charlie wonder whether their search

is focused on the wrong place and discuss the possibility of re-targeting their attention. Charlie mentions that he's heard of a 'town' in South America where the women outnumber the men by eight to one. He says it's called Caracas. The closing moments of the play show the pair hitch-hiking on a road in Scotland, holding a sign for 'Caracus'. Great stuff.

And Tim thought so too. Indeed, Tim thought it so amusing that when the three-night run of *Gregory's Girl* was over and we'd all gone out to celebrate, he suggested it was the place for me.

That last night Tim had been outstanding, and he knew it. He was thrilled that he'd made me cry. *Gregory's Girl* is hardly what you'd call a tear-jerker, but it was the last-night tangle of emotions – the climax of our hard work, the end of the road, the breaking-up of our little team – that got to me and when Gregory finally got the girl, I turned to Sophie, who was sitting with me backstage, and pointed, grinning, to the tears in my eyes. They returned when my players came off-stage after the curtain call and for once the girls, briefly, found me more inter-esting than Tim.

Naturally, Tim soon regained the ascendancy and much later his performance peaked again. In between, we celebrated in the Shakespeare and outside the Shakespeare, where he reeled off some of his favourite Sinatra.

'What shall we do now?' I asked, when he was finally done.

'Party back at my college,' said Sophie, with alcoholic enthu-siasm. 'Come on, you lovely people, everyone's invited!'

Sounded good, so we agreed unanimously. And it was then that Tim draped an arm round my shoulders. 'If I was you,' he said, with a beery grin, 'I'd be setting off for Caracas.'

How drunk were we? We always knew when Sophie was drunk because she went round hugging everyone and telling them how much she admired them, that she'd always been in awe of them and how wonderful they were. I had already been informed at least twice that I was a man of great intelligence. And we always

knew when Lucy was pissed because her omnipresent corduroy cap got turned back to front, as it was that night. It was like a warning to everyone that she might do something silly. Tim was probably the soberest of the four of us. And me? I was so perfectly, cheerfully pissed that I let Tim get away unchallenged with the Caracas comment. It hurt, but no one else heard it or saw the wound he'd inflicted. And anyway, *en route* to Sophie's college, Lucy slipped her arm through mine. I didn't feel as if I was *en route* to the capital of Venezuela at all.

'Grey-grey!' she called, later that night, from the centre of a room where a coffee-stained carpet had become a dance-floor. Some twenty swaying drunks were sort of dancing, sort of stumbling, sort of linking arms and taking turns to swig that old student favourite, the Bulgarian red wine that cost £2.49 a bottle. At Lucy's command, I joined the swirling swiggers, linking arms with her. God knows what music was playing – it might have been Deep Purple or Prokofiev but our sort-of dancing wouldn't have changed.

'Grey-grey!' she shouted again, when it ended. One of Sophie's friends was digging around in a record collection beside the turntable, looking for a replacement, and Lucy had sat down on a long chair with thin cushioning and an ugly green woollen cover. 'Grey-grey, come over here,' she patted the seat next to her, 'and bring some of that gorgeous wine with you.'

I obeyed, and we slouched in the seat, shoulder to shoulder.

'Grey, you're lovely,' she said.

'Stop it. You sound like Sophie.'

'No, I mean it, Grey.'

'You can stop calling me that too.'

'It's your name now, I'm afraid. And I do mean it, you know.'

'Really?' I sat up with my left leg tucked under me so I was looking slightly down on her. The music started again but we didn't hear it. At least, I didn't.

'Yeah. You seemed such a serious guy to me at first. And I

don't mind serious – but not too serious! But you're not really like that, are you? It's just your front.'

'You're coming dangerously close to understanding me, aren't you?' We were almost whispering now.

Lucy caressed my left cheek with the fingertips of her right hand. 'There's quite a lot of drama going on in there, isn't there?' She tapped my forehead. 'It's interesting. I like that.'

Her finger remained on my forehead, then slid slowly round my eyebrow, down my cheek and neck. Our eye-contact remained unbroken, and the way she was looking at me, it felt as if she was checking that the finger-sliding met with my approval. This heralded the moment I will never forget: my left leg was aching, because I was sitting on it and had cut off the blood circulation, and I was ignoring the pain because to reposition myself might have broken the spell. I also remember Lucy holding her cap to her head as if it was going to slip forward into my face, and I remember the anticipation as our faces seemed to converge. This was it! It was happening! It was going to happen! It really was!

That was the moment when the world stopped spinning and water glasses in Dorking teetered on bedside tables, then clattered to the floor.

I don't know how close we got. To within an inch, lip to lip? Definitely. A centimetre? Possibly. A tantalising matter of millimetres. But somehow our mouths never met. The kiss was ruled incomplete. It didn't count. It didn't happen. Instead, I felt a heavy slap on my shoulder and the feeling of immense weight as a large person sank down on the seat next to us, half on top of me. It was Tim.

'What on earth is going on here?' he asked, in a loud, drunken slur. 'Dom, I hope you're not harassing a member of your cast. That would be terribly unprofessional.'

'I'd never do such a thing, Tim. You know me.' I stood up, embarrassed, a schoolboy caught in the act. I'd already been accused of being a non-starter with girls, and here I was, just a few hours later, caught in the attempt to get off the mark.

'I'm going to see if I can find any more booze,' I said, and left him on the green chair next to Lucy, exactly where I had been.

The following day I met Tim for coffee and post-match analysis.

'How's your head today?' he asked.

'It's got the familiar Bulgarian throb. Otherwise it's empty. I've got complete memory loss. What happened to you? What time d'you get home from Sophie's?'

'Between you and me,' he replied conspiratorially, 'I didn't go home at all.'

'You and Sophie? At bloody last!'

'Ah, no. Late change of plan. Not me and Sophie. Me and Lucy.'

3

Sixteen years is some wait to make up for a missed opportunity. Indeed, up here on Greenwich Hill, I don't know if there's any making up to be done. It is two minutes before midday, and all we have to show for that night is a newspaper cutting. The damp patches at Dorking bedsides have long since dried up. In fact, what didn't happen – the non-kiss, that millimetre or two that we came up short – was tidily forgotten thereafter and swept away into an undisturbed corner of the past. And there it has remained, gathering dust, never mentioned, so perfectly untouched that Lucy and I have never shared a kiss or even another near-miss. I don't think we've even held hands. Hugged? Yes. Many times. We go for pizza together too, but that is about as erotic as it gets.

Yet Lucy had always insisted she would be up here to meet me. Even as the years passed and she and Tim stayed together, she said she'd make her millennium date with me. She would tease Tim that time was running out for him, that if he didn't propose in the next ten years – nine, eight, whatever – he would lose her and she would end up on Greenwich Hill with me for good. Tim would laugh dismissively and this was the way our game went, until the day he really did ask her to marry him. And she, of course, said yes. She had given her answer almost before he had completed the question. Yet still she persisted with the plan. She and I would be up here on Greenwich Hill, she said, sad singletons together. She and Tim would never last – at least, that was how the joke went, and she would prod him in the ribs as she made it.

Lucy and I were 'made for each other' – that was another of her lines. 'You and me, babe,' she would say flirtatiously, batting

21

her long eyelashes. Was there ever a semblance of seriousness in her voice? Did she ever remotely mean it?

Here, on the hill, it seems I have my answer. It is midday on the dot, it says so on the Observatory clock. And here she is. Smiling, dark eyes burning with amusement and disbelief, wandering slowly up the Tarmac path, just as I had always imagined.

But it's not as though I've spent the last decade and a half in limbo. I'm not desperate, really I'm not. It's just that while I always liked the idea of sleeping around, I ultimately found that it wasn't for me. It didn't make me happy, even on the rare occasions when I got to try it. At the very least I've got Nadia to show for my troubles – though some trophy wife she turned out to be.

At Durham, my mother used to ask me on the phone if I'd met anyone to write home about and the result was that she barely ever got a letter. The term after *Gregory's Girl*, I finally jotted her a line. Or a word. On the back of a postcard of Durham Cathedral, I wrote 'Daisy'. It was with her that I lost my virginity, and if *she* hadn't been someone worth writing home about, I'd never have troubled the postman.

Daisy was reasonable-looking, a biology student with a Roman nose and a delightful, if domineering manner though anyone who's prepared to take their clothes off and do stuff to a nineteen-year-old virgin would have seemed domineering. And delightful. She gave me the impression that we were having regular sex – at least, she did for about seventy-two hours; we had it three nights in a row, sometimes more than once, until suddenly she decided it was time to stop. Hardly had my mother received her missive than another was travelling south-bound: 'Previous card sent in error.' My mother enjoyed this form of cryptic information-sharing and sent a postcard back, picturing a shoal of angel fish: 'Plenty more of these in the sea,' she wrote.

It may have taken me nineteen years to lose my virginity and I may never quite have made up for my slow start. And I will probably never sleep with as many women as Tim. But to suggest I was a case for hitch-hiking to Caracas seems unfairly wide of the mark. I never considered myself thumbs-out *en route* to South America. As I had said in the rehearsal room, I thought I was Gregory, stumbling with absolute uncertainty in more or less the right direction. Not Andy or Charlie.

The problem, of course, was that I wasn't Gregory. Tim was Gregory, and Lucy was Gregory's girl. But Lucy has finally made it here to be with me. As hill walks go, this is about as symbolic as they come.

'What the hell are you doing here?' I'm on my feet. Lucy is puffing a little. My smile is ear-to-ear.

'What the hell are *you* doing here?' she replies, almost shouting, red-faced and delighted.

She spreads her arms wide and we collapse into each other. I can feel ripples of laughter moving through her small body. She is still so light. I pick her up and spin her round. 'I can't believe you've come!' How many hours have I spent imagining this very spin on top of this very hill?

'Grey?' She pulls back her head, looking at me as if I'd gone mad. 'You think I'd break the promise of a lifetime? I just can't believe you've kept it too.'

I put Lucy down and we look into each other's faces, our arms still round each other's waists. She looks . . . she looks as she always has: young, small, boyish, with laughing eyes and those lashes that always seemed unusually long. Her hair looks grown-up, funny – because grown-up doesn't suit her – but attractive, dark, wavy, to just above her shoulders. But I need to know what her eyes are saying. I need to know why they're laughing and, whether they're *just* laughing or she's taking any of this seriously. I need to know why she is here.

'So, what now, Grey?' she asks, frowning, eyebrows raised,

shaking her head very slightly, amazement and disbelief coupled on her pretty, elfin face.

'Dunno. It's happy-ever-after time, I suppose, isn't it? Doesn't the fact that we're both here imply that we're going to spend the rest of our lives together? That's the deal, isn't it? Made for each other, we are.'

'Oh, yeah?' Questioning, smiling, spirited Lucy.

I can't tell for certain whether or not that comment had a question mark appended. 'You're looking good, you know,' I tell her.

'Stop it.'

'You are. I like your hair.'

'I like your old grey sweater.' She smiles up at me. 'I like the fact that you've come.'

'Stop shaking your head.'

'I can't help it.' She shrugs her shoulders in response. 'I can't believe we're both here.'

We sit down together on the bench. She looks tired, hung-over probably, but the lines around her eyes do her no disservice. Her distinctive gamine features have aged well. She looks more feminine, but still matchbox cute. Me? Such is the recession of my hairline that I've opted for the last-resort crew-cut. Captain Average in the looks department. Smily eyes, not apparently overweight. Nice arse, I'm told, after a drink. But doing pretty well to be discussing marriage with someone as uniquely attractive as Lucy. Even if the conversation isn't serious.

I still can't believe we're here. Before us is the green slope of Greenwich Hill, the Thames, the high-rises of Canary Wharf and the Millennium Dome, designed to salute the march of time. And next to me is Lucy, exactly as planned on that drunken night all those years ago. Between us there is a moment's silence. An edgy silence? 'Lula! Lula! Lula!' I say to fill it, extending the astonishment theme.

'So why *are* you here?' she asks, turning to me.

'I don't know. Not much else to do today.'

'Bollocks. Not much else to do? You high-flying bloody you! Bollocks!'

'Yeah. I came to get married too.' And I said that with irony.

'And me,' she replies, ironic too, grinning.

'What a great little arrangement!' More irony. How else do you discuss marriage with your best friend's wife?

Another short silence.

'What sort of a wedding do you fancy?' she asks.

'What sort of wedding do *you* fancy?'

'I asked first.'

'OK. Any sort, just as long as you're there.' I pause to crank up the irony even further. 'My darling.'

'How sweet!' She bats her eyelids at me. Then she drops her head and laughs, as if she can't sustain the joke any more. She puts her right hand on my left knee and shakes it. 'This is so funny! What would dear old Tim make of it?'

'Tim wouldn't understand.' And I know I got the tone all wrong there. Too serious. Far too serious.

We talk about last night. The last night of the millennium. I spent it on a boat on the Thames, the guest of a partner at work. Five hundred pounds a ticket, dead posh, two hundred people, six courses, a rare hedonistic atmosphere, sensational jazz band, sensational women in sensational dresses, lurching around pissed and throwing themselves at high-earners who were too pissed to catch them.

'Your sort of people these days, Grey?'

'Oh, purr-lease. The sort of people I see too much of, I'll grant you that.'

'I'd imagine you fit in very well.'

'Stop teasing! I'm trying to get out.' I pull my right leg up in front of me on the bench. 'I'd much rather have been singing "Hi! Ho! Silver Lining" under the paper chains and streamers in the village hall with you.'

Lucy's New Year's Eve: a church hall in Richmond-upon-Thames, just down the road from her house, lots of local couples

dancing to their favourites from the seventies and eighties when they used to dance more often, their children allowed to stay up late and themselves struggling to embrace the occasion and get past midnight.

'I made it to quarter past three,' she says proudly. 'How about that?'

'Amazing! Those Richmond party animals sure know how to rock.'

'You're not far wrong. I even did one of those pop-star dives off the stage.'

'Sensible as ever! How did it go?'

'Well, no one knew what was going on so they didn't catch me properly. A bloke in corduroys broke my fall but I hit my head rather hard and had to sit down for five minutes.'

I laugh. Lucy wraps her arms round my knee, rests her head on it and gazes down on the greyness that has enveloped London. This is natural, peaceful. At least, that's how it feels to me. Life continuing down there before us; Lucy and I sitting up here, together, set apart.

'Here,' she says, sitting up. 'I've got you a present.' From her handbag she presents me with a small, delicately wrapped cube.

'I haven't got you anything, which isn't a very impressive start to a marriage.'

'It doesn't matter. Open it.'

I untie the bow and unwrap the paper. Inside is a small box that contains a pair of cufflinks with, inset into each, a picture of John Gordon Sinclair as Gregory.

'Lucy! Amazing! Come here.' I hug her. 'Where on earth did you find them?'

'I got them made for you.'

'How wonderful.'

'You are Grey-grey after all . . .'

'As, to this very day, you keep reminding me.'

Lucy beams, delighted with herself, and rests her chin on my knee again. Then she cocks her head up to face me, her eyes

full of laughter. 'So, come on, what *are* we doing here?' she asks, but softly this time, as if she is genuinely interested in the answer.

'We're here for the new start, aren't we? We've staggered to the end of the bloodiest and most miserable century in human history. The age of Hitler and Stalin, "The Birdie Song" and the Thompson Twins is behind us. Time begins again now and the fact that we're here, at the Greenwich Observatory, the centre of time and space, couldn't be more symbolic. We've got a clean slate, a second chance. We can forge ahead, learn from our mistakes, set new standards. Save the world, make it a better place. That's what Michael Jackson said, didn't he? I've always said he was a smart guy. But here we are, Lucy, right at the beginning of it all. It's a great opportunity.'

'Grey, how is it that you always had the knack of making huge, ridiculously profound and sarcastic statements in such a way that it's impossible to know if you mean them? Did you mean that? It sounded ludicrous.' She pauses. 'It sounded lovely.'

'Of course it sounded ludicrous. This *is* ludicrous. *This* – you, me – is like the ultimate dare of our lives. And I don't really know if I meant it. I know it's a nice idea. But, Lula, I'm scared of giving too much away here. If I thought *you* thought it was a nice idea too, I might be able to give you an answer.'

'We're really discussing it,' she shakes her head with incredulity, 'aren't we?'

'I know I am. I don't know about you. Are you?' And then, repeating myself, changing the tone, as serious as I'm prepared to risk: 'Are you?'

'Grey,' she gazes across the cityscape before us, 'I don't know. OK. I *have* wondered about it. The thought *has* ambled into my mind once or twice and parked up for a while. But – Christ – you should see some of the other stuff in there. But, yes, *something* dragged me and a major hangover across London. If all I'd wanted was some fresh air and a stretch of my legs, there are a hundred more convenient places I could have gone. But I

couldn't not come. And yet I know that coming here is, as you say, completely ludicrous . . .'

'We're both here. Isn't that the point?'

'Grey! Stop it!' She laughs, then stops. 'You're joking, aren't you?'

I pause. 'Want a straight answer? Not completely, Lula.'

'Grey!' She strokes my left cheek.

'You give me a straight answer, then. You're joking, aren't you?'

She looks at me, confounded. She makes as if to reply, then swallows the words. She repeats the whole charade. 'Oh, Grey!' Exasperation fills her voice. 'Come on. It's lovely up here with you but I'm afraid I've got to go back to real life.'

'Lula, that wasn't a no.'

'C'mon, ridiculous man.' She's on her feet, but a smile is sufficient to show that she heard my last comment and chose to ignore it. 'Let's go.'

'Where to?'

'To meet the other man in my life.'

'Oh, yeah?'

'Josh. He's waiting for me in a café down in the village.'

'OK, hang on a sec.' I stand up and, from my side of the bench, pick up a suitcase that Lucy hasn't noticed.

'What are you doing with that?'

I'd been waiting for this. 'Well, if we're going to get married, we've got to do it properly. Most of my stuff is in New York, but I can start by moving in with these things.'

She says nothing as she reads my face, but it's straight now. She laughs – but nervously. 'I don't believe this is happening.'

'Why not?' I'm smiling again.

'Grey! You mean this, don't you?'

'Don't you?'

She shakes her head, gesticulates with her hands, and takes a deep breath, as if about to deliver her answer.

'Look, it's no problem,' I say calmly. 'I'm not turning psycho

on you. I've just checked out of a hotel – that's why I've got my suitcase. I'm in limbo. Less than a week ago I lived in New York. There's plenty of places I could go. To my mum's, to Bill and Alice's. Or another hotel.'

Her mouth is gaping, amusement and exasperation written across her face. 'OK. You win, Grey. You're coming back to mine.'

'I knew you'd see sense.'

'You're mad.'

'How d'you like your tea in the morning?'

4

Where were you when you heard Princess Diana had died, or that John Lennon or JFK had been shot? There are people who know exactly where they were when they heard about Tim.

I was in the middle of a fight with Nadia at our flat in SoHo, Manhattan. It was January, early evening. Nadia had said we were going out for dinner with her parents; I'd just got back from work, knackered, and I told her I hadn't known about it because she hadn't told me, and that a friend had offered to take me to the Knicks game at Madison Square Garden and that was where I intended to go.

Nadia was right, of course. She *had* told me about dinner. And I was lying: there was no Knicks ticket. But I had lost patience with her parents and I knew the bar where my Knicks friend would be watching the game. Our conversation – if you could call it that – was following the familiar path down which I would often find myself pushing her.

'Of course I like seeing your parents, Nadia,' I said, letting the killer blow hang in mid-air. 'I love it when your mother's dog jumps on to my lap in smart restaurants.' I used the lap-dog line, but I had countless other put-down references to her parents that would trigger her fury. Her mother's dog, her mother's weight in jewellery, her mother's weight in makeup, her mother's weight, the long, long hugs I had to endure from her mother whenever we had the pleasure of seeing her. Easy lines, cheap lines, same reaction. That evening, after the lap-dog reference, Nadia tried to hit me and failed. She was turned away from me on the sofa, whimpering, and I was coldly enjoying the fruits of my work when the phone rang. It was Lucy.

Nadia answered and held out the receiver for me.

'Hello, you tartan lovely,' I said to Lucy. As if, in the context, I could forget a comment like that.

From the other end came muffled sobbing. 'Grey . . . Grey . . .'

'Lucy?'

'Grey . . . This is the call I've been dreading most. But I had to do it myself.'

In quiet but determined tones, broken by audible sobs, she explained. Just after midnight last night the phone had woken her. It was the police. There had been an accident in Wittingsfold in Buckinghamshire. A car had gone over a humpback bridge, slipped off the road on the bend the other side, spun forty-five degrees anti-clockwise and hit a tree. Tim. He had been badly hurt. He was in the High Wycombe general hospital. Come quickly. She had bundled Josh into her car and driven like hell to High Wycombe. By the time she got there Tim had died.

'Grey, I'm in fucking pieces here.'

'I don't know what to—'

'You can't. Don't even try. There's nothing anyone can say. They've tried already. Don't you try too. Just share it with me.'

'Oh, Lucy! I – I – I – oh, fuck, Lucy. No! Tell me it's not true.'

'I'm so sorry, Grey.'

'*You*'re sorry!'

'Yes, I am.'

'Christ. And how's little Josh?'

'Don't ask. I can barely look the wee man in the eye. He's just mastered two-word sentences, and every sentence has now become a question that ends in "Daddy". "Where Daddy?" "When Daddy?" "What Daddy?" "No Daddy?" Oh, Grey, I tell you, I'm trying to hold him together but I'm falling apart myself. There's one other question he's got that is directed particularly at me. "Why crying?" Why fucking crying?' Lucy sobbed. 'God! He's not stupid, you know, Grey. He knows perfectly well there's something up.'

'Can anyone help with him?'

'The whole bloody world's rallying round. No problem there. My parents are flying down first thing in the morning. But it's unbearable here, Grey, that's all, just unbearable.'

There was momentary silence.

'What was Tim doing in Wittingsfold?'

'On his way back from seeing a client.'

'Oh, Lula! I'm so—'

'Grey,' I could hear her weeping, 'can I ask you something?'

'Sure.'

'Do you think there's any chance you could come back for a bit? Just a couple of days.'

'Sure.'

'It's just . . . you know . . . I need to share this. I can't do it on my own. And you and I, we knew Tim together.'

'I know.'

'Will you?'

'Of course.'

'Good. So you'll be able to make the funeral, then?'

'I guess so. Do you know when it is?'

'I think next Monday.'

'I'll be with you as soon as I can.'

'Thanks, Grey.'

'You know I'm here for you, don't you?'

'You're going to have to be, Grey.'

'OK. Listen, call me whenever you want.'

'Thanks, Grey.'

And she did. Two hours later. 'Could you speak at the funeral?' she asked, voice wobbling.

Of course I would, I said reassuringly, unaware that it would be one of the toughest assignments of my life. I would spend the best part of the next day in my large Manhattan office sitting in front of a computer with the word 'Tim' at the top of an otherwise empty screen.

It wasn't because I knew I would be standing before a church dripping with tears that the speech was so tough, or that the

aisles would be packed with ladies he had charmed and whose hearts he had broken or who knew their hearts would have been broken had they got close enough. And neither was it tough because I knew the church wouldn't be large enough to hold all the men who, like me, had followed him, be it on to the stage, the cricket pitch, into the meeting room or the pub. For some reason, team mates in his various cricket sides had long made a habit of pointing out to me that he was one of the most natural talents they had ever played alongside and they would often add, unprompted, with a jocular you-know-what-I-mean raising of an eyebrow, that he played an outstanding game off the pitch too. I guess the message was that they had a claim to his friend-ship too; his charisma was such that people noticed him, relished him and didn't forget him. So, even without the widow and the two-year-old son standing side by side at the front of the church, the funeral could only be a titanic, draining experience.

But it wasn't the prospect of all this that made my address so hard to write. I had known Tim better than almost everyone else inside that church, but as I sat in front of my computer screen, I found myself wishing I could pull some of the tricks that we advertising people are accustomed to. Should I sell them the image they wanted to buy into? Should I paint Tim as they saw him? The golden child, magnificent in mind and body, one of nature's most wondrous creations? Tim was great product, they were my target market and, if I so desired, I could make this the easiest campaign of my career.

Two windows into the mind of my dead friend, though what we see is only obfuscation.

One. When Tim lost his job, his confrontation with failure was a strange one.

When we had left Durham and were cast into that scary place called the Real World, Lucy remained true to herself and worked in theatre PR. I struggled for a while and eventually got my first job in advertising.

Tim waltzed confidently into the working environment: he applied for jobs at six banks and got offers from five. We told him that he was selling out, that his was a cheap soul flogged off to the world of commercialism, but when he started making serious money, we forgot our ethics, especially when he was spending it too. He was not only wealthy, he was generous.

Then one day, some seven years ago, he came home to the flat in Putney he shared with Lucy and told her he'd been fired. Something about a 'personality clash'. 'Ignorant arseholes' were the words he used. He hadn't been given any warning, he was just told to clear his desk and go. He didn't want to talk about it, he wanted to go to the pub. He rang me, and the three of us went out and he got drunk and sang 'Jetplane' as we left, and it was as if nothing had happened. I'd tried to ask him about it but he wouldn't give away anything beyond 'personality clash' with someone higher up the ladder. All I got, I remember, was a sympathetic raising-of-eyebrows from Lucy, a fleeting acknowledgement that this was an issue on which we shared similar feelings and which we couldn't understand.

Everything did remain pretty normal because Tim went off on a three-week cricket tour with one of his clubs, then returned and started chiselling away at his golf handicap. Within a month and a half, he was in a new job with another bank, on a slightly higher salary, which he breezed through for three years before setting himself up as a financial consultant.

However, the sacking was something he hated talking about, he loathed so much as a mention. I had tried to discuss it with him again when he was between jobs. I thought – as a friend – that he might appreciate the opportunity to get it off his chest, a problem shared, that sort of thing.

Also I was beginning to make some sort of a name for myself in advertising. My agency, Dylan and Duffy, had given me a huge break: they'd made me the copywriter on a campaign for Peachey's, a new ice-cream brand, and they'd given me an open cheque book to hire a creative partner. I

went straight for Jerry Sweet, a splendid, licentious whisky-drinking insomniac whom I'd known, admired and been nurtured by at my previous agency. As I expected, Jerry came and, as I also expected, he and I gelled. Our brief was to make Peachey's sexy and we came up with a shamelessly derivative soap-opera-type campaign, involving two drop-dead-gorgeous twentysomethings, boy and girl, who, we decided, should live in neighbouring houseboats on the Thames under the yellow lights of Battersea bridge. Instead of borrowing the traditional cup of sugar from each other, our hero and heroine would ask for ice-cream and the implication was always that they'd want a lot more on the side. The campaign went so well that Jerry and I were the blue-eyed boys, a team tipped to go far. Sweet and Lord: create an agency one day around those names and it couldn't fail.

It was when this campaign was taking off that Tim got the sack. At the same time, Dylan and Duffy was looking for a new financial director; I thought he would be perfect and also that my rise at the agency might help me help him to land the job. But my altruism was misplaced. Tim thought the idea preposterous, almost insulting. He put up barriers and I was made to feel that I was intruding for even going near them.

'It's not your problem,' he said sternly. 'Don't let it concern you. I'm quite capable of looking after myself, thank you very much.' Which killed the conversation dead.

Maybe I shouldn't have been surprised. This was, as far as I knew, Tim's worst – maybe first – setback, his maiden brush with concepts like mortality and failure. Maybe he had started to believe his own publicity. Most people – the Gregorys of this world – spend their life learning the art of coping with disappointment; it was one skill that Tim didn't have, simply because he'd never required it. He'd only ever acted Gregory, never *been* him.

Two. The following year Tim and Lucy got married. It happened to be a pretty good year for me too because Peachey's

sales were booming, my horny houseboaters were sharing their bodies and their ice-cream, their corny chat-up lines were purposefully cornier and their relationship was even discussed in tabloid gossip columns. At the height of the campaign, we had the hero knocking on the door of the heroine's cabin in the middle of the night, holding up a pot of the new pecan-flavour Peachey's and asking, 'Want to try my nuts?' The line acquired a notoriety of its own, my status at Dylan and Duffy swelled, and Jerry and I were asked to transfer to New York and head up the creative team there.

We shared a leaving party. It wasn't opulent but we took over a wine bar and put a fat cheque behind the bar, which our friends and colleagues drank their way through rather more quickly than I'd imagined. It was a good occasion, and though speeches were not intended, Jerry stood on a chair and told everyone that I was going places and they should watch out. He told them about this young lad with a silly haircut and no idea about life who had started working under him seven years ago with a few strong ideas and no confidence that they were any good. He told them how the boy would shove his hands into his pockets and shuffle from foot to foot, and how he stayed late in the office because he wanted to toy with ideas without worrying about anyone looking over his shoulder and seeing what he was doing. And then Jerry turned to me, put an arm round my shoulders and said, 'And can you believe what he's turned into?' He said he was proud of me, and although I felt embarrassed, I treasured his words.

They seemed to make an impression on others too. 'You're so naughty, Grey,' said Lucy, who accosted me afterwards with Sophie, both of them inebriated, each putting an arm round me. 'You never told us you were doing so bloody well.'

'I thought you were going to New York to be the coffee boy and help with the photocopying,' said Sophie, spilling her wine. 'But you're bloody famous, aren't you?'

'We're so proud.'

Indeed, almost everyone left me feeling a little special, everyone who counted, that was, except Tim. I hardly saw him that night until the wine bar closed and we were all on the pavement saying goodbye.

'What happened to you tonight?' I asked him.

'It was your night,' he said, a little soberly.

'Tim?' I couldn't catch his meaning.

'Your night, mate.'

'Yeah, but it's over now. Aren't you going to cry on my shoulder and tell me how much you're going to miss me?'

'You've done really well,' he said, looking me firmly in the eye, shaking my hand and missing the opportunity to make light of my comment. 'Good for you.'

And then he turned to go. But as he wandered off down the street in search of a taxi with Lucy under his arm, I watched him, thinking about what he had just said to me and the way he had said it, and wondering if it was unfair of me to question whether he had meant it.

Nadia didn't come with me for the funeral. I insisted on that. I stayed for four days, the penultimate day being that of the funeral.

The climax of the service took place, characteristically, at Tim's command. It turned out that he had requested in his will that 'Jetplane' be sung, and although the words were printed in the service sheet, I would guess that half the congregation had learned them from him anyway. But never had any of us pondered those lyrics so deeply or attributed to them such significance. We all understood them to be about packing your bags and bidding *au revoir* to a lover; we hadn't thought of them as a way of saying goodbye for ever.

My address came straight after 'Jetplane', and when I had finished, Lucy, who had insisted that I sat with her, Josh and Tim's parents, took my hand and squeezed it so tightly that I could still see the marks after the service.

The address went down well. People approached me afterwards and told me I had captured Tim perfectly. I had given them the Tim they had wanted, of course. What right had I, then, to question his authenticity?

5

Lucy opens the door to the Galley, a café in Greenwich village. As its name suggests, it has a nautical theme; the ceiling and walls are adorned with ropes and webbing, the till is built over an anchor and the tables are designed to look like dinghies.

'Hoist up the sail,' yells a little boy in a denim jacket and a baseball cap. He is jumping up and down at the helm of his dinghy. 'C'mon, Mummy. All aboard. Sv'ana says we're going to sail to Croatia to say Happy New Year to her mummy and daddy. All aboard.'

This is Josh: blond hair, dark brown eyes, the same bright face as his mother, without – to Tim's dismay – the slightest resemblance to his father. He is loud and squeaky of voice, and keen that we should board the ship for Croatia. So we do.

'Here,' he says, thrusting a plastic beaker into my hand. 'That's a bucket for you to use if any water comes over the sides. It's a very important job.'

On the other side of the dinghy, the girl whose parents we are sailing to see in Croatia is also bailing out imaginary water with a beaker.

'This is Svetlana,' says Lucy, trying not to disturb the captain of the ship in the process. 'She's Josh's nanny and my saviour and she's going home for two weeks this afternoon. What am I going to do without her?'

'I'm sure you'll find me a very adequate replacement,' I answer, with a grin. Did I really say that?

Svetlana flashes me a smile and gets back to bailing out our ship.

'Josh darling,' says Lucy, 'are you going to say hello to Godfather Dominic?'

39

'Is he the one who didn't come to my christening, Mummy?'

'That's right.' Lucy rolls her eyes at me apologetically. 'The lovely one who was stuck in America where the Red Injuns come from.'

Josh lets go of the wheel and turns to me. 'Hello, Dominic. Do you have any friends who are Red Injuns?'

'No. There aren't many living in New York, these days.'

'Why?'

'Well,' I get a supportive smile from Lucy, 'there's nowhere to park their horses.'

'Why?'

'Horses don't like multi-storey car parks.'

'Why?'

'Josh!' Lucy is stern-voiced. 'He likes the Why game,' she explains to me, 'and I suspect that's largely because I told him that I don't.'

'A-why, why, why, why, why, why . . .' Josh starts singing 'The Why Song' to the tune of 'Away In A Manger'.

'Josh! Please!' Lucy feigns despair. 'Did you go to see the *Cutty Sark*?'

'I think it's sunk, Mummy.'

'How did that happen?'

'I think some Red Injuns did it, so we've got to sail to Croatia in this boat instead.'

Lucy turns to me. 'Annoyingly sharp, isn't he? Still keen to move in, Grey?'

'Absolutely.' Which isn't entirely mendacious. The one comes with the other; apparently that is generally the way when you propose to a single mother. But an encounter with Josh is a sobering experience, especially when you've seen him roughly once in his four and a half years. A spirited chap who likes to have his own way and, as one of a family of two, tends to get it. But I've thought about this and I'd still rather go to Croatia with Josh than Caracas on my own. And if I ever get there, I really would have something to write home about.

We order some lunch and Josh is brought to heel on the promise that if he is a good boy and finishes two of his three fish-fingers and at least three of his five potato-skin boats, then Godfather Dominic – the one who didn't attend the christening – will produce a late Christmas present.

'It seems that Dom thinks he might be coming to stay with us, Josh,' says Lucy, which is a fairly loaded but noncommittal response to the marriage question.

'Where's he going to sleep?'

'In Svetlana's room,' she replies. Which was predictable, and begs the question: what if Svetlana hadn't been going away?

'Um, Dom, does that mean you could play dinosaurs with me in the morning?'

'I suppose it does.'

'Yeah!' Josh flourishes his fork and a piece of potato boat falls on to the floor. 'Every morning?'

'I don't see why not.'

'Yeah!' Another piece of potato boat hits the floor. 'Only one more potato boat till present-time, Mummy.'

So, it's not long before Josh has a present in front of him. Its wrapping is unimpressive as it has been in my suitcase for over a week since I left New York, but he doesn't register this, just rips gleefully into it. What he discovers inside makes his eyes light up. Lucy tipped me off well.

'Red Injuns! Hey, cool! Can I take them out of the box, Mummy?'

They are on the table before she has time to answer: five Red Injuns on horseback, two carrying spears, two mid-action with bow-and-arrow and one with an axe in his hand. When you click back the feathers on their heads, they emit a Red Injun war cry, which has Josh in raptures. 'They're so cool,' he says. 'Thank you, Dom.'

'Do you like them?' I reply, milking my moment of triumph.

He looks at me strangely and then at Lucy, as if he doesn't understand the question. 'But I already said thank you, Mummy.'

'I know, you're a good boy.'

'Do you think these are the Injuns that sank the *Cutty Sark*?' I ask, in an attempt to win back some ground. Josh looks at me as if I'm the school dunce and says nothing. Lucy giggles. Josh spares me the embarrassing silence by picking up one of the spear-carrying Injuns and, complete with sound effects, guides him through the air at some speed towards my nose. With no time or room to move, I am forced to take the blow, and feign what seems to me an impressively dramatic death. Josh is convinced by it anyway, because the sight of me dead – or, at the very least, unconscious – in the back of the boat reduces him to a rare state of silence.

'I didn't hit him very hard, Mummy,' he says eventually, clambering over me. When I feel his breath on my cheek and it is clear that our faces are centimetres apart, I decide it is time to come back to life.

'Ha!' I shout, simultaneously getting to my feet and hoisting Josh above my head. It's not textbook Greenwich-café behaviour, but Josh finds it funny, his laughter is interspersed with gasps to be put down.

He returns to playing with the Injuns. 'Dadadadadiddly-diddlyda,' he half mumbles, half sings.

'What's he singing?' I ask Lucy.

'It's good news. He always does that when he's happy.'

Coffee arrives and a strawberry ice-cream for Josh. Everyone seems happy. I get the bill. Svetlana has to leave for the airport.

'What did you get for Christmas?' I ask Josh.

'Red Injuns.'

'Anything else?'

'Not much,' he replies, without looking away from the spear-carrying Injun in his hand.

'I bet you did.'

'I didn't get what I wanted.'

'What did you want?'

'Don't, Josh,' Lucy interrupts.

There is a brief silence as Josh contemplates his response. 'I wanted a new daddy. I told Mummy that and she wrote it for me in the letter we sent up the chimney to Father Christmas.' The spear-carrier has now been discarded and Josh is talking loudly at Lucy with blame clear in his voice. 'And I didn't get one, did I, Mummy? And I've tried to be a good boy about it and not complain, but that was the only thing I really wanted. Wasn't it, Mummy?' Josh stops. He looks on the verge of tears. 'Wasn't it, Mummy?'

6

We leave the Galley as a family. We jump into Lucy's family car and drive back to Lucy's place – our family home, for now, anyway – in Richmond. Number thirty-eight, Archdeacon Avenue, three bedrooms and a decent garden in a cosy, peaceful street; a nice place for families. Svetlana departs in a taxi for the airport, and Josh shows me to my room – Svetlana's room – which will do for now.

Then it's off to the party. Our first family party. And it is a fantastic, no-expense-spared party with which to kick off family life.

The hosts are Sophie (lovely Sophie née Chamberlain of old) and Marco, her husband, whom she met through Tim. Marco is stinking rich. He is filthy rich too, if it's possible to be both. Whichever is worse – or better – he's it.

Marco was Tim's big mate at the bank that fired him, and his confidant in all matters financial. Marco and Tim could talk share prices and money markets all night, and they'd do so with unconcealed mouth-frothing eagerness and dollar signs spinning in their eyes. And they were welcome to it. They loved sailing too – it was their special thing: weekends on boats talking money, planning their fiscal futures. It had been on one such weekend that they hatched their greatest plan of all, one that would have made Tim a millionaire many times over too had his car not gone off the road.

Marco's speciality was computer systems and before anyone else had thought of it, it seemed, he had started researching rumours of a possible cataclysmic threat to the world's computers that was poised to strike at midnight on the turn of

the millennium. He became king of what came to be known as the Millennium Bug. He told anyone in business who was wealthy enough to listen that, at midnight on New Year's Eve – last night – when they were at their most inebriated, and dancing round in circles trying to recall the words of Auld Lang Syne, calamity would strike and his invisible Millennium Bug would render their computer systems ga-ga and their businesses inoperable. The fat cats believed him. It was brilliant.

Marco was thus one of the leaders of an industry born of their fear. He employed computer technicians to make their computers bug-proof and, if they paid him enough, he gave them a millennium-night guarantee: his army of technicians would remain sober, he told them, and if any bugs were to strike on the night, SWAT teams would be dispatched to do battle with them.

If Tim's car hadn't gone off the road, he'd have been in there with Marco, fifty-fifty. As it was, Marco took all the profit for himself. He moved his family to Bermuda as tax exiles and from there he marketed and masterminded the Millennium Bug, returning to head office in London for the ninety days a year he was allowed in the country.

There was only one minor drawback in all this: Marco missed last night. He missed the Auld Lang Syne and the dancing around in circles because he had to sit in head office with his SWAT teams on the slim off-chance that the Bug might materialise. Funnily enough, it never did. And there was one major plus in all this: because he had missed last night, and because he was suddenly ludicrously wealthy, he decided to throw his own new-millennium party. Not that he would do the throwing himself, he would get others to organise everything, from the sending of the invitations to the personalised 'Marco and Sophie wish you a Happy New Millennium' message on the loo roll. He would just write the cheque. It would be a huge party, a no-expense-spared party, a day late. And here we are, in the Kensington Roof Gardens and it looks like money well spent.

'Bloody Mary, sir?' asks the waiter in attendance at the top of the lifts. 'Or something else for the hangover? Champagne cocktail? Resolve? Paracetamol? Guinness?'

I take the Bloody Mary, Lucy the champagne, Josh an orange juice and we walk through to a large room stylishly decorated in red and black: every inch of the ceiling is covered with red and black helium balloons, huge red and black crêpe flowers obscure the walls, while the waiters and waitresses are in black and red outfits. I have no idea what the red and black theme is intended to signify.

Although it's pleasure to be the beneficiary of some of Marco's wealth, I find it hard to focus on the party because I've just moved in with Lucy. That's all I can really focus on. It's surreal, unthinkable, and I'm buzzing inside. I'm inside the bloody house! With my own clothes and underwear! I don't want to be at the party, no matter if it is Marco whose Bloody Marys we're drinking: I want us to be back at the cosy homestead together. And I've no idea what I'd do if we were there. Would I play it cool or would I play the nervous teenager, tentatively dangling an arm round her on the sofa? I don't know. An arm? Round my best friend? All I know is that I'm not the only one bending the rules here. It's not just me. I'm *sure* it's not just me. I *think* it's not just me. Or maybe I'm wrong. But it feels as though I'm not the only one who's slightly tight, emotionally high, strangely excited, looking for reassurance, glancing furtively to see if there might just be something genuine in all this or whether it's just the punchline of a fourteen-year-old joke.

So, the party's an ordeal. Because Lucy is gregarious, popular, interesting, inspiring and a glittering party guest, she will be a social butterfly. And I, because I'm still self-conscious in company, especially among people I knew at university with whom I've lost touch but who remember me as the quiet one Tim rescued from the road to Caracas, will shift from foot to foot, thinking of our family home. I'll put on a good show, though: it's not as if I've learned nothing in advertising.

First, we sort out Josh. Along a walkway, there is a large marquee over the Spanish Garden and it looks like kids' heaven: bouncy castle, entertainer, a bloke on stilts with a red plastic nose, and a corner with sofas, cushions and a big-screen television showing cartoons. Josh spies Sam, his best friend, and that is the last we see of him.

We walk back to the main party. 'Our first social engagement as a couple,' I say, not entirely seriously.

Lucy laughs. 'We're a couple, are we?'

'I don't bloody know.'

'Well, don't mention a word of it. OK?'

'Why? Are you ashamed of me?'

'No.' She shoves me amicably. 'I'm actually very proud of you.'

'You sound serious.'

'I *am* serious. But I still don't want a word of it mentioned.'

'Fine.' I decide to do the teenage arm-round-the-shoulders trick – but only for laughs. And it works. We walk towards the mêlée of people, Lucy giggling as we go.

We immediately locate Bill and Alice. Good old Bill and Alice who met in a Jane Austen tutorial and married two years after we left, then reproduced in quadruplicate, two boys, two girls, two blonde, two dark, with exactly two years and two months between each arrival, the youngest and blondest being Josh's friend, Sam. Despite the four-child burden, Bill and Alice remain about as solid and reliable a unit as I have ever known. When divorce has finished reaping its unpleasant harvest of our generation, Bill and Alice will be the last couple left standing, Bill with his sweaty complexion, his safe job as a solicitor and his Volvo estate, and Alice forever chiding him for telling bad jokes and showering him with affection. Splendid, warm Bill and Alice, already middle-aged, always middle class and about as perfect a blueprint as I could hope to find. Maybe Lucy and I will be left standing too.

'Hello, darling.' Lucy slips out from under my arm and greets Alice, her best friend, with a kiss.

We all kiss. Then Bill tells me how sorry he is about Nadia and me. 'Final nail in the coffin and all that, is it? Really? God, she was bloody lovely, but I don't suppose you need me to tell you that.'

'Not really.'

'You all right? It must be a nightmare.'

'Yeah, I'm fine, actually.' I should, I suppose, be knee-deep in mourning, but the grief hasn't even reached my ankles and I just had my arm round Lucy. 'But obviously it's been hard.'

'Poor old you, Dom,' Alice chimes in.

'Oh, don't worry about me.' I try to play the brave wounded soldier.

'Of course we worry about you! I mean, what are you going to do with yourself now?'

'I'm moving in with Lucy.'

The comment has the desired effect. Bill almost spills his drink, and Alice, aghast, turns to Lucy. Lucy stares at me with incredulity, but she's smiling too.

'Yes, aren't I lucky?' she says. 'Dominic's come to help around the house while my au pair's on holiday. You must come round. I'm sure he'll cook for us too.'

'Of course,' I respond. 'What night are we free, darling?'

'Not sure, darling. Alice and I'll do diaries.'

And so Alice and my little darling go into a huddle and Bill starts quizzing me on my career. Where is it going? What am I doing? How important am I?

'I'm not sure,' I tell him. I'm not. Neither do I know, I explain, where I'm going to be working or in what direction my career's going. I don't add that part of the reason I'm not sure is because I haven't a clue whether Lucy sees me as the fill-in au pair or the future husband. So I tell him about my book. 'It's fiction.'

'What's it about?'

'Love.'

Bill laughs disbelievingly.

'I promise you.'

'What about love?'

'That's all the information I'm prepared to give, mate. Sorry.'

'Well, what's the storyline?'

'Sorry. Not telling.'

'Why not?'

'I haven't told anyone. I guess I'm too self-conscious.'

'Does it contain fantastically dirty sex scenes?'

'Would you buy it if I promised you it did?'

'Of course I bloody would. We've got four children, don't forget. Fantastically dirty sex scenes – if I shut my eyes and think hard, I can just about remember them. When can I read it?'

'If it's ever published, I'm sure you'll find a shop that will sell you a copy.'

'Oh, great, thanks! Well, tell me this, do I appear in it?'

'My lips are sealed.'

'Do I feature in the sex scenes?'

I shake my head.

'Give up, Bill!' Lucy has overheard the conversation and can't resist joining in. 'You're not going to get anywhere! I've tried – and he's bloody impossible to prise open. He won't tell anyone. Not even his new landlady. God, it's so infuriating!'

'Would it make it any easier for you if I paid you rent?' I ask teasingly.

'No, it would not. I don't want a rent-boy. I want to read your manuscript.'

'I'd rather be your rent-boy.'

'But seriously,' interrupts Bill, with seriousness in his voice, 'is this a new career for you, Dom?'

And that's a hard question to answer. Because I don't know whether I'm still an advertising star or not; I don't know whether I want to be. Some people – people in finance – want Jerry and me to start our own agency. Dylan and Duffy have given me three months' sabbatical with an office in their London head-quarters to work out my future, but what they really want is for Jerry and me to come up with another world-famous ad

campaign, most probably with a trite catchphrase involving the word 'testicles'. What I *really* want is to get my book published.

'Hello, darling.' It's Sophie – tanned, Bermudan, well-groomed Sophie – with a timely intervention. 'So sorry about Nadia.'

'Thanks. It's been hell, you know.' I'm quickly learning the role I'm expected to play.

'Poor thing.'

A hand presses my shoulder and I spin round. 'Hi Marco.' The host, far balder than I am and fuller in the waist than he was when I last saw him, shakes me firmly by the hand.

'Good Lordy, Lordy.' He likes to call me 'Lordy Lordy'.

'Great party,' I say, ignoring the long-running and never notably amusing joke.

'Thanks, Dom. Good of you to come, you know, what with that bloody Nadia thing going on.'

'Oh, fuck it. That's what I say. Might find someone else here, you never know.'

'Quite right.'

The sarcasm was lost on him.

'Want any introductions?'

'Err . . .'

'Not many singletons left, actually. Couple of second-time-rounders, though.' Marco, generosity personified, scans the room for a replacement wife and I watch Lucy, her eyes glittering, effortlessly exercising her mastery of small-talk with Sophie.

'Clean up big time last night did you?' I ask Marco. But he is already looking for someone better to talk to. I'll never be as good at this as Lucy, I think, and attach myself to her side.

'When are you coming to Bermuda?' Sophie asks.

'As soon as I have the money and a spare week, I'm there,' Lucy replies.

'I've heard that before, Lucy.'

'I'm not just saying it this time. It's really, honestly one of my New Year's resolutions, I promise.'

'Fantastic. I'll warn the island.'

And so on and so on. More small-talk. We meet Ross and Jo, good old faces, and Rhys – whom I like – and Emily, whose fantastic figure has gone AWOL, and the bloke whose name I've forgotten who somehow managed to marry Sarah. Emily drapes a maternal arm round me and serves up another dose of post-Nadia medicine. Rhys is far too frivolous to offer sympathy – which is probably why I like him – and asks if my impending divorce is part of a grand plan designed to hitch myself up to the girl in the Peachey's ice-cream ad. Then he launches into an impassioned defence of the single life and reels off his top five girls whom he would go out with if he wasn't married to Emily. The Peachey's girl is at number three, Lucy comes in at number five, and Emily smiles throughout at her endearing fool of a husband. She has clearly heard all this before.

But at least Rhys is a variation on the theme of the evening: more old faces, more questions about my future, more caring, sharing questions about the death of my marriage, which are followed by wincing expressions of sympathy. Lovely people who care, I suppose. But I whisper in Lucy's ear that I think I'll go and check up on Josh. She is surprised and impressed.

Three-quarters of an hour later, Lucy finds me. I'm still checking up on Josh, I explain to her from the depths of a plastic-covered sofa where I'm involved with him, Sam and about twenty-five other children in a hot debate about whether we should have a rerun of *Toy Story* or go for *The Jungle Book*. I am all in favour of *The Jungle Book* – famous old tunes, bare necessities and all that – I explain. But Lucy's scowl and her crossed arms suggest that she's not convinced either way.

'Come on, we're going home.' Her voice is uncharacteristically hard.

'Oh, Mum!'

'Don't start, Josh.' The instruction is accompanied by a wagging index finger. 'Come on, boys.'

And that's that. It is a tone with which you don't argue. You

get up and leave. You do as you're told. You say thank you politely to your hosts. And Josh understands it better than I do.

Lucy, however, takes rather longer to say goodbye than we do. Indeed, her goodbye to Sophie is lengthy and initially less than cordial and, though I cannot hear her words, her tone has that same hardness.

She looks lovely, though. Even when she's cross.

7

Lucy leads a hasty retreat up the road to her car, her right hand on the back of Josh's head ensuring that he keeps up. Josh doesn't like being frog-marched so I pick him up and put him on my shoulders, which he thinks is fun, especially when I take large, skipping strides so that he wobbles. Lucy, however, remains half a yard in front of us, impervious to fun.

'My mummy can walk very quickly, can't she?' says Josh, unaware of the scowl on her face.

'Yes, you must be proud of her,' I reply. Lucy's expression softens.

But she remains in an efficient, business-like mood all the way home, telling Josh that it's late, past his bed-time, that it's straight into the bath and bed when we get back and that, no, no matter if he is a good boy and puts on his pyjamas without having to be asked seventeen times, there will still be no time for telly. Or dinosaurs. Or even Red Injuns. Maybe, just maybe, if he asks very nicely, Dom will read him a story before he goes to sleep.

So this is what happens. Lucy gets Josh ready for bed, I am summoned to read him a book. Just one, she says – but I read him two and make him promise not to tell. And when I go downstairs, it occurs to me that I'm getting on better with Josh than I am with his mother.

'You're smoking!' I say, with surprise. Lucy doesn't smoke.

She is sitting in the kitchen, an elbow leaning on the table, her forehead resting in the palm of her hand and there is a far-off look in her eyes. She has changed into jeans and a cream woollen cardigan with a red flower woven into the back. She hasn't answered me.

I decide to break the silence again. 'You don't seem to be enjoying much the first day of our new life together.'

Suddenly she smiles. 'Sorry,' she says, shaking her head and widening her eyes, as if to wake herself up. 'These,' she holds up the cigarette guiltily, 'I know.' She shrugs. 'Here.' She pats the place at the table next to her. 'Our new life together, eh?' she says, and drifts off again, then snaps back. 'Do you want one?'

'A new life together?'

'No, a fag!' She laughs.

'Can I have both?'

'A fag would be easier.'

'Easy's boring. And since when have you been smoking?'

'I don't know – not since Tim, if that's what you're thinking. I don't really smoke. My current packet's lasted since November. Just one every now and then when I need it.'

'And why do you need one now?'

'That's why I want you to come and sit here so I can tell you.'

I take my place at the table. Lucy has one last puff on her cigarette before she stubs it out and turns to face me.

'I don't like this subject, Grey – in fact, I hate it, and with Tim gone it's barely possible to deal with it.' Her words are measured. 'So I don't deal with it. I don't even talk about it. I pass by on the other side. But with you being you, and you knowing Tim, and you being here, and this being the first day of our wonderful new life together . . .' She raises her eyebrows and the corners of her mouth and God knows what that means. 'Here's what I'm talking about.

'Did you see that girl Vicky tonight?' she asks. And then she describes her. Short dark hair, probably slightly older than us, good-looking in a not-too-obvious way, wearing a straight blue sleeve-less dress. Arrived on her own about twenty minutes before we left, didn't look particularly comfortable, talked to Marco for a bit.

'Sorry,' I reply. 'Don't know who you mean. I was watching *Toy Story*.'

'Yes. Doesn't matter. Anyway, the point is this. She used to work at the bank with Tim. I met her a couple of times, on those Friday nights back when I would go drinking with him and his workmates. She seemed quite nice, actually. Anyway, about a year and a half before he left the bank, Tim was staying overnight in Peterborough – I know, the glamour of it – because he had some business with clients up there. Anyway, I rang him at his hotel, the Peterborough Radisson, late that night and got Vicky's bloody voice at the end of the line. The stupid tart answered his phone. Tim's probably told you all this, hasn't he?'

I shake my head.

'The bastard was playing around. That's the long and the short of it. He didn't try to deny it – at least he was honest about it. Did he really not tell you?'

'I was probably the last person Tim would tell if he'd done something to upset you.'

Lucy puts her left hand on my right. 'Anyway, after that we were bloody awful for a while. Not surprising, really. I did the drama-queen bit, told him I'd had enough and that it was all over. But he swore it'd never happen again and did his hand-some, charming, gorgeous, all-too-believable and here's-yet-another-bunch-of-bloody-flowers Tim act on me and persuaded me that we should move in together. So we did . . .' she stops, a watery glaze in her eyes, and manages an unconvincing smile '. . . and got married two and a half years later.'

'Come here.' I put my right arm round her and pull her towards me so that I can feel her tears on my neck.

'So why does she have to fucking turn up at the party today? That's what I want to fucking know,' she says, with a hardness that surprises me. She sits up suddenly and thumps the table hard. 'Jesus Christ. The bitch.'

'Was that what was up between you and Sophie at the end?'

'Yes. Sophie said Marco invited her. She'd never even met her – she certainly didn't know the history.'

I get up out of my chair and lean against the sink. 'But, Lucy,

isn't that what this is? History? You're beating yourself up over something that must have taken place about nine years ago.'

'I know.' She swivels round to face me, dabbing her eyes and trying to smile. 'But . . .' she sighs '. . . I find it hard – because there's an image of Tim that I want to remember. You know the one: great, lovely, swashbuckling Tim, my Tim, Tim the entertainer, Tim the lead man. I have mental pictures of him with Josh on his shoulders or singing his song at the end of a party. And because he's dead, that shouldn't change. I should be able to treasure it, shouldn't I? Isn't that my right?'

'I suppose so.'

'So I find it really hard when evidence like Vicky strays into view. It distorts my picture. I want to be at peace with Tim – I've got to be, for my sake. I'm perfectly aware of that, as you know rather better than anyone. So, Grey,' she stops and shakes her head and continues gently, 'I'm sorry to have been so twisted and angry, but when Vicky walked into that party, it just stirred up stuff that I'd tried to lay to rest.'

I say nothing. I know Lucy well enough not to. She doesn't want advice, top tips on emotion management or even clumsy male sympathy. She just wants me to look into her eyes and show that I understand.

Suddenly her face changes. 'Were you ever unfaithful to Nadia?'

'No.' My answer is almost too quick.

'Even though you never really loved her?'

'No!' Defiance is in my voice. It's too late to change my tune. 'Not until I'd given up trying to love her and told her I was leaving.'

'Good.' She smiles. 'That's important.' And with that she stands up purposefully, takes a bottle of white wine from the fridge and two glasses from a cabinet next to it. 'Come on,' she says cheerily, and walks through to the sitting room.

'So,' she settles back into a dark blue sofa, her eyes smiling, 'what about that new life of ours?'

'Oh, Christmas.' I pour the wine to buy me some time.

'Tell me about it,' she says, amused to be putting me under pressure.

'I have. Christmas. It'll be like Christmas every day.'

'Very good. Anything else in your sales pitch?'

'Hmm. The brochure says it's sunny every day too ... that there's world peace – at least, there is in Archdeacon Avenue – that the trains start running efficiently and hospital waiting lists go down, my hairline stops receding –'

'Thank goodness for that!'

'– England win the World Cup, Josh scores the winning goal, and there is no dispute over whether the ball crossed the line. That point probably went over your head. Um, what else? I become a best-selling author, television chiefs decide to ban reality TV shows, the Rolling Stones come out of retirement again and are banned from drawing a pension unless they carry on playing until Mick Jagger reaches a hundred and fifty. Sounds pretty reasonable to me.'

Lucy is still laughing. I'm doing a good job.

'So what's in all this for me?' she demands.

I sit back on the sofa while I ponder my reply. Her dark eyes are full of life again.

'You?' I answer, as if surprised that she should be concerned about herself. And then, without having intended it, I realise I'm about to be sincere. 'You,' I say gently, 'find happiness.'

And suddenly everything's different. Because we both know that I have changed the tone: a slight inflection and this isn't a joke any more. I have been the first to show my hand. And I don't mind. I guess I was prepared for this – I couldn't keep my cards secret for the rest of my life. But that doesn't make the act of declaration any easier. I am out of the closet, self-conscious, aware of the touch of our legs, my heartbeat quickening. Part of me wants to look away because I still don't feel I belong in this situation, but I don't, I gaze confidently at Lucy. I want it too much.

And she doesn't recoil. Which is good news because, of all scenarios, that is the one I have imagined most. Instead Lucy does a Lucy. She narrows her eyes, as if she is asking whether I really meant that.

I nod.

She smiles. We're having a Dominic-Lucy conversation without words.

Really? she asks. But she doesn't say it: the question is in the slight raising of her eyebrows.

I nod again.

She drops her head, as if pausing for thought, then meets my gaze again and brushes her hand across the back of my head, letting her fingers run through my hair. She never does that. 'Tell me,' she says softly, 'do you really, *really* think we could be happy?'

'Why else do you think I was waiting for you up that hill today?'

Again, the narrowing of the eyes, those minute movements of her face. You can't be serious, she is saying.

Again I nod, because I can.

'You really think this outrageous plan could work?'

'I think we'd be tossing away the chance of a lifetime if we didn't try.'

'And,' she pauses, 'do you think it would stop you going bald?'

'I'm prepared to give it a go.'

Lucy's face breaks into a grin and I can withhold mine no longer. She collapses into me, laughing, her head against my chest as I laugh too.

But the laughter dies and all that is left to fill a pregnant pause is Lucy, lying almost across me, looking into my face, those large dark eyes narrowed again and brimming with meaning. She caresses my face and I brush away the dark hair that has fallen across hers and slide it behind her ear, stroking her temple as I firm it into place. And then in one same movement, I find myself gently pressing my lips to her ear.

This hadn't been remotely planned. At least, not the ear element. As passes at women go, it would never make it into the coaching manuals, the move in on the ear is not a clever one, it isn't one I've employed before and it came from nowhere, pure instinct. From temple-stroking to ear-kissing in one unpredictable move. But again, to my surprise, Lucy doesn't recoil. Indeed, she remains unmoved, almost as if to let the ear-kiss linger.

'You like my left ear?' she asks.

'My secret is out.'

She tuts and sits back against me, laughing. 'You should have told me. I'd have made more effort with it, given it a sunbed session or something.'

'Don't be ridiculous,' I reply. 'It's a very reasonable left ear just as it is.'

'And what was that thing about the ball crossing the line?' she asks.

'It's a reference to the 1966 World Cup final. Geoff Hurst appeared to have scored a goal for England but no one was sure if it had crossed the line.'

'Goodness! How exciting! What happened?'

'The Russian linesman awarded the goal. He decided that the ball *had* crossed.'

'And is that kind of metaphorical?' she asks.

'What do you mean?'

'Well, do you think maybe you crossed the line with that assault on my left ear?'

'Sorry.'

'Don't be.' She takes my left hand and squeezes it. 'But I think I'd better go to bed. Otherwise, if I've got anything to do with it, that Russian linesman really will be waving his flag.'

8

A history of infidelity in two short parts.

PART ONE: MINE

My watch said it was just before one o'clock when I slipped out of bed – Svetlana's, that is – walked lightly past Lucy's bedroom and came downstairs.

I can't sleep. Too much in my head. I poured myself an orange juice, came into the sitting room and am now leaning against the back of the sofa, taking in the photographs of Tim that fill the antique card table, a little shrine of seven black-and-white portraits in seven silver frames. And I'm feeling guilty. Guilty because the new millennium, the rebirth of me and Lucy, which found 'us' on this sofa flirting like nervous teenagers, and me diving in for that ear-kiss – had begun with a lie.

'Were you ever unfaithful to Nadia?' she asked.

The first time I was unfaithful to Nadia – I might have said – was eight months into our marriage one boozy night after a girl from work called Kathy had pulled up her shirt, lain back on a bar in Manhattan and insisted I lick the salt for a tequila shot off her tummy. Kathy was a third-generation Irish American from Boston, dyed blonde, young, sassy, a few rungs into an impressive ascent of the ladder at Duffy's. Nice tanned and toned tummy too, but that detail wouldn't have endeared me to Lucy much either.

I could also have said that the second time I was unfaithful was a week later. With Kathy. No tequila required. I could have added that I cooled it with her after that, steeled with

60

determination to make my marriage work. I could have added further that I'd had little choice but to cool it with Kathy because she had worked up an enthusiasm for me and started telephoning me at home. As if I had shared the whole truth and nothing but, I could have thrown in the fact that my steely pro-Nadia resolve held for just three and a half months. Different girl that time. Not that it mattered.

But I don't think I'm a serial adulterer. I just married badly.

America fitted the bill for me: the land of opportunity. Caracas? Who needed it? I was English, earning well, self-assured at last, I could sing 'Jetplane' all on my own, and my success in advertising had given me confidence and the awareness that I could be fast with language, witty – I could say the right things easily and with conviction – exactly as I have with Lucy just now. It seemed that I was suddenly reasonably desirable. And with plenty to write home about, pre-Nadia, two postcards home in one month. Felicity, then Grace. My mother sent back a card with a cartoon drawing of a man who had lined up five pairs of shoes and was filling them with water from a kettle. 'George had heard it was good to fill his boots,' was the caption under-neath. My mother's note was two-worded. 'Take care.'

But I didn't require her counsel. I wasn't interested in making up for lost time. I settled: first with Joy, then with Grace and in between with Felicity. Given the precedent, I was waiting, natu-rally, for someone called Bonnie, Bella, Gloria, Lifelong Happiness or Drop Dead Gorgeous to come along next. So there was no irony lost when I took a shine to Nadia. In our happier times, I would stress the second syllable of her name – 'Nad-ir, you are my Nad-ir.' But I was being sarcastic then.

We met through the ad agency. She was an assistant producer in a TV production company we'd employed to shoot an ad. Italian, long black wavy hair, lips that looked implanted but weren't, had done some modelling but was told she wasn't tall enough to succeed: my fantasy girl. Or so I thought. The shoot was in California and on the last night Nadia and I stayed up

until breakfast sharing life stories and each other's bodies. Later she would introduce me to cocaine, Brooklyn and an undiscovered erogenous zone in the small of my back. I was so swept off my feet that by the time I was back on them, she was pregnant and I'd agreed to marry her.

In the eleventh week of the pregnancy, Nadia lost the baby. She was consumed by guilt and a desperate longing. The guilt was the Italian Catholic in her. She barely left our flat for three weeks. I would come home from work to find her crying, still in the black silk dressing-gown she had been wearing when I left. My sympathy was nevertheless so deep that it carried me up to the wedding and out the other side.

It was only when we had settled down as husband and wife that Nadia was herself again. And it was then I realised that I wasn't as fond of her as I had previously imagined. Ours was an intensely physical relationship, so much so that at our worst times she would hit me and throw at me items that had recently arrived from our wedding list. The barbecue tongs hurt. But she was small and generally a bad shot, so wounds were rare and, anyway, my self-defence improved as I learned to second-guess her explosions of fury. I also mastered the art of riling her – she was a simple tease – but she would infuriate me by running back to her parents. I felt as if I was taking on the whole family each time we rowed.

I didn't like myself much in all this. I didn't recognise or approve of the behaviour it brought out in me, though taking that tequila shot, and everything that followed, was a weight on my conscience that I found surprisingly easy to bear. What depressed me was not that I had become an adulterer but the knowledge, so early in our time together, that I had got my choice of life-partner so wrong. It irked me that I was thirty-two years old and yet, like some innocent, I had failed to see beyond the obvious two dimensions of the girl I married. I suspected, too, that Tim knew I'd been fooled and that irked me too.

So, I don't believe that infidelity is in my genes. I knew that

Nadia was a mistake, so cheating on her seemed not to matter. But I was unfaithful nevertheless. And I had lied to Lucy.

PART TWO: TIM'S

In the yellow light from the lamps of Lucy's sitting room, those seven smiling images of Tim on the card table make him look so handsome, noble and god-like that you would never believe he might have strayed with a girl called Vicky, or Penny or Dolores or whatever.

I hadn't known about Vicky but I can believe it. I certainly couldn't believe it when I first witnessed it, with Penny, and challenged him over it.

'What the fuck do you think you're doing?' I remonstrated. It was a Sunday at Durham, it was Tim's birthday and he was excited about it. One of the many elements of his boyish charm was that he never seemed to grow out of birthdays. Especially when they were his own. He happened to share his with Lucy's mother and, because she was turning fifty, Lucy had chosen to go to Scotland for the weekend. He didn't like that and viewed it as justification for sauntering into the pub at lunch-time, grinning widely, and announcing that he had come fresh from a long morning's lie-in with the newspapers and a blond Mancunian law student called Penny. I remember that grin, which suggested he had done something clever, and even after I'd challenged him it remained.

I came back at him a second time, poking him on the sternum as I spoke: 'Tim, what on earth are you playing at?'

'Come on, Dom,' he replied. 'Don't be so harsh. It's my birthday.'

'Don't be *so* pathetic,' I replied. My tone finally registered with him. Tim wasn't used to being spoken to like that, certainly not by me. He saw that I wasn't going to let the subject rest and his face darkened. He motioned me towards the door and took me outside for a lesson in the facts of life. 'Noble Dominic,' he

called me, 'Lucy's puppy.' He told me that what he did was none of my business, that I should wise up, and that just because I'd shaken off the shackles of virginity, it didn't mean I'd lost my innocence. 'I suppose,' he said, 'you still believe in Father Christmas?'

'It's not about Father Christmas!' I objected. 'It's about Lucy. Don't you respect her?'

'Oh, leave it out.'

'No, I won't!'

'Look,' Tim placed his hands firmly on my shoulders, 'sweet, noble Dominic. You don't understand. Butt out. It's nothing to do with you.'

'But it's very much to do with Lucy.'

'Dom, listen.' Tim's eyes burned threateningly into mine. 'Leave it out.' With that, he turned back into the pub.

So I did. I left it alone. But Tim knew thereafter that infidelity and Lucy was not a subject to share over a jovial pint. He couldn't, of course, keep it from me, we operated too closely for that, but he was discreet, never mentioned it, and when we shared a house together, he never brought strange girls home. Always played away.

'I really do love Lucy, you know,' he said to me, when he returned home guilty one morning. And, in his way, I believe he meant it.

I never knew how often Tim cheated on Lucy. It might have been four times a month or just four times in their time together, and neither do I know if the cheating continued after they were married. All I know for sure is that when Tim, Marco and Bill came to New York for a mini-stag weekend three weeks before his wedding, I found Joy and temporary rapture, and he found one last temptation and couldn't resist it. That was Dolores. She had a stud in the side of her nose, gaps in her teeth and a figure that made jaws drop. To Tim, she was irresistible.

'Come on,' he said that night, again sensing my disdain, even after three hours in a Manhattan vodka bar. 'It *is* my stag.'

And given that I had found Joy, that Marco was pawing a surgically enhanced pair of breasts owned by a girl called Sandy, and that Bill, who would never have contemplated cheating on Alice, was too drunk to register any moral objection, I got into the cab to the nightclub with them and our girls, thus swallowing my one pathetic statement of silent censure. It was easier to participate and let myself be swept along on Tim's irresistible tide than to object. And it *was* his stag.

Neither do I know how much Lucy was aware of all this. The stag weekend never leaked out. Mancunian Penny did, though, and Tim was *persona non grata* for two weeks while Lucy insisted that it was all over between them, staunchly fending off his efforts at a rapprochement. She succeeded until one Sunday night, at about half past twelve, when she – with the rest of the girls in the wing of her hall of residence – was awoken by the Frank Sinatra soundalike serenading her from the grassy bank below her window. Tim had sung 'Fly Me To The Moon' and was half-way through 'I've Got You Under My Skin' when she relented.

I remember the conviction with which she told me the next day that she knew Tim would never stray again. I replied meekly that she was probably right, but I suspected that if he was in for the proverbial Penny, riches were yet to come.

9

A sudden sharp pain in my temple wakes me. It's a stabbing sensation that I feel a second time, as I hear a high-pitched yodel. This is 'Good morning' Josh style, with one of the spear-carrying Red Injuns. I sit up in bed quickly, to save myself from the rest of the fighting force. It is exactly seven o'clock. The axe-wielding Injun, the pair with bow-and-arrow, two plastic dinosaurs, a Spider-Man figurine and a plastic chicken are lined up in my doorway, facing me as if for battle.

'Mummy said you'd play Red Injuns with me!' says Josh.

'She did, did she?'

'Yes. And she said that I'm to give you a T. Rex because otherwise you'll lose and you might be sad.'

'How thoughtful of her. And she's going to bring me coffee and get breakfast, is she?'

'No. She's going back to sleep. She says I need time with my godfather who didn't come to my christening.'

So Red Injuns commences. I am directed to the battlefield, which is stretched across Josh's bedroom floor. A shoe-box of other plastic models is emptied and divided between our two sides, and I am handed the chicken and told to protect it because it isn't very strong. There are no apparent rules to the game but Josh plays a masterstroke from the off by laying my tyrannosaurus on its side and explaining that the poor chap has been up all night, is tired and needs to go to sleep. Moments later, it is no surprise to find one of his Red Injuns steaming across the room and descending upon my defenceless chicken. The poultry was my army's Achilles heel.

'That'll be straight to the battle hospital for your chicken,' he says earnestly.

'Ah, yes, of course. Poor chicken. And it's not as if you didn't warn me.'

'Um, Dominic,' he says, 'do you think a Red Injun would win in a fight with Spider-Man?'

'Only the Red Injun with the axe would stand a chance,' is my considered reply, 'because he needs to be able to chop Spider-Man's arm off to stop him spinning webs.' That, however, turns out to be a forlorn hope: Spider-Man is on Josh's side so he is immediately in the fray and, with all the appropriate sound effects, annihilates my spear-carrying Injun.

It is a somewhat one-sided battle. I am continually ferrying my injured men/chickens/whatever to where Josh instructs me is the hospital at the corner of his Lego box. I am forbidden to wake my dinosaur, and when I improvise by commandeering a truck from the Lego box, Josh furrows his brow and shakes his head. Eventually, however – operating under the certainty that it would be good for Josh's upbringing and understanding of the world if he were to sustain some collateral damage – I reinvent my chicken as 'the wonder-hen with super-rooster powers' and bring it down on the head of Josh's axe-wielding Red Injun.

'Dominic!' yells Josh with the despair of a wronged man. 'The wonder-hen can't kill an Ind— Oh, Dominic!' He glares at me, eyes welling. 'Look what you've done!' He's shaking with fury. He picks up the Injun by its feather. The wonder-hen has inflicted on it a horrible injury: it has broken the electrical connection and deprived the proud man of his war cry. 'Oh, Dominic!' Tears are now spilling out of Josh's eyes and he hurls the Injun angrily across the room.

Not good. Any more volume from Josh, Lucy will wake up and my use as a surrogate father will be negated. I beseech Josh to pipe down but the effect is the opposite. 'Please, Josh, I'm really sorry.'

'It's your fault!'

'I know – but the wonder-hen can't be absolved of all responsibility.'

He glares at me. Does he know what absolved means? Or responsibility?

'I'm terribly sorry.'

Still glaring.

'We'll definitely get you another.'

'Really?'

'Yup.'

'When?' I've hit the right spot.

'Soon. Promise.'

'OK. Don't do that again with the wonder-hen.'

We agree to postpone the battle and go downstairs for breakfast. Before long, following Josh's instructions to the word, I have produced a breakfast of boiled egg and soldiers to be washed down with a can of Diet Coke. Really a can of Diet Coke? Yes, really, he insists, with certainty in his voice. He always has Diet Coke for breakfast.

'Come on, then,' I urge. 'Let's have it in front of the telly.'

Breakfast with television hadn't struck me as the height of liberty but Josh is delighted with the idea and we settle down to watch cartoons, the delicate bond of friendship restored.

It is about an hour later when Lucy appears. I am greeted with a big thank-you, a peck on the cheek and no indication that the status quo between us might have changed. She removes Josh's Diet Coke with an amused tut and joins us in the sitting room with a glass of orange juice.

'Few problems on the battlefield earlier, were there?' she asks.

'Oh, you heard.'

'I went back to sleep. It was wonderful.'

'And how's your left ear?'

'After the sleep I've had? Just about recovered from the shock.'

'Good. And what do you want to do now?'

'I think I'll wear ear-muffs.'

'I mean . . .'

'I know what you mean.' She smiles encouragingly. 'Swings and slides? What do you fancy? Walk in the park? Family swim? Domestic life? That's what you want, isn't it?'

We opt for Richmond Park. We dress warmly, take the football,

tell Josh how clever he is when he points out the deer to us, find Josh's favourite spot by a stream, which is good for throwing stones, and gambol about rosy-cheeked and brimful of fresh air, with all the apparent happiness of a nuclear family togged up for a knitwear ad.

The commercial, however, comes to an end when Josh runs ahead with the football and, after some forethought, I put out my right hand and clasp Lucy's left.

'Aaah!' Lucy immediately rips hers away with shock and embarrassment on her face. She is as surprised by her reaction as I am. 'Hmmm. That was a funny thing to do, Grey.'

'Was it?'

'Well . . . yes . . . It did sort of take me by surprise.'

'Sorry.'

'Don't be.'

'I thought your hand might be cold.'

'Oh, yes. How thoughtful . . . Yes, actually, it is.' She turns away as if she can't bear to look and puts it out, inviting me to hold it. I take it with uncertainty. 'Right,' she says, barely two seconds later. 'That's fine now. Hand nice and warm, thank you very much.' She shoves it rapidly into her coat pocket.

'Good hand-holding, Lula.' I put my arm round her waist, but only in jest. She studies my hand carefully and removes it with her thumb and forefinger as if it is infected. She laughs. The moment's awkwardness has evaporated.

'What *are* we doing?' Lucy muses rhetorically.

'We're like the breasts in the Wonderbra campaign.'

'Pardon?'

'Uplifted, slightly unnatural, possessed of a daring, go-for-it mentality. I don't know about you but that's how I'm feeling. The great thing about that pair was that everyone thought they looked splendid together. And, if I remember rightly, they didn't seem too unhappy about it.'

'Hmmm. They didn't have much choice, did they?'

'I'd say they were probably meant to be together. Like . . .'

I change to the cheesiest tone I can muster '. . . like you and me, remember!'

'Grey,' she kisses my cheek, 'you are a complete and utter tit.'

Back at Archdeacon Avenue, I am once again the entertainment for Josh – Red Injuns and then more Red Injuns – and this remains the case until the tea-bath-book-bed process takes over. This is an early-evening ritual that nothing can disturb. Whether or not there is a frisson of something – anything, surely something, it wasn't just me who noticed something, was it? – between Lucy and me, the electricity is cut off for the hour and a half it takes to rule Josh out of the evening equation. That is non-negotiable. In Archdeacon Avenue, even the most passionate love scenes would be suspended at five thirty p.m. and not resumed until three chapters of *Fantastic Mister Fox* have been read and Josh's light turned out.

While Lucy does the Roald Dahl bit upstairs, I sink into the deep blue sofa downstairs, listening to the last CD she had on, relaxing, enjoying some piano music I had never previously heard, and thinking about the electricity. I have a half-decent bottle of Pouilly Fumé and two healthy-sized wine glasses in front of me to help end the power cut.

I am almost half-way through the bottle when Lucy appears in the doorway, grinning. 'You!' She takes a running jump at the sofa and lands in a tiny bundle next to me. 'Stop it!'

'Stop what?'

'I dunno. Whatever you were doing. What were you doing?'

'Thinking about you.' That half-decent half-bottle makes such confessions easier.

'Oh. Don't stop, then. Carry on. But I'd better pour myself a drink. Thinking anything nice, were you?' The delicate, boyish contours of her face beam at me with encouragement.

I say nothing in response but her answer is in my smile.

'No? Nothing nice?' she probes, trying to wring a compliment from me.

I shake my head.

'You weren't thinking about my ears, then, I hope . . . or particularly my favoured left ear?'

'No. Not ears, really.'

'I could always tape them up.' She cups her hands over them. 'That'd protect them.'

'Right! Enough!' I bark, trying not to laugh. I wallop her gently with a cushion and she tumbles, giggling, into me. Suddenly our faces are inches away and we hold each other's gaze, recognising that we are pausing where we paused last night. Last night hadn't been an aberration, then.

'What do you want?' I ask provocatively.

'I want to be able to curl up next to you on the sofa and watch telly without thinking about what you're thinking or whether you're going to start nibbling my earlobe.' There is not an ounce of sincerity in her voice, but I tease her by taking her at her word. I turn on the television. She grabs the remote control from my hand and turns it off. I snatch it back and turn it on again, pretend to watch a home-improvement programme, despite the challenge of the lilting piano on the music system.

'Right, that's it.' Lucy walks over to the television, turns it off manually, then comes back to sit next to me. 'Come here,' she whispers, and pulls me towards her. Our mouths meet.

And suddenly, now, it's happening. Sixteen years on, the kiss. Our kiss. And it's no ordinary kiss, as if it could be when it's been sixteen years in the waiting and it involves me kissing my dead best friend's wife. She looks as if she means it, though. Her eyes are tightly shut, and I know mine should be too, but I'm looking to check that this is really happening. But over her shoulder I can see the rows of photo-frames with Tim smiling at me. And I'm looking at the clock behind her too, wondering if this is a long kiss – which I think it is. But the point is not how long it is – although long is clearly better than short – but that I don't normally kiss like this.

In my brief history of kissing, I've always done a pretty good

job of it, I think. I've focused on the job in hand, nothing too fancy, but I've put my mouth in the right place and got on with it properly. Instinctively, sensually. It's better that way. I've never done it with so much clatter, hope, wonder, anticipation, and sixteen years of subtext to distract me.

I guess I'm like an Olympic gold-medallist. 'How does it feel?' they are asked, after the culmination of their life's work. 'It hasn't quite sunk in yet,' is invariably the answer. So I close my eyes, too, to let a natural sinking-in process take hold. Lucy kisses me beautifully.

Then our faces are about three inches apart. Lucy narrows her eyes as if to determine my thoughts. But my thoughts are clear. There's probably a bit of feline Cheshire in my features. Lucy smiles too, a can-you-believe-we-did-that smile.

'What's that bloody music?' I ask, breaking the moment.

'Erik Satie. *Gymnopédie* No. 1. Do you like it?' I can feel her breath on my face as she talks.

'I like kissing you.'

'Smoothie!'

'You started it.'

'What?'

'The kissing.'

'I had to.'

'Why?'

'Do you want to talk?'

'Isn't that what we're doing? I'd rather kiss.' And with her lips just three inches away, I mean it.

And we do. Again. All very gentle. It's not an explosion of lust. It's not as if the cork has just popped on sixteen years' suppressed desire. It's not Tchaikovsky's 1812 with fireworks blasting. It's more *Gymnopédie* No. 1. It's gentle. Out of respect? I don't know. I caress her cheek, brushing her ear gently, and move my hand over her shoulder and down her arm until it touches hers and she clasps it. She squeezes my hand, then opens hers so that the tips of our fingers and our palms are

touching. I move my hand up her arm again, then slowly down her side so that it rests on the curve of her hip. She opens an eye quizzically.

I slip the hand further down, by barely an inch. It's gone too far. Lucy pushes me back with a sharp intake of breath.

I stick my hands up, as if held at gunpoint. 'Sorry!'

'No, I'm sorry. It just didn't feel right.'

'Too much?'

Lucy nods.

'Queensberry rules, then?'

'What?'

'Anything below the belt is illegal.'

She nods and her face brightens. 'Yes.'

We sit facing each other, wondering what comes next. 'Good kissing, though,' I say optimistically. 'What a day. Hand-holding in the morning and kissing later.'

'It just suddenly felt wrong. Weird. Didn't it?' There is a contrasting seriousness in Lucy's voice. 'I don't know, Grey. You suddenly made me feel . . .' she gesticulates '. . . like a physical object.'

'Sorry.'

'No! You mustn't be. It's so hypocritical of me.' She pauses, as if she's building up to something significant. 'I've been thinking of you like that all day. I've been thinking all day of what it would be like to kiss you. I've been waiting all day for it. I had to kiss you.'

'Why?'

She sighs, composes herself. 'Grey, listen.' She screws up her face and pounds her chest, then stops and looks pleadingly at me. 'Fuck, I don't know what to say.' She pounds her chest again. 'Look, Grey, there's stuff, real stuff, big stuff, going on in here. I can't articulate it. It's weird. But it's there, and I guess that's why I went up that hill yesterday, because I knew it was there. And I can't say I understand it. I know I couldn't feel more differently about you than I did about Tim. It's a totally different

feeling. Obviously. Yet it's as positive a feeling as I've had since he died and I don't feel I should just cast it aside. This, us, it's not based on physical attraction, is it? It's something deeper. I mean, it wouldn't have been a sixteen-year thing if it was purely physical, would it?' She looks at me for encouragement, and I feel obliged to give it. 'And that's why I had to kiss you. I had to know how it felt, the physical thing. I had to see if I could tick the final box. I had to know if there really could be more with you. I guess this is what I'm saying. Because maybe there could be some kind of an "us". I dunno. Maybe, just maybe. Because there could never be an "us" otherwise.'

'You mean without tipping me off you let our entire future hang on a single kiss!'

'Two kisses.'

'Smartarse!'

'Grey!' She thumps my shoulder playfully. 'I'm being serious!'

'I should hope so.' And I'm serious now too. I pull her towards me so that our legs are entwined and our faces just inches apart again. 'It's not very often that someone tells me so eloquently and with such precision that they think maybe they might kind of like me.'

Lucy chuckles and drops her head on to my shoulder. 'Sorry.'

'Don't be. And don't think of me as a series of ticks in bloody square boxes. Can't I be triangles? Or hexagons? Can't we be different? Isn't that what we're about?'

'It was only an expression.'

'I know.'

'And, yes, we are different.'

'But did I get the tick?'

'Oh, God! I don't know!'

'I can do better, you know, on the kissing front. I was a little distracted.'

'Stop teasing!' She smiles coyly. 'The kissing. Yes, nice. Can I decide my whole future on the back of one – sorry, two kisses? Of course I can't.'

Still only inches apart, we stare into each other's eyes. Does she like me? How can I be thirty-five and turning over thoughts I had at nineteen?

'Great bit of Erik Satie,' I say, as the music ends.

So, what now? Queensberry rules on the sofa. Nerves, Pouilly Fumé, fumbling, edging self-consciously ahead, carefully watching out so as not to break any boundaries or tiptoe unawares over each other's feelings. We watch the news on television and it's like a welcome break, but then it's over and we're back in this situation of our own creation.

'I can't believe we're doing this,' Lucy says.

'I know,' I reply. 'Isn't it bloody wonderful?'

'I hope so. C'mon. Let's go to bed.'

I raise my eyebrows suggestively.

'I mean, let's go to our bedrooms,' she clarifies.

We kiss goodnight outside hers, a proper kiss, but not a great one and not a long one, definitely a 'goodbye' rather than a 'hello' kiss and certainly not an 1812 overture with cannons and fireworks, not even a *Gymnopédie* No. 1, more a kiss to the accompaniment of a grade-one pianist trotting out the theme tune to *The Sting*.

Lucy closes her door, leaving me in the corridor outside. She seems happy. Which is good. I remain standing outside her bedroom – we're like stifled would-be lovers in a film, one on either side of the door, each listening, wondering if they should make a move – but then I hear her brushing her teeth in her bathroom. Stifled doorway love is not reciprocated. At least I left her ears alone tonight. Christ, please don't tag me an ears man!

Suddenly the door opens. Lucy is standing there with her toothbrush in her hand, a dribble of white froth running down the side of her chin. She's caught me – at least, that's how it feels – but she looks at me lovingly as if it's alright to have been caught.

'I've worked it out,' she says. 'Can't we be like the Labour Party?'

'Eh?'

'No real conviction about what we're doing, where we're going or how we're going to get there, just making it up as we go along to see if we can keep everyone happy.'

'OK. Labour Party it is.'

10

The morning after. A trip to Sainsbury's. Could there be a better start to family life? Unless you've got a different supermarket preference, that is . . .

Josh derives boundless fun from running away and hiding, particularly in aisle eight behind a mountain of cut-price chocolate Santas. I can play his game: I'm brilliant at being a hopeless finder. Lucy ticks me off, but I can tell that inwardly she is in full approval of all this man-and-boy bonding. There is little that makes her happier than the sound of Josh da-da-diddly-diddly-da-da-da-ing and now his mumbo-song is in full flow. This remains the case when he elects to sit in the trolley and I spin him round as if he was on a playground carousel. Then I push him at top speed, complete with racing-car noises, straight at the crates of semi-skimmed milk, and bring the trolley to a standstill just inches short.

Me the fun guy; Josh the playmate. Some team. Meanwhile Lucy is able to select her shopping and fills the trolley with an impressive number of two-for-one bargains. Indeed this heralds the only cloud on Josh's sunny horizon. He is now out of the trolley and approaching us bearing a cereal packet plastered with pictures of Michael Owen. 'No, you can't have that, Josh,' Lucy says.

'Oh, Mum! Sam has these. He told me that this is what makes him bigger than me.'

'Sam's full of porkie-pies, Josh.'

'No, Mum, he doesn't like porkie-pies. Whenever we get them at school lunch, he cries.'

'I was speaking metaphorically, darling.'

'Why, Mum?'

'I just was.'

'Why?'

'Don't you start that "why" thing, Josh.'

I intervene. I whisper in Josh's ear and he likes the plan. He starts da-da-diddly-da-ing again and when Lucy's back is turned, he slips the Michael Owen cereal into the trolley.

'You're very naughty,' Lucy whispers to me, aware of the game, but she's enjoying the sight of Josh and me teaming up to play it together.

'C'mon! You'd have bought it if it'd been on a two-for-one.'

'You cheeky bugger.' She squeezes me under the ribs, laughing. All is well.

But we can do this. We can do Sainsbury's, fun, interaction, laughter. There's never been a problem here: this is the high ground for us and our occupation of it has been long and is well established. It's our strength, our foundation stone, our *raison d'être*.

The tricky bit comes about twelve hours later when Lucy is looking cosy and cuddly in stripy pink pyjamas in the corridor outside her room. This is the new ground, the recently annexed territory, the new *us*: The Sexual Life of Dominic L.

So here we are in the corridor, Lucy in pyjamas, not sex-bomb pin-up but wholesome, good, right for me, and we are facing each other outside her bedroom door. We smile, acknowledging where we are: back in this foreign land, back here at bedtime where the *us* thing comes most sharply into focus. Lucy moves to me, slides her hands up my chest, sweeps them across my shoulders, then up to my cheeks, caressing them. Nice move. Bodes well. Her hands slip down the back of my head, her fingers wrap themselves in my hair, and she pulls me down for the kiss. Our eyes meet, hers are laughing, and then she checks. 'Sorry! It just feels funny.'

She's spot on.

'I think it feels right.' I'm being sincere but dishonest.

'I know. I want it to be.'

'It'll happen, Lucy. Don't worry.' I'm not sure if I mean that but anyway . . .

'I know. OK. But not tonight.'

The next night? Lucy exhibits a blatant disregard for the Queensberry rules, but we are still left embarrassed. We are back in the Corridor of Uncertainty and – blimey – it's her hand that's found its way on to my groin. Right there. Fantastic. So I break the rules too. I put mine on her bottom. And she pulls away, laughing.

The night after that we don't even get to break the rules.

And I find myself having to make a mental note. I'm not in this for a fleeting moment's physical gratification. Not with Lucy, never with Lucy. Come on, I'm way above that. I'm here for the long haul. And yet this Corridor thing is hard, it's making us feel awkward. And it was the opposite – the sense of being deeply at ease with each other – that brought us together. We had never previously known awkwardness.

At least, it makes *me* feel awkward. Lucy is more relaxed. 'Ha, ha! We've done it again!' She laughs, shaking her head and simultaneously cupping mine in her hands after our third comedy failure on the landing. 'Bloody useless, we are, aren't we?'

I frown longingly.

'Look, Mister!' She wags her finger at my nose. 'You'll just have to wait.'

'Fine, fine, no problem, honestly.'

'Good.' She raises her eyebrows seductively and closes her bedroom door behind her.

And there's another thing. We're into day five of the new millennium, and Lucy said that Svetlana was going to be away for a couple of weeks. Where will I sleep in ten or so days' time? Will my residency be over? Am I on a two-week trial period? Two weeks to make the short move down the Corridor of Uncertainty, in through Lucy's door and there to stay? That's real pressure. And a decent would-be couple like us could do

without it. We're trying to focus on the job in hand. Or, at least, I am. Has Lucy thought about the Svetlana Predicament? Maybe she's being like the Labour Party and making it up as she goes along.

But I don't find being Labour quite so easy. At least Labour eventually got elected. I've done the kissing thing, but I feel as if I'm still out there campaigning. And I've got ten days to get voted in. Or am I already down to nine?

January 6. I thought I'd take the whole week off, but have reassessed. It might not be a bad thing to get out of the house for a bit. It might be a relief for Lucy too.

'Here.' Lucy pulls me towards her on the front doorstep as I make to leave. She straightens my tie, not because it needed it but to show that the situation amuses her too. Here am I, a regular guy leaving a regular family for a regular job. Kind of. 'You'd better come back,' she says, eyes narrowed with the familiar, laughing suspicion. 'A new family's not just for Christmas.' She kisses me goodbye. And I like it. And I ask myself why I'm going.

I set off for limbo, because I haven't got a regular job. I've just got limbo. My choice. But that was why I was pitching up at the office, and I knew it.

The Dylan and Duffy building is just off Regent Street, an impressive five storeys with a cool designer interior and a receptionist who doesn't know me. The offices are almost all bright and modern, but the one they have found for me is a modest cubbyhole with a single small window that provides me with an excellent view, ten yards away, of the brickwork of a neighbouring building. It is here that I shall spend three months of unpaid sabbatical, trying to suss out which strand of my life – my career in advertising, my career as a writer, my future with Lucy – is going to come out ahead.

But day one doesn't provide any answers, just a liquid lunch at the regular old haunt, the Three Feathers, with Ray, the

agency's creative head. He wears his glasses on a cord and flips them back on to his nose whenever he's trying to express enthusiasm. At lunch with me, the glasses are barely allowed a chance to dangle. The London end of the agency is really going places – at least, that's the message he wants to convey – and he seems particularly excited about the possibility of winning an account with the National Birth Control Association.

'Come on, Dom, why don't you hop up off your arse and come back now?' he asks. 'It's so ripe for you. Stop all this fannying about.'

But one man's fannying about is another's mid-life crisis.

I leave work early. Back to Lucy. After all, we're entertaining tonight, aren't we?

And we do. Brilliantly. As a team. There's native understanding here. We produce three courses. I prove myself notably capable around the kitchen and Lucy is impressed. Bill and Alice seem to enjoy themselves, basking in the wine and, more importantly, my lemon tart.

'Tell us about the book,' they implore me.

'Bugger off!' I reply.

Perfect couple, Bill and Alice. And I get the impression that they quite like being around us too.

'Go on.' Bill's forehead is shiny with sweat. 'Go on. Just a teensy-weensy smidgen of information.'

'I said, bugger off!' I reply, and get back to my role of replenishing everyone's glasses. Wine is consumed copiously, and long before they are gone, Lucy is wearing a hat, turned, in time-honoured fashion, back to front. It's from Josh's dressing-up box, a yellow *Bob the Builder* helmet. That's how drunk she is.

Bill and Alice finish their coffee and bid us farewell. The moment the front door closes behind them, Lucy and I rush breathlessly up the stairs, stopping half-way, as if in a scene from a film, to tear at each other's clothing. Then down the Corridor of Uncertainty and straight in through the bedroom door. At last. Without a second thought. Alcohol and inhibitions. Why didn't

we think of this earlier? We even circumvented the washing-up.

I'm staring at the intricacies of her bedroom, the photos of the ubiquitous Tim, when Lucy jumps off the bed and on to my back. She's so light. I swing her round and we collapse on to the bed together, laughing, Lucy's helmet slipping over her face. I pull it off and our eyes meet. I know I'm somewhat fallible when it comes to reading behaviour, but her smile of approval suggests that it's here-we-go time. Lucy rolls round so that she is lying on top of me. She caresses my forehead then kisses me hard. Suddenly she hops off.

'Wait there!' she orders, wagging a finger. 'Need the loo. Don't budge an inch!'

She skips to the bathroom, and when I hear the flush I turn. Fantastic! There she is in the doorway, grinning self-consciously, one arm against the door frame, a hand on her hip, posing, naked.

She's beautiful in a tiny, fragile, scrawny way. I want to look after and care for her.

My silence, as I watch and admire her, makes her more self-conscious. She clasps her hands protectively in front of herself and gazes meekly at the floor.

'Come here.' I get up, usher her over and lay her on the bed. 'My turn.' I head for the bathroom and turn to mimic her. I wag a finger and repeat, 'Don't budge an inch!'

In less than a minute I am naked in the bathroom doorway. Lucy, I am pleased to see, hasn't budged. But she has fallen fast asleep.

'Morning, boys.'

Lucy is sitting at the kitchen table in her dressing-gown. It is half past ten the following morning. Josh and I have just returned from a lads' breakfast down the road. More male-bonding while Lucy had a lie-in. What more could a man do? I did something else, though: I popped a one-word card in the post to my mother: 'Lucy'. After all, last night's was the sort of progress that's

worth writing home about, wasn't it? At least, that what I thought.

'Morning, Lucy.' I'm offered a cheek to kiss. I linger momentarily in the application but the cheek turns away.

'Josh, could you go and tidy your room, please?' she asks.

'Oh, Mum!'

'Go on, darling.' So he does, and she gestures to me to sit down. 'Sorry about last night, Dom.'

'Don't be.'

'I am.'

'I'm not.' I try to catch her eye but she looks down. 'It was . . .' I shrug '. . . an amusing incident?'

'Look,' she glances up, swallows. 'Grey. It's just a little hard, all this, isn't it?'

'Agreed.'

'I thought maybe getting drunk would make it easier.'

'It nearly did!'

My exclamation mark is unappreciated. 'Well, it hasn't.'

And so, that night, I sidestep the Corridor of Uncertainty in favour of the early-to-bed option. 'Sorry, Lucy, I'm knackered,' I explain. She doesn't try to persuade me otherwise.

11

It was when we were at Durham, and Tim and Lucy were the golden couple, that Lucy and I really got started. The problem with Tim and Lucy was that while they were both golden, to everyone apart from me, I suspect, he seemed the more golden of the two. He partied the hardest and drank the latest yet always seemed the freshest-faced and quickest-witted the next day. Lucy was never an introvert, nowhere near, she didn't trail along in his wake the way I sometimes would do, but that was how she appeared sometimes in comparison, and while Tim was performing – drinking, holding court, leaving on his jetplane – she graduated towards me.

One evening in the first term of our last year, Lucy and I struck out for ourselves. We were in the back room of the Shakespeare. Tim was in his familiar position at the centre of a large group of acolytes and Lucy and I were on the edge of it. Lucy asked if I fancied going out for something to eat. Nothing special. A pizza? Sure. We said goodnight, Tim raised an eyebrow of concern, then smiled approval. We made our escape.

We didn't say as much but I was sure Lucy felt liberated in the same way that I did. We didn't have to sing or drink or perform. Instead we went to a pizza place where we drank and talked until we were, by some distance, the last to leave. Somewhere in this marathon, I told her about my father, how I believed my life had been shaped by his early death. She told me about 'wee Carrie', her younger sister who had died of leukemia when she was two. After we left the restaurant, we continued talking and laughing over a bottle of wine at the cottage in which she lived under the viaduct.

That night Lucy said two things that stuck with me: first, in passing, that she hardly ever talked so openly and personally with Tim. She had never told Tim about wee Carrie, for instance. When she said this, her intention was not to draw a comparison between Tim and me but to demonstrate how much she had enjoyed the evening. Yet it was the comparison that stuck with me.

Second, at around half past midnight when I pulled myself to my feet to go home, she grabbed my hand, clasped it in both of hers and made me swear that we'd go out for dinner together regularly. It was a promise I found easy to make. Until my departure for New York, I kept it three or four times a year. I'd turn up on Tim's doorstep to take his girlfriend/wife out for a pizza – always a pizza – and he would greet my arrival with affectionate mockery. 'How sweet', 'I don't want her out after half past ten', or 'You two and your special relationship. Like Britain and America. You'd bloody go to war for each other.'

But his spirit was so generous that he never begrudged our outings, never questioned them. After they'd moved into Archdeacon Avenue, he asked once, though not entirely seriously, if he could come too. And Lucy chided him tenderly in her reply. 'Now, now, Tim. You know that all Dom and I do is girly talk. You'd never enjoy it.'

Now that I am living in Archdeacon Avenue and have my own room – albeit only for another eight days and hell knows what happens after that – I feel that the girly talk should be getting girlier, the special relationship should be getting stronger and the land masses of Britain and America should be merging (God help us).

Yet in the space of a week, the opposite appears to have happened. We once went out for special pizza nights, now we have TV dinners. A week ago, this wonderfully perceptive, vivacious, scrawny creature had the key to my soul, could unlock it and scrutinise whatever she found inside. Now I have three horrible secrets. I can't tell her about about Nadia, and my life as an adulterer. I can't tell her about being the Labour Party: I

can't tell her that I don't feel I'm very good at it, that I'm not enjoying making it up as we go along, that I hate the awkwardness we've created for ourselves in the Corridor of Uncertainty, that I never know whether the Queensberry rules are on or off, and I haven't a clue whether we've passed the Geoff Hurst test of crossing the line. Because if I did tell her, I'm scared she'd declare that our marriage – which isn't on anyway – is most definitely off. And because of this strange distance between us, I find myself asking what made her set foot on Greenwich Hill. Which is the cause of the third, and most poisonous, thought: maybe she's only interested in my money.

So I decide to get out of town, put some distance between us. Running away is not the most mature response for a young man with a new family, and it is certainly one that surprises my mother, who is waiting for me, in her white Vauxhall outside the station in Tunbridge Wells.

'Where's Lucy?' she asks, disappointment ringing in her voice.

'Ah, yes.'

'And where's Josh?'

'Hello, Mum. *Hello. Nice to see you. How are you?* What happened to the traditional form of greeting?'

'Yes, hello, my darling. But I've only this morning received your postcard. Now you tell me you're coming to stay for the weekend and you're on your own. Don't tell me you got my hopes up for nothing.'

'Mother!'

'Sorry, darling. It's lovely to see you. And I've got you for two nights! This will be the longest you've stayed at home since – I don't know – since you married that Nadia.'

'*That* Nadia?'

'Well, don't tell me there's another.'

'No, I can thank my lucky stars that she is unique.'

'Ah, yes, your lucky stars. Are they of the especially lucky variety today? Or have they lost their shine now that you've come without Lucy and Josh?'

'Am I not good enough on my own?'

'Now, now, darling, let's not wander off along any dark alleys. I've got my own garden path to lead you down. Some splendid new arrivals to introduce you to.'

We pick up where we left off. My mother, her mind a complex filter for the minutiae of words, becomes what I call 'the language police', picking up on the mistakes and banalities that most people take for straightforward English. She does it to me as a way of asserting herself, of reminding me who is the more intelligent. Which is why the language police are always out in force for the first hour or so of our infrequent reunions. It's her bizarre form of 'welcome home'.

'*Sarcococca confusa*,' my mother explains, at home in her garden, pointing to some clustered white flowers.

'They're all shrubs to me, Mother,' I reply.

'And *Chimonanthus praecox*. Wintersweet to you, darling,' she continues, unabashed, determinedly forgetting that although she was once successful in selling me the idea that gardening was a cool, acceptable forum for mother–son bonding, she couldn't keep me teenaged and geeky for ever.

I might not have been geeky at all, had I had a father to balance my mother's idiosyncratic approach to parenting. At least – as I explained to Lucy on our first pizza night – that was a recurring thought I harboured when I met Tim and became aware of the stark differences between us. My father had died of cancer when I was four, leaving the responsibility for my development in the hands of an intellectual, infuriatingly well-read, bridge-playing, once-retired literary agent. Here I am, thirty-one years later, still talking plants with her in the garden where so much of our mutual fondness was forged.

'You see how the cold has killed that camellia right at the base?' she says, kneeling down beside a small wilted evergreen.

'Aha.'

'Is that like you and Nadia?'

As sharp as ever. 'Back in the Garden of Life, are we, Mother?'

'All the world's a garden, I've told you that, and the bulbs and pot plants merely players.'

'Shakespeare?'

'You *are* coming along, darling.'

'*All's Well That Ends Well*?'

'That's wishful thinking, I'm afraid. *As You Like It*.'

'I like it strong with milk and one sugar, actually.'

'OK. Let's go inside.'

We have a cup of tea. 'Do you want to talk about it, then?' she asks.

'About what? My lucky stars? Your garden?'

'The other thing.'

I shrug nonchalantly.

My mother leaves the room and returns a minute later with a red wallet folder.

The *other thing* is my book. And the other thing about the other thing is that my mother renounced retirement to work as my literary agent and this makes her the one person in the world who knows the book's contents. This renders our unusual mother–son relationship even more unusual. It re-empowers my mother. Having spent my entire adult life asserting my independence from her, I am now in need of her again. I weaned myself off and now, at the age of thirty-five, I am weaned back on again. I have suddenly become doubly reliant on her: her knowledge of my novel gives her a degree of ownership of me and my thoughts, and her role as my agent gives her an influence over me and my future. If she wasn't so damn good at her job, if it hadn't been her who persuaded me to write the book and nursed me through the pain of producing it, I would have gone to another agent.

But there was something more complicated to it than that. My mother had always told me I could write, and when I started producing copy for ads she suggested I could do better, more and better. She never bothered with the soft touch: she didn't mind letting me know that she didn't think writing copy to sell

ice-cream was proper writing. Love in a cold climate was the way I had it, but it kept me interested, keen to impress, even from a long distance, even in my thirties. And so when I told her I was ready to write something that she considered proper, she announced that she would come out of retirement to sell me to the bookshelves of the world. And although I contemplated saying no, I didn't.

'Now.' She pushes her half-moon glasses up on her nose. 'You know I think this is good, darling, don't you? And you know I'm not saying that just because I'm your mother.'

'Perish the thought, Mother.'

'Well, the publishers I sent those first five chapters to didn't universally agree.'

'Oh. Why didn't you tell me they'd got back to you?'

'I'm telling you now.'

'Why didn't they like it? It wasn't the title, was it? Tell me it wasn't the title.'

'No. You're safe with the title.'

The title is my pride and joy, an advertising man's joke that I couldn't leave alone. *Book of the Month*. My mother hated it. She thought it a gimmick. I told her that that was the point, that the whole story had been shoehorned neatly into the space of thirty-one days almost entirely for that reason. She told me you shouldn't write a book around a title. I said I agreed with her, but it was too late to go back. We fought over it, I threatened to sack her. She told me I was getting 'bolshy and het-up'. No other agent would have used verbiage as familiar and humiliating in professional circumstances, but she was right. I *was* bolshy and het-up, and I insisted that the title remained unchanged. To my astonishment, my mother acquiesced.

'So what's the problem with it, then?' I ask.

'I'm afraid they don't specify. But your rejection, darling, wasn't universal.'

'Explain.'

'How much of the book is written now?'

'It's finished. I still tinker but, to all intents and purposes, it's done.'

'Good. Because, of the ten publishers I sent it to, two have come back saying that their interest has been aroused but that they'd like to see the completed manuscript.'

'That's good news, isn't it?'

'It gives us a modicum of encouragement. But it also means they're not convinced.'

'Can't you persuade them to throw caution to the wind?'

'I could, but it's not an expression I've had much fondness for. Throwing caution to the wind is all very well, but what if the wind is too strong? What if it's blowing the wrong way? What if it's a completely calm day and there's no wind at all? It seems unwise to take a gamble with a party as unpredictable as the wind, don't you think?'

'I do think, Mother, but not like that.'

'I know. It's long been a source of disappointment to me, darling.'

'Thanks, Mother, you're a brick.'

'Ooh. I'm not sure about that.'

I put up my hands, as if in self-defence. 'Oh, don't start again.' I'm out of practice. 'One needs to limber up before having a conversation with you, Mother.'

'You're very kind. I've missed you too.' With that she gets up and kisses the top of my head.

That, at least, is confirmation that business is done. The red folder, which was never opened, is put away and then, rather sweetly, we follow tradition and exchange Christmas presents. I give my mother an all-mod-cons cappuccino-maker and she gives me a beautiful early-edition, illustrated copy of *The Rubáiyát* by Omar Khayyám. We thank each other and I feel boosted by the renewal of our unusual form of affection.

But my mother wants more from me and, over dinner, she manages to extract a few nuggets of information. She asks about Lucy, and I tell her about New York; she talks about advertising

and what-the-hell-am-I-doing-with-my-life, and I tell her a bit about Lucy. It's a little game that's been played out for years between us, about ownership of information and ownership of one another. If I tell her about Lucy, she owns a little part of me. And I think that's OK. At thirty-five I'm happy to go along with it, as long as I can control the information exchange, give information when I want to on my terms. At least that way I retain a bit of ownership too.

I say goodnight and I'm heading up the stairs when my mother stops me. 'Dominic.'

'Yes, Mother.'

'I'm not sure about this, and I don't think that what I'm saying has anything to do with where your job is going next or whether your book is ever going to be published, but, darling, you don't seem very happy.'

This astonishes me. She is straying into territory where we rarely ever go.

'Tell me I'm wrong,' she says, staring at me over her half-moons.

'I'm not sure I can.'

'Well, sit down, then.' I take a pew on the bottom step. 'Tell me, Dominic. It'll be good for you. What's the matter with you and Lucy? I thought she was worth writing home about.'

I pause. This is an essay question and, to my mother above all, I am attuned to giving cop-out answers. 'She's obsessed with two-for-one deals in Sainsbury's.'

'Hmmm.' She waits for further information. I withhold. 'There are worse offences than that, darling.'

'I know.' Then I decide to allow her a victory. 'We have a "relationship",' I do the inverted commas with my fingers, 'that is, hmm, six days old. I have had purer and deeper thoughts for this girl than I have had for any other ever in my life. No one has ever come close. Nadia was bollocks, we all know that. Lucy isn't.' I pause. 'But it's not easy. Me and Lucy? There's still Tim. Heaps of bloody history. I want this so much, and yet I find I'm

asking myself if she does, or if she's just going through the motions and, if so why? And yet, on Day Six, the most impure thoughts of all. I hate myself for this, Mother, but I find myself wondering if she needs me for my money.'

And I cannot stop there.

Earlier that afternoon, as I explain to my mother, I had been to a meeting with Tim's accountant, Richard Wright. As one of the two executors of Tim's will – Marco was the other – I'd had dealings with him a couple of times before and they had been so yawningly dull that I hadn't bothered telling Lucy that I was going back for more. I didn't think she'd be interested. But I was wrong.

The situation was this: as well as being executors of the will, Marco and I had also found ourselves executors of the trust that Tim had left for Lucy and Josh. We were thus obliged to file the trust's annual tax return and, because I was living in New York and Marco was mostly in Bermuda, this was a duty in which we had failed, so we eventually handed it to the right person, Richard.

So, I'd thought I was meeting Richard at his offices in the City today for a standard signing-off of Inland Revenue documentation. However, he explained that he had seen Marco the previous day and that he had told him exactly what he was telling me: that he suspected something was amiss.

'It's nothing that the taxman would pursue anyone for,' he explained, in easy, layman's English. 'I don't imagine anything remiss can come of this. But it seems to me that a large part of Tim's estate has gone missing.'

He studied my face as if in search of an answer to the following question: 'I don't suppose you'd happen to know where it might have gone?'

All he got was a blank expression. 'Marco neither?' I asked.

'No. He was particularly surprised, and, as I'm sure you know, he was very *au fait* with Tim's finances.'

'Are you sure of this?'

'I am. You see, it's rather simple,' he said. 'I did Tim's previous three tax returns. I know what his estate was worth. When I was doing the tax return for the trust, the natural thing for me to do was use Tim's last return as a checklist. He hadn't been having a great time business-wise, but nevertheless, almost half his estate appears to be unaccounted-for.'

'How much are we talking about?' I asked.

'About four hundred and fifty thousand pounds.'

'Do you see what I mean, Mother?'

'Not really. The story you told me is hardly a tale of plotting and deception by Lucy.'

'Not remotely?'

'No.'

'Well, I want nothing more than to believe you're right.'

'I think, Dominic, you should be supporting her, helping her with this problem, showing her the commitment that someone with the feelings to which you have just paid lip service should want to show.'

'Two-for-one in Sainsbury's?'

'You may joke about it, Dominic, but I think, with Lucy you're desperate for something here and yet you're simultaneously looking for an excuse to fail. That was how you used to be sometimes as a boy, scared of flying high. I thought you'd risen above it, darling, but I suppose success and ice-cream awards don't change you deep down, do they?' She studies me for an answer, but I am stunned into silence. 'Goodnight, then, dear.' She kisses me and disappears upstairs to bed.

A considerable victory, then, for my mother. She never was a graceful winner, which was why I always ducked her invitation to learn bridge. The upshot, though, is that the Lucy subject is firmly off the conversation menu. By the following evening I'm bored. And still not happy. And although my mother and I had a perfectly pleasant time together at a garden centre, she was a

little disappointed because they didn't have any of the new winter-flowerers she wanted. She seemed to have forgotten the previous night's conversation. I, too, left the garden centre empty-handed. It didn't seem sensible to start buying plants when, in a week's time, I may not have a garden to put them in.

Then it was home for snooker on TV. My mother has a strange affection for the game; she's not a sports fan, but snooker's quiet intensity appeals to her and the mathematics fascinates her. It's the angles – she purrs at angles. She purred at Terry Griffiths in his heyday too. Tea, crumpets and the perfectly coiffured Welshman. A strange vice for an academic – and, incredibly, it had once seemed normal.

But today it has no appeal for me. I opt out, leave my mother to enjoy it, and sit down at the kitchen table with my laptop open in front of me. I fidget, stare at a blinking cursor for half an hour, fidget a bit more, start to create a presentation, stare more at the cursor, then finally do the sensible thing. I pick up the phone and dial Lucy.

'Lula! It's me.'

'I know it's you. You haven't called me Lula since New Year's Day.'

'That's one of the reasons I was ringing.'

'Go on.'

'Well, let's face it, we haven't been very cool, have we?'

'Is that why you ran away?'

'Pardon?'

'Is that why you ran away?'

'I s'pose so.'

'Marvellous!'

'Well, another reason I was ringing was to say I miss you.'

She sighs heavily. 'You miss me? Wonderful! Grey, how am I supposed to feel? You make me believe I should take the whole "us" thing seriously, then you run away, and now you say you miss me.'

'I miss us. You know, the real *us*.'

'Well, don't disappear on me, then. There's no *us* that way, Grey. I'm a widow, remember? I'm not used to being out there playing the game, courting, dating, looking for a husband. I'm terrified of it. And I know I'm not the ideal bedmate right now. I know I'm not dragging you upstairs the moment you get in from work, demanding that you satisfy me. But I'm a bit scared, Grey. Remember that. I even got drunk to see if it would be any easier and that misfired too. And that's not how we're supposed to be. You're my best friend! I need you to help me, be patient with me, not run away from me.'

'Sorry.'

'And – hang on a sec.' The phone goes quiet. 'Hi, sorry, I've got someone here who wants to talk to you.'

'Dominic!' It's Josh. Bright and squeaky. 'Where are you?'

'Hello, Josh. I've just come to pay my mum a visit.'

'Are you going to come back here ever?'

'Of course I am.'

'Great!' Brighter and squeakier. 'Can we play Red Injuns again?'

'Sure.'

'Promise?'

'Absolutely.'

'Cool! I think maybe your tyrannosaurus can wake up this time.'

'What splendid news. I'll see you tomorrow, OK?'

'Yes. See you tomorrow.'

'Right.' Lucy is back on. 'That's a date, is it?'

'Yup.'

'Good. You can run, but you just can't hide.'

'I don't want to. And, Lucy?'

'What?'

'Oh . . . nothing. I'd better tell you tomorrow.'

'Well, there's something else I want to say and I've got to say it quietly because I don't want the little chap to hear.'

'Go on.'

'I told Svetlana to take an extra week off.'

'So my trial period's extended?'

'Is that how you see it?'

'No, no, no! Joking. But you want me to stay?'

'No. That's not what I said. I said I'd told Svetlana to take an extra week off.'

'You want me to stay.'

'Stop it.'

'You want me to stay, don't you?'

'I'll see you tomorrow.'

12

'He's here, he's here, Mummy!' is the cry from Josh the moment I put my key in the door.

He's waiting for me. And the Red Injuns are waiting just inside the door in their field positions for battle along with the attendant prehistorics, Spider-Man, the chicken and a couple of new players: a winged car – presumably Chitty Chitty Bang Bang, therefore extremely dangerous – and a goat that looks as though it comes from the same farmyard collection as the hapless hen.

'Someone's very pleased to see you,' is Lucy's pointed greeting, delivered with a chuckle and an air-kiss.

'Not both of you?'

She responds with the eyes, half smiling, half telling me not to push my luck. 'He's had the battlefield ready for two hours now.'

'Here you go, Josh.' I toss him a small paper bag. 'I brought you some new troops.'

He eagerly reveals three plastic Red Injuns on horseback. I had found them in the toyshop in Tunbridge Wells and knew I was literally looking a gift horse in the mouth. Three gift horses. And I was right.

'Da-da-da-diddly-da,' mumbles Josh. 'Come on, Dom, let's get going.'

So we do. This is by far the easiest part of my charm offensive. I'm so high on Josh's list of favourite people that I can't put a foot wrong. In fact, he likes me so much that I get presented with a half-decent army and my goat is even allowed to play a blinder. But I know the boundaries of the game now, and after a good half an hour's fierce fighting, I ensure that the goat and the rest of my battle-weary mob go down valiantly in defeat.

Josh is the victor and he is so delighted that he agrees to let me cook his tea. Even better, he agrees to eat it, and when I turn down his request for one of his mother's Diet Cokes, he doesn't complain. Then he lets me chase him upstairs. We have at least fifteen minutes' wrestling – 'rough-and-tumble', he calls it – followed by bathtime, books and bed.

I turn out his bedroom light. 'Da-da-da-diddly-da,' comes from within the room.

When I return, victorious, from my childcare duties, Lucy is reading on the deep blue sofa with a cigarette burning in an ashtray next to her. 'You're wonderful with him,' she says. And that's exactly the kind of thing I was hoping she'd say. For all his non-stop energy, volume and, yes, occasional tiresomeness, there is no doubt that Josh has the potential to be useful to me. Is that cynical? I suppose so, but I've got a marriage to rescue here, haven't I? Is Josh being ruthlessly exploited? Only if you're too grown-up for fifteen minutes' rough-and-tumble. And I'm not.

'Shall I open a bottle of wine?'

Lucy lowers her book, props her glasses on her forehead and takes a drag of the cigarette. 'Not for me, thanks, but help yourself.' She goes back to her book.

'Pizza?'

She looks up again. 'No thanks, Grey. I had a big lunch.' And returns to her book.

'OK. Well, I want your attention anyway.'

'Why?' She frowns.

'Because I've got a presentation to make to you.'

'A presentation?'

'Yup.'

'Isn't that the sort of thing you do at work?'

'Yup.'

'So you're bringing your work home with you already. You must be feeling settled. What's a presentation got to do with me?'

'I'll get that bottle of wine first.'

Soon we're set up. Two glasses of wine after all, the cigarette stubbed out, Lucy, intrigued, on the sofa, and me on the floor in front of her. Next to me is the coffee-table on which sits my open laptop, about to lay bare the hard work I started yesterday at my mother's and completed this morning.

'Here we go.' I press the return button on the keyboard. 'This is an extension of what we were talking about last night. It's a product of us. It's how I feel. There's so much I want to say to you, Lula, and I kind of felt that this was a fun way of doing so.'

At the centre of the screen a slow-rotating headline comes to a halt. It reads: 'You and Me'. The screen clears and another headline spins to a halt: 'The Marriage of the Millennium'.

'Bloody hell, Grey!' She recoils, as if in shock. 'Go easy on me.'

The screen clears for the arrival of a third headline: 'Or Is It?'

'Thank you!' Lucy laughs. 'Is this the advertising man's way of having a wee personal conversation?'

'No. It's a one-off, especially for you.'

I press return. 'SWOT analysis' appears on the screen.

'What the hell's that?' asks Lucy.

I press return and the answer appears. Under the title, 'Marriage of the Millennium', vertically down the screen is the word 'SWOT'; then horizontally, next to the capital letters, four words: Strengths, Weaknesses, Opportunities and Threats.

'OK? Got it?' I am enjoying watching the delight and disbelief playing on Lucy's face.

'Yes. Go on.'

'Now, SWOT analyses are a much-used and highly valued system of assessment in the business world.' I'm trying to sound serious, and probably failing. 'So I thought I'd introduce the concept to Archdeacon Avenue. What we have here is a matter of great import: the assessment of the Marriage of the Millennium.'

Lucy giggles. I press return. The screen clears, then 'Strengths' spins to a halt. A number of bullet points appear below it.

I explain: 'These are the strengths of the marriage of the millennium.' And I read: '"One, great sex." OK, that's a little ironic, but I thought I'd get the awkward stuff out the way early.' Lucy smiles.

I continue: '"Two, bespoke marriage. Cool new concept." Because we're coming at the whole thing from an original angle, we get the chance to design our marriage from scratch. Modern marriage isn't a successful product, as you may have noticed. It comes burdened with expectations, obligations, matching bathrobes, joint bank accounts, and it's too much for many. The batteries die or it breaks and there's no guarantee. I understand that as well as any. We can redesign it. And who knows? Maybe one day we can repackage it and sell it. OK, joking, but seriously, Lucy, we're coming together from a different kind of start. We can decide how we're going to be, as I say, almost design our relationship.

'OK. "Three, my cooking." Well, sort of.

'"Four, solution to hair-loss problem." A happy marriage would do my barnet no end of good.'

I press return again and three more bullet points appear on the screen. 'We're getting serious here, so I'm going to read these out together.

'"Five, respect."

'"Six, affection."

'"Seven, love." The thing is, Lucy, I just think we've got something really, really strong. Different from your standard couple, but that's good. I'm sure you know this, I'm sure this comes as no surprise to you and it's a bizarre way to say it, but, Lucy,' I clear my throat, 'I do love you. I really do.' Lucy puts her hand up as if to request permission to speak. 'No, sorry, questions at the end. And I've got to move on. Otherwise I'll get too emotional.'

'You tell me you love me and you're not even prepared to talk about it?'

'Ssh! I'm trying to give a presentation.' I press return. The screen clears and the word 'Weaknesses' spins to a halt, followed

by another series of bullet points. 'OK. So these are the weak-nesses in the marriage. "One, we're a bit scared."

'"Two, well, I am anyway."

'"Three, yes, we're risking our friendship."

'"Four, didn't someone say: ''Tis better to have loved and lost than never to have loved at all.'"

'"Five, that was Tennyson. Clever old Tennyson."

'"Six, we're being a bit nervous around each other."

'"Seven, we must overcome the problem identified in point six."'

I press return again. Lucy chuckles and rubs my shoulder. 'This is so romantic, Grey. No one's ever done a SWOT analysis for me before.'

'Well, it's just a token of how much I care.'

She kisses the top of my head. And I continue: '"Oppor-tunities".

'"One, lifelong happiness." That's what we've got a shot at here, isn't it?

'"Two, a real structured family life."

'"Three, could possibly be so good that you won't want to smoke any more."

'"Four, get to know Richmond Park better."

'"Five, more games of dinosaurs with Josh."

'OK. Right. Moving on finally to "Threats". Threats to us.

'"One, nuclear war." Well, you've got to take these things seri-ously, haven't you? But I think we'd be strong enough together to survive.

'"Two, global famine." Ditto. "Vegetables." Vegetables? What did I mean there? Oh, yes, maybe we should start growing our own just in case. I've got a gardening background so I could handle that. And it'd be a positive, educational thing to get Josh involved in.

'"Three, the bedroom situation." I'd have to move out of Svetlana's room some time. Maybe that should be an item for further discussion.'

'Quite a big item, Grey.'

'Granted. But in its favour is the link with point one of Strengths – great sex. Anyway, more threats.

'"Four, Plato. What a tosser." Yes, he's only going to be bad news for us, Lucy. We've got to kick that Platonic love stuff into touch. I know it's the basis, the foundation stone of everything we're about and that's what makes us so good, but that's what it must remain: the foundation, the start. And then we've got to build on it. It's not enough on its own. I've done a spot of research on this. The God-awful theory of Platonic love comes from Plato's *Symposium*, but in it, Plato doesn't simply advocate chastity, purity, the end of reproduction and thus the human race. He only discusses this form of love as one of many. He's well into romance, physical attraction and bodily secretions too.'

Lucy lies lengthways on the sofa so that her head is right next to mine. 'Are you getting a bit desperate?' she asks, teasing.

'What? Desperate as in frustrated? As in wanting to jump on top of you?'

'Yes.'

'Um. Ah. A little. But not unhealthily so. It's not as if it's my prime driving force. It's just natural. I find you very attractive, Lula – you must have worked that out by now. It's a positive thing. It's good. Especially in a marriage.'

'Well, that's very nice of you.'

'And that's the end of the presentation.'

'So that's it, is it? Our lives summed up in advertising jargon on a hi-tech bloody laptop?'

'Didn't you like it?'

'I loved it. Aren't we supposed to discuss it now? Form a think-tank, have a brain-storming session or something? Come to conclusions? Draw up a lifeplan?'

'It . . . well . . . I just wanted to break the tension, to find a way to get us going again.'

Lucy pauses, rapt in thought. She hops to her feet and smiles

at me strangely. 'Come on, then, my darling. Let's break the tension for good.'

She takes my hand and leads me out of the sitting room. We go up the stairs and straight into her bedroom.

No word is exchanged. Lucy faces me. We are standing very close. She fixes me with a meaningful look and her fingers move to the buttons of my shirt. Three are undone when she takes my hands and instructs them to undress her. I tug lightly at her T-shirt, freeing it from her trousers and slide my right hand softly round her naked waist. Still in silence, we slowly, carefully, strip off the layers, kissing and caressing bare flesh as it appears until we are both naked. And it feels sensual, natural, right. There's no explosion of lust, no laughter, no lewd seduction, no groping, no one-way traffic, no frustration and panic in the corridor; Queensberry rules consigned to history. Just touching, stroking, exploring, sharing, a quickening of breath, a legitimising of sensations coursing through two bodies pressed against each other, welcoming the advent of physical harmony.

Lucy cups my face in her hands and kisses me long and deep. 'Come here,' she purrs into my ear. She takes my hand and guides me to the bed, her eyes never leaving mine.

And now everything seems right – natural – at last. I've told her that I love her and now there are clothes scattered with abandon, we're naked, she's got that unmistakable this-is-it-here-we-go look in her eye. There are no different conclusions to be drawn. And yet it's not good enough for me.

'Lucy.' I tumble backwards on to the bed so that I'm looking up to the ceiling. 'Sorry.' I know I'm killing the moment. 'But you've got to tell me something. Why?'

'Why what?'

'Why this? Why exactly are you doing this? I have to know what you're thinking.'

Lucy draws breath pensively. She lies down next to me, propped up on her elbows. 'Can I give the answer in bullet points?'

'Sure. It works for me.'

'OK. In no particular order. One, I haven't had sex since Tim died. Two, I haven't had sex with anyone who was not Tim since I was nineteen. Three, I'm thirty-five, Grey, and I'm scared of sex. Ridiculous, isn't it?' I shake my head. 'I just have to know if I can do it again, if it will work. And, four, there's no one else I could possibly feel comfortable with. It had to be you.' She pauses. 'Five, I don't know where we're going, Grey, I really don't, but there's no way we're ever going to get anywhere unless we give it a try. Six, I'm not sure how much – if any – of that presentation I was supposed to take seriously but some of it, the mushy bits about us and how we are together and how we can be kind of unique, that rang really true.'

'The nuclear war bit or growing our own vegetables?'

'You idiot!' She collapses on to me so that her chin is now on my chest. 'And there's something I want you to understand. I'm closer to Plato than you are. You have to know that. But at the same time I'm with Tennyson all the way. "'Tis better to have loved and lost . . ."'

There are times when Lucy reveals her strength and weakness all in one moment of honesty, and this is one. As she recites the line from Tennyson, eyes darting in a way that reflects her nervousness, she is inviting me to break the boundaries of friendship and become her lover. I roll over so that I am now looking down upon her. Our legs are now intertwined and my chest is brushing against her breasts. There is nothing to hold me back now and her smile, both self-conscious and encouraging, invites me to go on.

Of all the times I have imagined it, making love with Lucy was never like this. She is not feisty, challenging, brave or on top. The earth doesn't move – in fact, she barely moves and neither do I. We are quiet, careful, considerate with each other, the eye-contact unrelenting, checking we're OK, gently enjoying our complete togetherness. And at the end we're still friends, but lovers too.

Afterwards, our bodies curled together, it is Lucy who breaks the harmonious silence: 'There's an item in the SWOT analysis I want to discuss.'

'Go on.'

'Under Threats, I think it was point three. The bedroom situation. I lied to you yesterday when I said that Svetlana was taking an extra week off.'

'How?'

'She's not coming back at all. I'm going to ship her remaining stuff back to her. I told her on the phone yesterday morning.'

'Blimey. All to make way for me?'

'Largely for you.'

A pause. 'You can't afford her, can you?'

'No, I can't. It doesn't make sense. On my day-and-a-bit's work a week, I've been paying her more than I earn. She's not going to come back and I'm not going to work any more. If I can't afford to work, what's the point?'

'So it wasn't for me, was it, that you were getting rid of her?'

'Hey! Stop it! It was a combination of the two. If what you're asking is whether you're just some minor storyline in my life and have I therefore just made love with you for the hell of it, then the answer is no.'

13

Next to me, curled into my side, Lucy looks serene. But I can't sleep.

I go downstairs, pour myself a glass of milk and flick through the newspaper at the kitchen table. I wander through to the sitting room and focus fleetingly on the invitations on the mantelpiece, the photos of Tim on the antique card table, the eclectic range of reading matter on the bookshelves behind the television. French literature, the complete leatherbound Dickens, Tom Stoppard plays, Chekhov, an impressive collection of *Wisdens*, which presumably belonged to Tim, and, to my delight and surprise, thin and barely visible, the script of *Gregory's Girl*.

'What's on your mind?' Lucy's voice is soft yet she startles me.

'I didn't want to wake you,' I say apologetically.

'For the first time in years, I get a bloke in my bed and he does a runner!' She is smiling, arms crossed in her white dressing-gown. 'What am I supposed to make of that?'

'Nothing.' We converge on the sofa and she kisses me lightly on the lips.

'Come on.' She whispers into my ear: 'Answer my question, what's on your mind?'

'Hmm.'

'Grey. Now, of all times, there's no point in pretending that I don't know when something's clattering around in your head.'

'OK.' I sigh, and prepare to give an adulterated version of the truth. 'I wasn't completely joking when I said that thing about you not being able to afford Svetlana. I saw Richard Wright on Friday.'

'Oh, yeah?' She slips down in the sofa, a worry line creeping across her forehead.

'He suggested that perhaps you aren't as well-off as you might have expected to be. Or should be. He said I should talk you through it – "it" being that he can't trace part of Tim's estate. It's just that he has to declare it to the Inland Revenue, and if you know where it is you should tell him.'

'Pardon? Run that past me again.' Confusion is written across her face.

'A large part of Tim's estate is missing. He wants to know if you know where it is.'

Lucy shakes her head. 'Fuck me. I'm the most useless person in the whole world when it comes to finance. I'm allergic to the entire concept. And Wright thinks I'm smart enough to dodge the taxman?'

I shrug. 'It didn't seem likely, which is why I'm concerned.'

'Look, Grey,' she interrupts, 'I never touched our money. Tim did everything and that was an arrangement I couldn't have been happier about. But he didn't do it as well as I'd assumed. As you say, I'm not half as well-off as I thought I would be. Don't, for God's sake, mention a word of this to Josh, but our mortgage here is so frightening that I think we're going to have to move out of town. I can't come close to affording it, even without Svetlana. And Wright thinks I'm trying to play games?'

'No, no – listen. You didn't give me a chance to explain properly. Wright doesn't have a clue. He's not pointing fingers. The whole point of this is that the money must be somewhere and, without it, it's you who's out of pocket.'

'Why didn't he tell me?'

'I guess he was worried that he might do what I've just done and make it sound like you're some kind of a suspect.'

'Oh.' She pauses for thought. 'So why's it taken you two days and a particularly successful SWOT presentation to tell me?'

And here's the white lie. 'Because us – you and me – is precious. Losing half a million quid, or whatever it is, is a big thing. I wanted to tell you in the right way, and maybe help you find it.' No mention of my paranoia that Lucy might have an ulterior

motive in our relationship. Indeed, the suggestion seems more ridiculous than ever.

Lucy jumps up from the sofa as if unburdened, plants a kiss on my forehead and starts riffling through one of the drawers in her desk. 'I don't know,' she says, preoccupied, 'but maybe this will help.' She pulls out a wallet file and takes out a piece of paper. 'Here.'

It is a copy of a short, typed letter signed by Tim and sent to someone called Dolores Sands with the words 'Letter of Wishes' at the top. I scan it quickly.

Dear Dolores,

This letter of wishes confirms your role as trustee of trust fund No. 78475E. The trust is placed in your hands for you to run at your discretion with the intention of maximising revenue for the beneficiary, my son. The fund should be held in trust until the year 2017 when he is 21 years old. When he reaches the age of 21, the fund is to be handed into his full ownership.

Yours sincerely,

Tim

'So,' says Lucy, when it is clear that I've digested the letter, 'who the fuck is Dolores Sands?'

'You don't know?'

'No, and because I don't know, I can't get in touch. I don't even know what the fund is worth.'

'You've presumably tried to find her?'

'What do you think? Of course I have. I've asked my lawyer, who was Tim's lawyer, and he knew nothing. He did an exhaustive search on the name and didn't come up with anything. There is no single registered legal practitioner or financial adviser in the world who goes by that name. He said maybe it was a made-up name — apparently that's perfectly feasible. I asked Marco too. He was always in cahoots with Tim about money and if anyone knew it would be him. But he drew a massive blank. He

also said he'd ask the accountant, and it sounds as though the accountant knows diddly-squat too. And I was thinking of asking you, but I didn't think there was a chance you'd know. Tim never talked to you about finances, did he?'

'No.'

'I don't know what to do except wait until Josh is twenty-one. Any bright ideas?'

'Make him pay for his own twenty-first?'

'I didn't think so. Right. Is that conversation done then?' She leans over me and whispers in my ear, 'Well, come back to bed then, lover-boyo.'

And that's an invitation I can't refuse. It turns out to be an invitation to the sleep version of bed and Lucy is soon curled into my side again, looking serene again, purring soundly. And I am wide awake, wondering again about her money. Dolores Sands. Dolores and Sandy. A sleazy night's infidelity in a Manhattan vodka bar. Does Marco really know nothing of this mysterious trustee? And why had Marco not told Richard Wright about the Letter of Wishes?

14

Lucy and I: the honeymoon period. Here we are. God, how I love honeymoon periods. Finally you get the girl, the barriers are down, the wondering is done, the ball has officially crossed the line and the Russian linesman has indicated that you have scored. There's no more nervous dilemma over whether she likes you or whether you're misreading the signs, whether you're pushing the right buttons or you're coming over like a first-time flyer at the control panel of a fighter jet. Because when you've done it once, and you've chanced upon the right sequence of buttons on the control panel, there's nothing to stop you: you may as well do it again. At least, that's the theory.

That's what it was like with Daisy, the biology student with the Roman nose – only for three days, admittedly, but three heavenly days none the less. One day in heaven with Daisy was spent solely within the four walls of her digs. She popped out once for sandwiches and Coke. I hotfooted it to the general store and came back with prophylactics and one of those bottles of Bulgarian red. I missed three lectures and an English tutorial on the metaphysical poets. It would have been worth writing home about if there had been someone other than my mother at home to read the letter.

And that was what it was like on the odd occasion thereafter, though a funny thing happened to me after those ice-cream ads. Women started expecting things of me. They'd discover that I was the 'genius' – their word, not mine – behind the Peachey's horny houseboaters, then make a leap of thought: they'd assume that because I'd used sex in my ad campaign, I was immersed in bedroom wisdom, king of the four-poster, good at it. The few

who dared put the theory to the test were, of course, let down: if you're a virgin at the age of nineteen, you're never going to make the transformation into gigolo, the school stud . . . or Tim, come to that.

In the States, it was worse. Or better. The ad campaign was considerably larger. It was on network television. It won more awards because it combined sex and English accents. When Jerry and I arrived to work in New York, the gossipy corridors of the designer-beer-drinking ad world knew we were coming and hailed us as people who knew what we were doing, who knew about sex, who were good at it. And in the States, they *really* believed it.

They couldn't, of course, have been more mistaken. Jerry was asexual, more interested in malt whisky and the late-night haunts where he could drink it than any female he might meet in them. And I, at that stage, could still count my sexual encounters on the fingers of my hands. I was less impervious to the charms of American women than Jerry, and I believe I managed to bluff my way and persuade one or two that they'd had a good time. Generally, though, I was like a novice golfer, searching earnestly for some rhythm, but swinging too fast, and trying desperately to get round the course without letting down my playing partner.

Thankfully, by the time I required my toes to start counting my conquests, I had found Joy, who was joyful, and Felicity, who was felicitous, and I had real honeymoons with the pair of them. Though not together. When I met Nadia, I felt confident out on the golf course. And she took me on to it so often that it seemed the honeymoon would never end.

So, here we go again. Another honeymoon period. The me-and-Lucy long-awaited special. In theory I should be rubbing my hands together in a sensibly contained thirty-five-year-old's version of childish glee. But do you do honeymoon-period-all-day-sex when you're thirty-five and your hairline's retreating, when the girl in question happens to have a four-and-a-half-year-old son and happens to be the widow of your dead best mate? The answer's probably no.

And I also suspect that that is not what Lucy and I are about. We are, after all, the special relationship.

It is the night after the night before – the night of the fabulously naked union, that is. We've been out for a pizza. Lucy got a babysitter so we could 'celebrate'. Her word. I liked the idea of celebrating. I particularly liked the fact that it was her idea. And the pizza place, a decent, earthy, unpretentious local called Isabella's, was Lucy's suggestion too. 'C'mon,' she said, 'we're pizza people. It's our thing. We don't have to change and go all candle-lit and romantic just because we've started a . . . well . . .' She stumbled on the words and smiled in recognition of an unintended cul-de-sac. '. . . a thing.'

That's what we've got: a 'thing'.

She didn't dress up for me, which was important. She wore a fitted brown suede shirt with the top three buttons intriguingly undone – comfortable, stylish, not dazzling, but Lucy-like, which was important. Because if we are to take this lurch into unchartered Dom-and-Lucy territory, we have to remain the same people who went together to the brink.

So pizza is good. We feel at home with pizza. Lucy was fabulous, bright and so at home with the status quo that she wouldn't relent in her ceaseless inquisition about my novel and the reasons for my uncharacteristically steely determination to keep her in the dark.

'C'mon, Grey! There's nothing between us, and as of last night that's pretty much indisputable!' she teased. 'Tell me, tell me, tell me about the book.'

'Sorry. Can't. Won't.'

'I'll share my body with you if you share your plot with me.'

'Can't I just pay for the pizzas? Isn't that enough?'

'No.'

'Even though you ordered extra pepperoni?'

'Even with the extra pepperoni, mate.'

'Well, it's stalemate, then, mate. No plot. No mating.'

'Oh, ha-ha!' She sat back in her chair, her bottom lip jutting out, feigning fury and struggling not to smile. 'When am I ever going to see it?'

'When it's published.'

'Thanks! If it's ever published, I'll bloody marry you.'

'That's not fair.'

'Why? I thought you'd be pleased.'

'Because you've already promised to marry me. All I had to do, remember, was be at the top of Greenwich Hill, single, on New Year's Day and I've done that. You can't start setting more conditions.'

She sat forward so that her face was just inches from mine, impish delight settling charmingly on her face. 'I just have.'

'Well, you might end up losing your man.' And although I said that in jest, we were both lost for words because the temperature had changed. We might have slept with each other; done a SWOT analysis and agreed to grow vegetables, but suddenly we were back where we were when we met on Greenwich Hill, still not sure what we were doing, where we were going, or if both of us *really* wanted to go there.

I changed the subject. I decided to tell Lucy about how she had reached postcard-home status and how my mother clearly approved.

'I thought our *thing* was a secret,' Lucy responded.

'I thought you'd be pleased with my mother's seal of approval,' I replied. 'It's not easily come-by.'

With that, Lucy charged off with the conversation; she asked what about her might disappoint my mother – the poor state of her garden, her lack of knowledge of post-war American fiction, her soft spot for extra pepperoni? Which brought us back to the central issue: extra pizza topping for Lucy's body? A fair deal or not? The question sustained the rest of the evening. Would she withhold herself, even after extra pepperoni? Oh, the tension! Throughout the short walk home, she danced around me, insisting that she never came that cheaply. And, of course, I

played along, but it's not as if I was taking her seriously, or as if I was hell-bent on honeymoon-period, all-night, non-stop fulfilment. All I wanted to know was that I could hold her in my arms, stroke her, kiss her. Have our 'thing'.

We got back to Archdeacon Avenue, paid the babysitter, and the moment the door was closed, she pushed me backwards so I was sitting on one of the kitchen chairs, straddled me and kissed me. That seemed uncharacteristic – forceful, domineering – but, then, I don't know what's characteristic for Lucy when she's in a post-pepperoni relationship.

And now it's just after midnight and I'm propped up on one elbow, leaning over her in bed, watching her as she sleeps. She looks peaceful, ruddy-cheeked and boyish as she always used to.

We did make love. Once. But while I know I shouldn't judge and I shouldn't over-analyse, rewind and ponder, I also know that after all these years of keeping hope closeted away, I should be sitting up in bed with a fat cigar. But I'm not and I don't know why and it's only partly because I hate cigars. All I know is that when we made love, I was looking down into her lovely dark eyes but they wouldn't look up into mine.

Still, this is a honeymoon. And there's always tomorrow night.

15

The telephone rings. It is six fifteen a.m. Lucy sits up and rubs her face. At least the phone is on her side of the bed. Who rings at six fifteen?

'Alice?'

The look on Lucy's face doesn't suggest that this is normal. The Alice I know certainly isn't one to call up on the six-fifteen grief-line. Not stable, sensible, sorted Alice. Lucy frowns. She turns on the light next to the bed. That means it's serious. Lucy hardly contributes to the conversation. She's just listening and, between long pauses, making occasional comforting noises: 'Ah . . . Oh, no . . . Dear, dear . . . Really? Alice, surely not . . . Bill? Not Bill . . . Come on . . . Don't worry . . . Sorry, darling . . . Bloody hell . . . Really sorry, darling . . . It'll be all right . . . It will . . . It might be . . . You've got to believe in it . . . You have . . . Yes, I know . . . What a bastard . . . Yes, a complete bastard . . . All men are . . . Yes, I know . . .'

This is still going on after fifteen minutes by which time I am irretrievably awake – and, apparently, culpable too. I get up and have a shower, and even then Lucy is still on the phone making soothing, sympathetic noises. I dress and go downstairs, make coffee and return.

Lucy is off the phone at last. 'Thanks, Grey. You couldn't make one for Alice, could you?'

'Pardon?'

'She'll be here in a couple of minutes.'

'What's going on?'

'It's Bill.'

'What about Bill?'

'He's had an affair.'

'He's what?'

'You know, shagged someone who isn't his wife. The fucker.'

'He can't have.'

'Why not?' Lucy's voice is cold, accusatory.

'Because he's in the strongest, most successful, most leakproof marriage anyone's ever known. They're almost a celebrity couple because of it.'

'Not any more.'

'But Bill wouldn't know how to have an affair. He couldn't get some poor unsuspecting female into bed. He wouldn't know where to start.'

She shrugs. 'That's what I thought. But what do we know? Diddly-bloody-squat. Because he has. The fucker! I'd better get up.'

'Can I have a good-morning kiss?'

'No, you can go and make Alice that coffee.'

So I do, and no sooner has the kettle reboiled than she is at the front door, a weeping mess in navy blue tracksuit bottoms and a pale blue sweatshirt, collapsing forward into my arms so that I can feel the waves of grief pumping through her body and the wetness of her face against my neck.

Immediately Lucy is downstairs to relieve me. She peels Alice off me and bears the physical burden herself, patting and rubbing our visitor's back and doing more of those sympathetic, soothing sounds. Then she looks at her watch. 'Um, Grey, do you think you could possibly get Josh up?'

'Of course, no problem.'

'And could you by any chance take him to school?'

'Sure.'

'And could you make sure he takes his white outfit for his karate class? He needs a packed lunch too. Could you, please?'

'No probs.'

She kisses me. 'Thanks. My saviour. Oh, I forgot, it's show-and-tell day at school.'

'What's that?'

'They have to take something – anything – with them and in class they stand up and show it to their classmates and tell them what it is. Just don't take one of his Christmas Red Injuns. He took one last week.'

'What about the wonder-hen with the super-rooster powers?'

'Sounds perfect.'

It is just after midday when Bill answers his phone at work, and just after one o'clock when we're sitting down having lunch.

'Are you all right?' Stupid question, I know.

'No, I'm shit,' he replies. He looks it too. 'How was Alice when you left her this morning?'

'She was shit, too, actually. Crying a lot. I didn't talk to her much. Lucy and I split the responsibilities. I looked after Josh and Lucy looked after Alice. I think we maximised our skills that way.'

'Oh, Christ!' Bill thumps the table and groans like a wounded animal. I order a bottle of still water and settle in to listen to the confessional.

It was a woman he met at a large company-client weekend away in December, he says. They were in Dublin. She flirted with him and his defences were hopeless. They weren't much better the following night. She was older and 'beautifully preserved', but, he kept repeating, 'That's irrelevant, mate.' What *was* relevant was that he had come home and been feeling guilty ever since. Simple as that. It wasn't that Alice had done anything wrong or that his feelings towards her had changed. Not at all. It was just that he had felt flattered, turned on and weak. Simple as that. 'I just slipped into it,' he says. 'Slipped into it' – a phrase he uses repeatedly. 'I can't believe how easy it was. I just wandered down the path to infidelity, hardly even checking to see if I was going in the right direction.' He'd never done it before. He wouldn't be doing it again in a hurry, 'No way, fucking José.' Not even if he had a lot of time on his hands. He still loves Alice. He just couldn't bear the guilt any more. He couldn't

handle being so dishonest with her: their whole relationship was based on openness and, after sixteen years together, it had suddenly stopped working for him.

'So, let's get this right, Bill. You came clean with her? You confessed, completely unprompted?'

'Yes. Last night. I had to. I couldn't go on pretending.' He spreads his hands to convey that there was no alternative. His eyes are watery, his manner dramatic, his voice too loud, and he is so deep in woe that he doesn't notice the glances from the people at the next-door table, their raised eyebrows and that they move tables before their food arrives.

He continues: he and Alice argued. And their arguments come round about as often as a leap year. They tussled all night. Alice's mood swung from quiet and wounded to aggressive and physical. She didn't offer him the quick absolution he had hoped for. And, no, he hadn't thought it would be quite that easy. They finally went to sleep at three forty-five a.m. Then, two and a half hours later, she was on the phone to Lucy and on her way round to Archdeacon Avenue, barking at Bill that he could 'get the fucking kids up and off to fucking school on his fucking own for fucking once'. Slammed the door. That was it.

'Have you spoken to her since?'

'Christ, I've tried. She's got the mobile switched off. I rang Archdeacon Avenue a couple of hours ago and Lucy made it pretty clear that Alice wasn't ready to talk.'

'But, Bill, you're supposed to be the couple that goes on for ever.'

'I know, and I fucked it up.'

Alice is still there when I get back from work. Her eyes are red, but she is no longer in the tracksuit, no longer crying. She pulls a brave smile and gives me a hug.

'Your husband's a broken man, you know, Alice.'

'He did the breaking himself.'

'I know. And, boy, does he regret it.'

'You saw him today, did you?'

'D'you mind?'

'God, no. We need our friends right now. I still love him, you know. It's just that the love is heavily outweighed by hate at the moment.'

Lucy comes down from putting Josh to bed, greets me with an air-kiss and the news that Alice is staying the night. She doesn't tell me where Alice will be sleeping but, given that the most concrete union in the history of marriage has sustained a deathly looking fracture, I guess my own nocturnal activities aren't much of a priority.

We open a bottle of red and sit down for supper. Lucy has cooked shepherd's pie, comfort food for cuckolds.

'Alice and I were talking,' she says to me, 'about you blokes. We were recalling a conversation we'd had on her hen weekend. The question was: who, out of all the blokes we knew, would remain faithful in marriage?'

'I presume Bill was the winner.'

'You presume right.'

'And if Bill can't keep it in his trousers . . .' says Alice suggestively.

'Then there's only you left, Grey,' says Lucy, rubbing my shoulder affectionately. 'You were the other. Bill was the favourite and you came a close second. And look at you now. One marriage down and still never unfaithful. My money's all on you.'

'That's quite a responsibility to carry,' says Alice.

'No problem,' says Lucy.

And I say nothing. I just smile in a manner that I hope looks relaxed and I raise my glass as if I'm toasting Lucy's good judgement.

'Never unfaithful to Nadia?' asks Alice, a little too suspiciously. 'Even though you never *really* loved her?'

I shrug my shoulders as if to suggest that fidelity shouldn't be such a problem. 'You see, we're not all bad.'

'I wish I could believe you,' says Alice. Her head drops and

the fragile façade of strength and bravery slips from her face. 'Sorry, sorry. I thought I'd stopped all this.' There is a box of Kleenex on the kitchen table, which has clearly been in regular use all day. Lucy pulls out a tissue and, without looking, hands it mechanically to Alice in a way that suggests she has been doing it all day.

So Alice begins afresh the battle to choke back her tears. We try to help by talking about other things. We watch the news, we pretend life is normal. Then Alice says she's going to bed, Lucy says she's going to bed too, and she delivers the news to me with an expression whose meaning is clear. 'Sorry,' she mouths. I get a full kiss on the lips – thank heaven for small mercies. 'I'm sorry, darling,' she whispers into my ear. 'I'll miss you tonight.'

And that's that. Alice gets my spot in Lucy's bed. The honeymoon is postponed.

16

My natural response is to launch an ad campaign.

Here at Duffy's, my dark, airless office has become a quiet and unproductive place. If I was proud, I would probably be wondering if it's the sort of cubbyhole befitting an award-winning ice-cream salesman. And I'm probably being a bit paranoid – that wouldn't be out of character – but I have noticed that my colleagues, who had been smacking me on the back like an old chum and regularly inviting me out to lunch, have started to throw questioning glances my way, as if wondering what on earth I'm doing here, as you would of a retired musician who still turns up to band practice. The thing is, I know I can still play a bit, but can I be bothered to go in search of the right notes again?

Ray, the creative head, continues to pop into my diminutive domain with enthusiastic debriefs of forthcoming campaigns, transparently attempting to hook my involvement. Although I respond with raised eyebrows and murmurs of interest, I've been careful not to transmit any suggestion that I'm remotely close to taking the bait.

But now I have an ad campaign of my own. The product: me. The target market: Lucy. And I set to work.

Ad number one is a shameless rip-off of an old campaign for Brut, the aftershave. Two small tweaks make it an ad for me. 'Frequent use may result in sleepless nights', was the big, bold headline in the original, which I copy almost exactly. In the Brut ad, the *i* in 'nights' was replaced by an *i*-shaped Brut bottle; in my ad, however, the Brut bottle has a cheesy, smiling mug-shot of me superimposed in the middle. In the Brut ad, there was another copy line in a smaller typeface that read: 'Brut. The

essence of man.' In mine, it is altered to read 'Dominic Lord. The essence of man.' As if there might have been an element of doubt.

At six forty-five p.m., unseen because most of the creatives have finished work and gone to the pub, I get the artwork printed off, A3-size, with a nice glossy finish, then return to Archdeacon Avenue with a spring in my step.

Alice is still there, back in her tracksuit bottoms and pale blue sweatshirt, with the red rings still round her eyes. But when she is on a long telephone call, I present my ad to Lucy, whose response is to fill the house with a volume of laughter that it hadn't heard for some time.

'You're fantastic,' she says, arms tight round me. 'And you're definitely the essence of man.' Which is nice to hear, although I notice that she doesn't Blu-Tack my homework on the kitchen wall with a big tick and three gold stars as she does with Josh's. Nor does she show it to Alice. Anyone suffering from paranoia might have suspected that maybe she didn't want Alice to know that Dominic Lord was the essence of man, or, more to the point, that she was entertaining the thought that he might be.

Ad number two is a reworking of a campaign for Club 18–30. Set against a black background, in a funky clubby typeface, is the main copy-line: 'Discover your erogenous zone.' Below it, and next to the Club 18–30 logo, are four shapes, in different, garish colours, that are identified underneath as islands: Tenerife, Ibiza, Majorca and Corfu. But in Lucy's version Corfu has disappeared and in its place, next to the logo, is a silhou-etted profile of my face with my name underneath. It is simple, amusing. It has a single drawback in that the silhouetted profile of my head doesn't reflect particularly well on my hairline but, nevertheless, I like it.

I'm completing it when Bill rings.

'How are you?' I ask. 'Are you all right? Are you coping?'

My question is greeted by momentary silence, then a long

sigh. 'Not really. I did manage to get the kids up and off to school without having a breakdown or any of them spilling Frosties down their school clothes, if that's what you mean.'

'Sort of . . .'

'Though I forgot Sam's show-and-tell the other day. God, he was pissed off with me when he got home.'

'Doesn't sound like you're doing too badly.'

'I disagree. Funnily enough, coping doesn't come easily when you're wondering if you're ever going to see your wife again.'

Which is a reasonable point. Three nights have passed and Alice appears to have stolen my bird. I haven't slept with Lucy once. But for a series of apologies and earnest promises that we'll soon be reunited, it feels almost as if we never ascended Greenwich Hill and reached the heights beyond. But I know that's not quite what Bill has rung to discuss. But I was on a honeymoon, wasn't I?

'How is she?' he asks plaintively.

'I think she's turning, Bill. I can't say anything categorically, but she's definitely improving. She was talking last night about moving out of the house.'

'Where's she going to go?'

'Back home to you, I think. At least she's talking to you now, isn't she?'

'Yes.'

'Well, my guess is that she's decided she wants to put the fear of God into you and hurt you as much as she possibly can –'

'She's succeeded.'

'– and then I think she'll go back to you.'

'Dom, that's fucking brilliant. It's the best thing I've heard all week.'

'I might be wrong.'

'I don't want to hear that. You've got to be right. You lovely man, you've made my day. 'Bye.'

By seven o'clock I'm marching back into Archdeacon Avenue hoping to make my day too. My bribes: a plastic stegosaurus

for Josh, nothing for Alice, flowers for Lucy and the Club 18–30 ad, to be held back for the appropriate moment.

I am greeted with excitement by all three. Josh barely has time for his stegosaurus: there's something he has to show me. He rushes up to his bedroom to find it, and returns proudly with a piece of paper: 'Batman, Spider-Man and Dominic Lord are all superheroes,' reads the top line, in biro, clearly written by his teacher. The same words have been copied underneath, in pencil, four times, by Josh.

'That's brilliant, Josh, but why did it take you so long to work it out?'

The joke is lost on him but not on Lucy, who is beaming. 'How about that, then?' she crows, though I don't know whether it is Josh's mastery of handwriting – his Ms are particularly well formed – or that he has acknowledged my superhero powers that she's so thrilled about.

Alice is smiling too. At last. She has a date tonight with Bill. At last. And Lucy, it turns out, has a date too. With the gym. It's a workout class she particularly likes, she explains, wrapping herself round me and batting her eyelids in a clear request for a favour. She's booked a massage afterwards. Can I babysit?

Of course I can. I'm also informed that I'm allowed a five-minute window to play superheroes with Josh. The kindness is astonishing. 'Superheroes' is another of Josh's complicated games with a changing set of rules of which he is in sole control. Stripped down to its bare essentials, it involves a battle of the superheroes, Spider-Man (he always gets to be Spider-Man) versus Dominic Lord (I always get to be Dominic Lord), with Spider-Man cleverly tricking Dominic Lord, jumping on his back and wrestling him to the ground. Poor old Dominic Lord, I discover, is equipped with few superhero powers and suffers such a spate of grisly deaths-by-spiderweb that Josh is finally satisfied and agrees to go to bed.

Finally, after Alice's departure, I corner Lucy. 'Lula, I've

something to show you.' I produce it with a flourish. 'Ad number two.'

'Oh, Grey, it's brilliant.' She laughs, though not as heartily as I'd hoped. 'Look, sorry, I've got to go.'

And with that she is gone. Dispirited and underappreciated, I lift myself with one thought: if Alice's date with Bill goes well, maybe she will go home with him, thus freeing up Lucy for me.

And yes, I discover later, the date went well. But not well enough.

Two days later, Alice is ready to return home. We see her to the front door, I lift her bag into the back of her car and we all wave her off. I can tell that Josh is pleased: a house full of hormones and tears and marital stress is no place for superheroes like Spider-Man and Dominic Lord. Lucy is delighted too, but in her altruistic way: she is delighted that Alice and Bill are at least beginning to attempt to enter into a semblance of the relationship they had before. And I am thrilled to bits, but my pleasure is so egocentric that I keep it to myself.

'At last,' says Lucy, a few hours later. After a quiet, cosy Sunday as a threesome – we went to the supermarket (I paid, but that's a dead issue now) and then to the cinema (my shout again, and it's still dead) – Josh is in bed and we are too.

'Now,' she whispers, raising her eyebrows suggestively, 'where was it we got to?'

Ad number three remains a work in progress, but I am excited about it and feel it may be the best in the series so far. The ad is the brainchild of Jerry, whom I had enlisted to help with the campaign on an unpaid consultancy basis. He was intrigued and amused by it, although, given that he was supposed to be working on a campaign for a medical insurance company, that was hardly surprising. He stole the idea from a Daihatsu campaign but, because it requires careful use of computerised air-brushing techniques and the theft of a

couple of photographs from Archdeacon Avenue, it requires a little extra work and time.

The original Daihatsu ad pictured two vehicles next to each other as if at traffic-lights, one a sports car driven by a single man, the other a Daihatsu Hijet, a van-like people-carrier, with two parents in the front seat and four kids in the back. The sports-car driver looks sad, lonely and unloved; the Daihatsu family, particularly its driver, all look deliriously happy. The big bold copy-line above the two vehicles was: 'One makes you look virile. The other proves it.'

The Dominic Lord version of the ad will have changed only the faces in the Daihatsu Hijet. The father figure at the steering-wheel will, of course, be me, the mother will be Lucy and one of the kids in the back will be Josh. It plays again on the 'Dominic Lord, essence of man' theme, but will take the message further, touching on concepts such as family happiness and human repro-duction. Daring stuff. Same effect.

For Lucy and me, though, the full Daihatsu reality is still some way off.

17

The sexual life of Dominic L. Perhaps better known as: A Long Day's Journey into Night.

NIGHT ONE POST-ALICE

Lucy rolls towards me with those splendid words: 'Now where was it we got to?'

If I was back at school, I'd probably have replied that we'd got past all the bases and scored a home run, that the innings was going well and we were back in to bat. But as I am thirty-five and an award-winning ad-man, my reliably smooth and witty reply is a single word, a malapropism you'd call it, if you were being generous, that seems to combine the words 'hurray', 'glug', 'you're lovely' and 'I've missed you' and is pronounced 'Raymissougluv'.

It appears nevertheless to have the required effect: we do go back in to bat and we do score another home run. A pretty quick one too.

But two thoughts.

One. Despite being the brains behind Peachey's horny house-boaters, I've never seen myself as a bedroom genius. I've just done my honest best and gone out to bat with my mind focused on the job. However, when tonight's honest best innings is done, I'm not convinced that it was good enough. Lucy doesn't say so, but neither does she say the opposite, or respond as if the opposite might be true. She certainly doesn't punch the air shrieking that she's just been through the greatest experience known to womankind, an experience far beyond anything she'd known

with Tim. Nor does she look me lovingly in the eyes. Indeed, she turns away from me with nothing but a whispered 'G'night'.

Two. It doesn't help having Tim with us all the time. He looks on smilingly from the three photographs on Lucy's bedside table and it's impossible to pretend he's not there. The largest and most prominent of the three is black-and-white, and although you can only see his head and shoulders, it would appear that he's naked, or topless anyway. His hands are clasped together, chin resting on them, and he looks straight at you, with a re-assuring, self-confident smile. Hello, Tim. How wonderful to have you with us again today.

NIGHT TWO POST-ALICE

We're in bed and we're back in to bat when Lucy stiffens. 'Sorry, Grey – you've got to stop tickling me,' she says, giggling.

'I'm not,' I reply, slightly too uptight. 'I was stroking you gently. It's supposed to feel nice.'

'Well, it's ticklish,' she says, gentle laughter in her voice, trying not to make me feel as if I'm doing a bad job.

So I stop. Christ, I can't even get the stroking right.

Then we start again, and I try to avoid the stroking. Lucy's muscles tighten momentarily, but then she relaxes again and it seems I'm doing OK until she's suddenly laughing again.

'What is it?' I ask grumpily.

'It's the tickling.'

'I wasn't tickling.'

'Well, it felt ticklish.'

'I wasn't *fucking* tickling.'

'I'm sorry.'

'What are *you* apologising for?'

We lie there in silence. A long, awkward one. Eventually we complete the job, but it feels as though we were doing it out of a bizarre sense of duty.

And Tim, looking on from his photo-frame, has probably

enjoyed the entire charade. I bet he never had his stroking mistaken for a tickle.

NIGHT THREE POST-ALICE

We get into bed and Lucy does something new. She sits up, puts on her glasses and starts reading her book. What am I to do? I don't have a bedside book, I'm wondering how long she's going to be with hers: it seems as though she's intent on finishing it. I cuddle up to her in a childish attempt to remind her that I'm still there.

She puts the book down, rests her glasses on her bedside table, turns to me and sighs. 'You don't mind, do you?'

'Don't mind what?'

'If tonight . . . if we don't . . .' She leaves her sentence hanging.

'No, of course not,' I reply reassuringly.

After a moment's silence, she turns to me. 'Sorry, Dom.'

'Oh, Lula, don't apologise.'

'It's just . . . it's that it's not that easy, all this, is it?'

'No, it's not easy at all, but we mustn't be awkward about it.'

'I know, Grey, but it's hard not to be, isn't it? I mean, we're supposed to be brilliant together, best friends, all that stuff, and that's what got us here in the first place.'

'What got us into this mess, you mean.'

'No, that's not it at all. I just hate the fact that at night-time it feels sometimes as if we've become strangers.'

'I know what you mean.'

'And I'm not saying I don't want you in bed with me. I do. It's just that I'm not used to going to bed with people. It's hard . . . no, strange for me. I'm only used to going to bed with *him*.' She nods in the direction of the three photos. And Tim smiles back happily.

'Come here.' I put my arm round her and pull her towards me so that she is nestling into my shoulder. She brushes the hair away from my forehead and kisses my cheek. 'It's all right, you know.'

'What?'

'To feel like that. It'd probably be strange if you didn't.'

'You don't mind?'

'OK, I'd be lying if I didn't say I'd rather it was different, but . . .'

'What?' She kisses me again.

'We can only be realistic. We can only do this if we're both feeling happy. But, you know,' I chuckle under my breath, 'the best thing you've done is tell me how you're feeling. Just talking, letting each other inside . . . I feel close to you now. This is how I love to feel with you.'

'Me too.'

'We've got to be careful with each other.'

'And just because things have changed, it doesn't mean we don't talk to each other.'

'I know. A *thing* is supposed to bring us closer, not put distance between us.'

'You do understand, don't you, that deep down in a profound, inexplicably *different* kind of way, I love you?'

'Well, hang in there.' I squeeze her more tightly to me. 'Your love's supposed to be getting stronger, not the opposite.'

NIGHT FOUR POST-ALICE

Another night's reading. We feel safe with reading: we can do it without any stress. In fact, we're so safe with it that I now have my own bedside-table book. And I know you're not supposed to read a lot of books on honeymoon, but the rules are different on this one, aren't they? Because this is a *thing*. At least, that's what I'm continually reminding myself. Lucy certainly seems happy and at ease with the reading rules and, after lights out, she curls in towards me and falls asleep, purring peacefully with her head tucked next to my chest.

I have no idea how long we have been asleep in this position, but I'm awoken by the sound of a child crying. Lucy is already

sitting up. Morning hasn't broken, but any sense of harmony has. This is unexpected and unusual. It is a quarter to three. And it's Josh. Standing by the bed. But Josh never wakes in the night.

In fact, Lucy and I had talked about this very thing. We didn't want him to catch us in bed for the obvious reasons: something to do with rendering him mentally disturbed and carted off by social workers. And it hardly needed to be said that if Lucy tried to explain to Josh that all we did in bed was read books together and that I was a useless lover who couldn't stop tickling her, it wouldn't make it any easier for him to comprehend. So, based on the (wrong) premise that Josh wouldn't wake up in the night, this was the rule we made: bed-sharing was fine as long as I was up by ten to seven in the morning. This would work, Lucy explained, because Josh knew that when his digital clock said it was seven o'clock, it was morning time and he was allowed out of his bedroom. And that's pretty much the only rule he's been known to keep. At least, it was until now.

'Mummy,' he is sobbing hysterically, barely able to spit out his words, 'I had a bad dream. It was horrid.'

'What's the matter, Josh, sweetheart?'

'I had a bad dream. And Spider-Man couldn't save me. And they were coming to get me. And – and – Mummy – Mummy, it was really horrid. And – and – and what's Dom doing in here?'

'Come on, darling,' Lucy says soothingly. 'Shall I put you back to bed?'

'But – but – but – I want to sleep here with you.' His eyes are almost closed, it's not clear whether he's properly awake.

'Come on, darling.'

'No! Mummy!' Josh's voice hardens between the sobs. 'I want to sleep here.'

'Come on,' Lucy's voice is noticeably harder too, 'back to bed, young man.'

'Mummy!' Josh is almost screaming. He is awake, that much

131

is clear. 'Why is *he* allowed to sleep here and not me?' He points at me accusingly.

'Josh, come on now.'

'Mummy!' His voice is louder and angrier still.

Lucy looks at me apologetically. Not a word is required: the message is clear. Josh has won the battle of wills, the prize for which is my spot in his mother's bed. I hop out, pulling a towel round my waist as I go.

'Sorry,' whispers Lucy, and rolls her eyes as if to say that this is all a tiresome shame and that she's going to miss me dreadfully.

And I am back in Svetlana's room.

NIGHT FIVE POST-ALICE

Never underestimate the opposition. Josh's victory wasn't a fleeting skirmish with a minor casualty: it looks as though he's bedding in for a long campaign.

Not once all day did he refer to the events of the night before. At breakfast time, before school, he didn't treat me any differently. He didn't mention his bad dream or that he'd woken up in his mother's bed. Neither did he ask her what the hell she thought she was doing sleeping with a second-rate superhero like me.

But I get home that evening, slightly late after a drink, to find that he's already won tonight's battle.

'Sorry!' says Lucy, with the same rolling eyes. 'He said he was scared in his own room, that there were noises. I tried and tried and tried but I couldn't talk him out of it.'

And it wouldn't reflect well on me if I started bitching about the selfishness of a fatherless traumatised only child. So I shrug nonchalantly as if to suggest that it's no problem to me and that the prospect of missing a night's reading next to Lucy is something I can readily handle.

'I could always come to *your* room,' says Lucy, positively.

And so, later, she does. And because she could hardly bring a book with her, the pressure is automatically on us to do something other than read. At least there's no Tim, so we have a bit of privacy, but I can't help imagining what the great Adonis himself would do, what great bedroom stunts he would pull to satisfy the lovely white body next to me.

Svetlana's room is no love palace. It is painted an ugly dark green and the curtains are of a lighter, non-matching green, thinning in patches at the bottom. It's a shoe-box, too, not big enough for a full double bed, so when two people are in Svetlana's single, there's no avoiding each other. Also, the mattress is too soft, so while it's impossible to avoid a bedmate – if, of course, you're lucky enough to have one – it's also hard to manoeuvre your way round one. At least, this is what Lucy and I discover.

Lucy may be small and wafer-thin, but her weight added to mine forces the bed to dip in the middle so we roll into each other, with Lucy giggling. Now, I'm not so pent-up that I cannot see the funny side but, given recent precedent, giggling is not what I need to bolster my bedroom confidence. I require something a bit more basic and carnal, and the trouble with sleeping with your best friend – even when they're not prone to giggling – is that they're never going to treat you like some grade-A porn star. It just wouldn't seem right.

So we are probably best advised to opt for the gentle touch, a soft-focus relaxed harmony of minds and bodies – it sounds good, anyway. However, I seem to be in clumsy mode again. I move my right hand to caress her left cheek and my index finger almost pokes her in the eye. She's not hurt so she giggles again. And I've had enough of the giggling.

'What's the matter?' she asks. Are my moods *that* offensively strong?

I don't reply. I just grunt in a tone that's not as negative as I feel.

'Oh, come on, Grey,' she says patiently. 'Don't . . . you know . . . it doesn't matter.'

'What?'

'Remember what I said, Grey, this isn't that easy for me.'

'Sorry. I guess I just want an 1812 Overture too soon.'

'What do you mean?'

'You know, fireworks, all guns blazing. I want this, us, the *thing*, it, to be great, fantastic, wonderful, a full orchestra performance.'

She laughs affectionately. 'This isn't a bloody advert. You can't think in terms of soundtracks.'

'No one complained when we did it with ice-cream.'

'But what if we never get the 1812 Overture? What if we get stuck on the *Roobarb and Custard* soundtrack?'

'Oh, thanks!'

She nestles into me and we lie together in easy silence. It feels good to be together again. And here we are, useless at making love but perfectly capable of joking about it. I'd call it a crushing victory for Plato. There are no easy games at this level, but Tennyson's been played off the park. It may have been better to have loved and lost, but we've hardly even loved at all and we're staring at defeat.

'You don't want to give up on all this, do you?' I ask, without having thought through what I'm saying.

'No. Do you?'

'Not at all.'

'I want to progress slowly, naturally, without feeling any pressure to be doing it to the 1812 Overture.'

'OK. Me too.'

She squeezes closer to me, wrapping her arm round my torso. Silence. Another easy one.

'What soundtrack did you and Tim play to?' I ask.

By the time she has finished spitting out her furious response, Lucy is out of bed and almost through the door. 'That's such a stupid question it doesn't even warrant an answer.'

And she's right. As stupid questions go, that one takes some beating.

NIGHT SIX POST-ALICE

Josh is still scared of the noises in his room and again takes my spot next to Lucy. But this has no impact on my life. I don't think it'd be my spot even if he wasn't there.

NIGHT SEVEN POST-ALICE

I decide to let any remaining frostiness thaw by coming home late after a drink with Bill.

And the drink is useful too. Without making my own interest in the conversation too obvious, I get Bill on to the subject of sex and find his information comforting in a disturbing way. He and Alice have sex about once a week – and that's in a good week when they're living together and he's not making confessions of infidelity. They haven't made love since her return home, but he hopes they will by the end of the month. And he fervently believes that once a week is fine, perfectly healthy and nothing unusual for thirty-five-year-olds with children coming out of their ears. He says it's the media and the bloody advertising industry that make people think everyone else is doing it more often than they are.

I suppose this makes me hoist by my own wretched petard. But it also gives me succour: if no one else in the mid-thirties family bracket is having much sex, then maybe it doesn't matter that I'm not. Though it's a sad bracket to be in. If it wasn't for Lucy, I'd want out.

NIGHT EIGHT POST-ALICE

It's time to clear the air so I pull out all the stops. I fix up a babysitter, I present Lucy with the Daihatsu Hijet ad and she loves it. I take her out for a drink, we have a light supper and another drink, and when we return to Archdeacon Avenue, it's clear that the alcohol and the passage of seventy-two hours have done the trick.

The sleeping arrangements are still unsatisfactory. Josh seems to have moved into Lucy's bed for life – those bloody night-time noises – and I'm not sure how hard Lucy is trying to shift him. But, given how poorly I've played my hand recently, I decide it's best to say nothing.

I decide right. When we get home, I pay the babysitter, Lucy leads me straight upstairs to Svetlana's room and then something happens. The whole thing happens. It's a little alcoholic, blindly fumbled, very quick and there's no 1812, but we get to the end and, for now, that's what counts.

NIGHT NINE POST-ALICE

Tomorrow I leave on a week's business trip, so tonight is important. I want to go out on a good note.

I start with Josh and we go through the whole bed-time bonding experience: dinosaurs, rough-and-tumble, superheroes (which is rough-and-tumble by a different name) and I lose gallantly at all three. I then administer bath-time and book-time, and when I'm convinced that his esteem for me could be no higher, I broach the subject.

'Josh, you know you're growing up and you're quite a big boy now?'

'Yes, Dom.'

'Well, big boys shouldn't be scared of night-time noises. They're nothing to be scared of. It's probably just the wind blowing outside or something like that.'

'But Sam says there are quite a lot of monsters in his house at night.'

'Well, Sam's a bit silly. There are no monsters anywhere in our country, only in books.'

'But I've got lots of books.'

'Yes, I know. I mean they're only pictures in books, not real-life monsters. You tell Sam that – and that he shouldn't be scared either.'

'Oh. OK. I won't be scared any more, then.'

'Good. So will you sleep in your own bed tonight?'

'No. I like Mummy's bed.'

'Josh, you should really sleep in your own bed. Big boys don't sleep in their mummies' beds.'

'But what if I really want to?'

'Well, how about this? If you're really brave and sleep in your own bedroom tonight, when I get back from my trip I'll bring you a prize.'

Josh's eyes widen. 'Really?'

'Yup.'

'What's the prize?'

'What do you want?'

'A Spider-Man outfit.'

'OK. A Spider-Man outfit it is.'

'It's got to have a mask.'

'Of course. Mask too.'

'Great! That's so cool, Dom.'

'So you'll be brave and sleep in your bed tonight?'

'OK, Dom. I'll try and be brave.' With that, I tuck him up in his own bed and kiss him goodnight, The Battle for Lucy's Bed showing a minor victory for me at last.

'How did you get Josh back into his own bed?' asks Lucy, when we are finally together in hers.

'Oh, you know, just a little bit of bribery and arm-twisting. I told him big boys weren't scared of night noises.'

'Well done you.'

I roll on top of her and whisper: 'There's something in it for everyone.' Which is a little corny, I know, but Lucy takes it the right way, with an amused but nervous expression, the sort you'd pull at the start of a particularly terrifying rollercoaster ride. And that takes the pressure out of the situation. I collapse on top of her and for the first time ever we're in bed and we're *both* giggling.

For the first time too, I think, we make love without feeling burdened by self-consciousness. And it's wonderful.

18

An urgent job before Lucy and Josh take me to the airport: wrap her present. Her birthday is two days before I come back and this is a very important present: a copy of the manuscript of *Book of the Month*. Giving it to her is a gamble, an act of untold bravery, so brave that it may even backfire. It'll surprise her, I suspect it'll shock her to the core, or the pips, or the heart, or somewhere of deep and meaningful significance. But it's about time she saw it. I want her to see it. I'm done with pretending. So I wrap it, give it to her and make her swear not to open it before her birthday. And this is important, as I explain to her. I don't want her reading it right now, then waiting for a week for me to come back before she can talk about it. I want to be there, back home, stepping through the front door as she finishes the final page.

Lucy and Josh drive me to Heathrow. There is a nice warm family feeling in the car, with Josh chatting away about the Spider-Man suit I'm going to buy him and his fear that I might neglect to get the matching mask. I assure him that the matching mask couldn't possibly be forgotten, and maybe that contributes to the nice warm feeling at Terminal One when we say goodbye. I wave them off in the car and, rather than checking in for the flight to New York, as Lucy had believed, I find the BA desk for flights to Bermuda.

Seven hours later I am walking across the Tarmac at Bermuda airport. It is the Bermudan winter and towards the end of the afternoon, but I can feel a pleasing warmth on my face. I cannot help but smile too, although this is less to do with the climate and rather more with my plan. My hire-car is further cause to

smile – an open-top Audi TT should bring pleasure to anyone – and soon I am driving slowly (first impression: people drive slowly in Bermuda) round the winding, single-carriageway roads of a pristinely manicured island, past pastel-coloured houses with distinctive white roofs towards my hotel, the Reefs.

The Reefs is barely thirty-five minutes from the airport and a cause for happiness too: a small collection of buildings decorated in an attractive cross between colonial and Caribbean style, all in pastel pink, overlooking one of Bermuda's hallmark pink beaches. It has a relaxed atmosphere of privilege and smells faintly of the sort of wealth that a successful ad-man could only aspire to. I settle down with a rum punch at the bar overlooking the sea. I think of Lucy and feel content. If she and I ever came here, I suspect we'd manage an acceptably high degree of happiness; it may even be the sort of place where we wouldn't be doing too much reading. It's one of the most expensive hotels on the island – I'd done my research – and there are plenty of expensive hotels to choose from. Here, I reasoned, I'd be able to make an impression: I wanted to look like a high-roller too.

All I really know is that Marco is on the island as well and is set to remain here for the week. A phone conversation with his PA, a girl called Aloisia, established that. I said I was a friend, I didn't have to give my name. I didn't want him to know I was coming. I certainly didn't want Sophie to know because then Lucy would have found out, and that would have negated the reason for the trip. The idea is simple – to turn up on Marco's doorstep unannounced – and after a couple more rum punches and a good night's sleep, I hope to put it into action.

Monday morning, another cloudless winter day. It is eleven thirty, time to get going.

I call Marco's office and ask for Aloisia. 'Is Marco in?'

'Yes. Can I put you through?'

'No, it's OK. I'll pop round later.'

I grab a coffee, bid goodbye to my beach and set off for

Bermuda's main city, Hamilton, only twenty minutes away, and that's driving at Bermuda pace. Hamilton's tiny. Its financial district is just a small part of a small town and Marco's offices are in a set of buildings called the Waterfront, which makes them remarkably easy to find. The Waterfront looks shiny and new and, helpfully, there is a square stone column at the front with shiny metal plaques detailing where its inhabitants can be found. On one, towards the bottom on the right side, between Stockton Insurance and Nomura Securities, I find the name of Marco's little empire, Millennia Corp. So far so easy.

Another early impression: Bermuda shorts. They really do wear them. It shouldn't be so surprising, but I'm in the Bermudan capital surrounded by businessmen, policemen, whatever, and they're all wearing tailored shorts above dark socks and shoes. I can see why the fashion has never caught on in London.

'Hi.' I introduce myself at Reception. 'I'm here to see Marco Bury.'

'Do you have an appointment?'

'No, but I'm an old friend and I'm sure he'll be delighted to see me.'

At which point the receptionist frowns at me. 'I'm sorry, he's gone out.'

'Ah. Can I speak to Aloisia, please?'

I do. She tells me I've just missed him: he's gone for an early lunch and to do some work on his boat. Another piece of free information: the boat is moored at Tucker's Town. She still didn't ask my name. Splendid Aloisia.

On an island where poverty doesn't seem to exist, Tucker's Town is where the unfeasibly rich go to get away from everyday run-of-the-mill millionaires. It is no surprise that this is where Marco likes to hang out. The idea of being in the upper-class of a population where seven-figure earners occupy the middle ground would appeal to him hugely.

The drive is short. The road hugs the coastline, then rises through undulating golf courses, pink and white hibiscus lining

the way. As I near my destination, the houses and local earning capacity start to grow. Eventually the road peters out, leaving me perched above what I presume to be Tucker's Town Bay, a bijou expanse of light blue pond hemmed in by luscious green vegetation with a little yellow carpet of beach at one end, a thin corridor through to the Atlantic at the other and some of the most sought-after properties on the island stretching their heads majestically above the green as if to keep an eye on what is going on in the water below.

The fleet resembles a troop of supermodels lining up for a beauty contest, some thirty boats of varying shapes and sizes with two elements conspicuously in common: their style and immaculate splendour. Which of these is Marco's, I have no idea. The boats are moored to a series of mini-jetties, so I park and walk down to the first. There's no sign of him, no sign of anyone. No sign of him at the second either, or at the third. In fact, there is utter calm. No one is around at all.

I walk to the fourth, then the fifth, and then, in front of me on the sixth, I am confronted with a sixty-five-foot long yacht, an Oyster, according to the branding on the side. Painted in blue on the stern is its name, *Sophie's Choice*. There are signs of life too: a blue baseball cap on the deck and a pair of black socks and shoes. I climb on board. The hatch to the saloon is open.

'I'm looking for Dolores Sands!' I shout, directing my voice inside.

No reply.

'Dolores? Are you down there?'

No reply.

'Marco?'

Still no reply. Then I hear noise from within. At last, Marco's balding head – even more shiny than mine, I'm happy to see – pops up from below. He is wearing maroon Bermuda shorts.

'Dom!' Effusiveness fills his voice. 'Bloody hell! What the bloody hell are you doing here?'

'I was wondering if you could help me,' I reply with no sense

of familiarity. 'I'm looking for a Dolores Sands. Do you know where I might find her?'

'Lordy, Lordy! Crazy guy!' Still effusive, albeit slightly patronising. 'Why didn't you tell me you were coming?' He shakes my hand – he seems frightfully pleased to see me. 'When did you arrive? I'd have picked you up from the airport, you old bugger.'

'Now, Marco,' I'm still matter-of-fact, 'this Dolores Sands, d'you know where I might find her?'

Marco turns. 'Come on down, Dom. Come and meet my second wife.' He skips into the boat and disappears out of sight. 'The other love of my life, y'know,' he shouts up. 'I spend almost as much time with her as I do with Sophie. I'm just plotting the waypoints for our weekend trip.'

I remain on deck. I'm trying to play a tough-guy role and that doesn't allow me to go inside and buy into this joke about the second wife. There's a moment's silence. I'm toughing him out now.

'Listen,' he says, 'I know what you're referring to, Dom, but I don't know who Dolores Sands is.' He emerges again at the hatch. 'Don't you think I haven't tried to track her down too?'

'No.'

'Did you come all this way just to ask me if I knew Dolores Sands?'

'Yup.'

'D'you want a drink?'

'I'll have one when you come clean on Dolores.'

'I don't know who she is.'

'But you knew she existed?'

'Of course.'

'Why didn't you tell Richard Wright that when he asked you where Tim's missing half-million had waltzed off to?'

'No point. If you can't find her and I can't, how on earth could he?'

'I've found her.'

'Oh, really?' His surprise is transparent.

'C'mon, Marco. I was at Tim's stag too, you know. I might not have slept with them, but I know who Dolores and Sandy were.'

He sighs, turns, sits down on the deck so that he is almost at my feet and wipes the back of his right hand across his forehead. 'Dom,' his tone has clicked out of pleased-to-see-you-old-mate familiarity, 'you don't want to know about this.' He is all businesslike sincerity now. 'I promise you. You can achieve nothing by finding out.'

'Persuade me.'

'I promise you, mate.' Marco has never called me 'mate' before. I was never mate-worthy until now. 'You don't want to know.'

'Lucy has a right to. She's going to have to move house, leave London. She's got to downscale, *mate*, to find a way of living off less money than she always thought she had. Doesn't she have a right to know? And, more to the point, doesn't the trustee have a right to release some of the money now? If the duty of the trustee is to her son, if that trustee wasn't easy-lifing it on an Atlantic pleasure island, then he – she, Dolores, whatever you want to call yourself – should see that now is the time the son needs his fund.'

'Actually, Lucy doesn't have any rights in this at all.'

'Oh, fucking hell, Marco! Does it have to come to this?'

'To what?'

'Threats.'

He turns his face to me slowly, his gaze following behind. He looks aggravated. 'What do you mean?'

'Well, if Lucy so wanted, she could report you – or your pseudonym Dolores, or both of you together – to the Inland Revenue, because no one's paying tax on the trust's income. I've done my homework, Marco. Even if the trust is held over here, it doesn't make it tax-free.'

Marco gets up, locks the hatch and starts pulling on his shoes and socks. All done with efficient swiftness and not so much as

a word. Not even eye-contact. Then he climbs off the side of the boat, still without speaking, and I stand still, watching him go. He is ten strides up the jetty when he turns back.

'Where are you staying?'

'The Reefs.'

His face takes in the information. It's clear he's impressed. 'Let's talk about this properly, then. I'll come and find you this evening. Six thirty good?'

I nod. And he is off.

Before six thirty, I have another appointment. Back on the other side of Hamilton, on Harbour Road, at a quarter past four, at Ceremonies by the Sea, Bermuda's finest bespoke wedding-planning service. 'Great weddings don't just happen,' at least so Ceremonies by the Sea told me on its website, 'they take planning.'

'When are you thinking of having the wedding?' asks Dinny, Bermuda's finest wedding-planner, placing a tea tray on the desk. Bermuda's finest wedding-planner also has one of Bermuda's finest views: her office is situated high above Harbour Road, and a huge ceiling-to-floor window offers a panoramic vista of Hamilton, its bay and the ocean beyond.

'Ah. Good question,' I reply. 'I'm not a hundred per cent sure about that.'

'Fine. No problem.' Dinny flashes me a warm, reassuring smile. 'May I ask what are the variables we're dealing with?'

'Sure. Hmm. Yes. Well, I haven't got round to the crucial bit, you know, the proposing bit. Not properly, anyway. It's kind of hard to explain. I'm sorry, I imagine it's probably better for you to plan weddings when you know there's definitely going to be one.'

'No problem, Mr Lord.' Another of those long, understanding smiles. 'I'm sure that the crucial proposing bit won't be a problem. But how do you wish to proceed?'

'Well, can you tell me how long it takes you to fix a wedding?'

'We generally need two weeks' warning, but I've done it in forty-eight hours. Would that be fast enough?'

'I don't think we'll need anything quite that fast.'

'Shall I take you through some popular venues, then?'

The photograph album comes out and Dinny shows me a hundred and one happy couples on myriad pink beaches by the sea. It doesn't seem too bad a way of doing it. At least, that's what I tell her as I leave.

'Good luck!' she says at the door. 'Propose well!'

Six thirty. From the corner of the Sand bar, on the veranda at the Reefs, the ice tinkling in my gin and tonic, I watch Marco, his eyes scanning his surroundings before he weaves his way between the tables to me. 'Not a bad old spot you've found here, mate,' he says, patting me on the back. I never used to get the warm back-pat treatment.

'I'd love to be able to stay. Please, do sit down.'

'Oh, come on, mate. If you're going to be here longer, I insist you move into ours.'

'You're amazingly kind,' I reply, although the sarcasm is wasted, 'but I've got to be in New York tomorrow and I see no reason why we can't get all our business concluded today. And please remember, Marco, it's best that Sophie remains unaware of my visit.'

We order drinks, Sam Adams for him, another G&T for me, and we do small-talk while we wait for them to come. Bermuda's the only place in the world for him now, he tells me. I can understand why, I reply, when you can wear those lovely shorts to work every day. How did you find the Reefs? he asks, oblivious again. I always stay here, I lie.

'Right then, *mate*.' Our drinks have arrived. 'If we're now agreed that Dolores Sands is you, tell me where Tim's money's gone.'

Marco sips his beer, playing for time. Then he places the glass assertively on the table, as if his mind is made up. 'OK. I'll tell

you, but there's one rule, and if you want Tim to rest peacefully, you'll stick to it. And if you care at all for Lucy, you'll definitely stick to it. I have no hold over you, I can't *make* you stick to it, but I can't see how it would benefit anyone if you didn't. If you really want to know about Tim's money, this is the only rule: that you never tell Lucy where it went.'

'But if I give you my word, how can you guarantee I'll never break it?'

'As I said, I can't enforce your promise.'

He stares at me straight-faced. Eventually I shrug, and he takes that as his cue. He rubs his brow wearily, as if this is an ordeal he would rather not endure, perches forward on his chair and begins.

'Tim didn't intend for it to happen this way. He didn't intend to die. He thought he was invincible – you know that better than anyone, Dom. Even when he was losing money, his confidence didn't allow him to consider that the losing streak wouldn't end.'

'I didn't know he was losing money.'

'Of course you didn't. He was too proud, wasn't he? He couldn't admit failure, not to Lucy and certainly not to someone as successful as you.'

'How much money did he lose?'

'I don't know exactly. He had a lot when he stopped banking. He continued doing pretty well as a consultant. But he got too brave. As I said, he didn't think he could lose. That was his problem. His investments started growing. We did a lot together and that's the only reason I knew what he was up to. He became a gambler rather than an investor. I'd try to rein him in, but he wasn't interested in advice. And gamblers lose, don't they? We went into a few ventures together and it got to the stage where he was putting in five, ten times as much as me.'

'Silly amounts?'

'Again, you've got to remember that this guy thought he was immortal. Some investments worked really well, and one in particular, a property deal for a conversion job on a small block

of flats in Borough, looked as if it would reap about half a million – until we were told, despite the assurances of our architect, we had never had planning permission to do the work and that we never would because there were all sorts of problems with the foundations. Subsidence, I think it was. That was the biggest mistake of Tim's life and you could hardly blame him because he made it when the Borough flats had all the hallmarks of an early-retirement ticket.

'And Tim was too impatient, especially in this incident where he really got ahead of himself. About six months before we realised that the Borough-flats project was going arse-end up, he started working on a start-up company mass-producing a new line of baby-food. It was newer and fresher baby-food, better than anything you could buy on supermarket shelves – at least, that was its USP – and Tim had just had a baby so he thought he knew what he was talking about. I was intrigued by the idea and put some cash into it. With Tim, however, there was no holding back. He decided to go in big-time and invested the profit that he was assuming would be coming his way from the Borough flats. Huge mistake. The baby-food business lasted barely six months, and the week after it folded the Borough-flats project went the same way. So he'd spent money he'd never had, lots and lots and lots of it.'

'And that's why Lucy's struggling?'

'Basically. And you know what he left, it's not as if he was broke, far from it. But, as you'd expect, he brushed it off. He thought it'd be no time before he recovered his losses and was flying high again. As I said, Dom, he didn't mean to die.'

'And he fucked up monumentally.'

'You could say so . . .'

I sit back in my chair, absorbing the information. 'OK, Marco, I'm not sure I get this. Tim played it a bit fast, he made a couple of fat mistakes and died before he had a chance to mend them. But where's the crime in that? Why not tell Lucy? Why not tell the accountant?'

Marco puts his glass to his lips and doesn't answer.

'It's not as if he left her in debt,' I continue. 'And there's a trust fund going to Josh anyway, so I can't see the problem.'

'I'm about to tell you what the problem is, Dom.' He leans further forward towards me and lowers his voice. 'And believe me, once you've heard what I have to say, you'll understand exactly why Lucy must never be allowed to know.'

19

When I think of Tim, I remember the night in Trinidad when we stole a twenty-five-foot boat.

We were twenty-four. More to the point, Tim was turning twenty-five. He had been in the Caribbean on a week's cricket tour and I'd flown out to meet him on the penultimate day. Lucy was to arrive the day after in Kingston, Jamaica, where the three of us would unite for an extended celebration of Tim's birthday. Tim had certainly shown no signs of growing out of celebrating his own birthday, and the idea was to have a party that stretched over an entire week, living cheaply on beaches, discovering rum, learning how to buy weed without looking too much like schoolboy Englishmen there for the taking, and dining royally on the odd occasion when Tim fancied paying.

But it's the recollection of the night in Trinidad that gives me most pleasure. Tim came to pick me up from the airport in the beach buggy he was renting and I have a snapshot in my mind of the delight on his handsome features as he saw me appear from Customs. He put an arm round me, told me how delighted he was to see me and insisted on carrying my bags to the car. All the way to the hotel, he kept telling me how pleased he was that I'd come out to join him, that I was invited to the last-night-of-the-tour dinner and that, when the formalities were completed, we would jettison the squad to attack the bars and the rum together.

And that was how it went until we finished up at a quarter past two, giggling and whispering in the quiet darkness of a small marina on Chaguaramas Bay, treading soft-footed up and down wooden jetties while Tim studied the boats because he said he fancied taking one for a spin. I was giggling at his

audacity. He was giggling because he wanted to go out on the water and genuinely thought he was going to get us there. And we were both giggling because we were pissed.

What we needed to pinpoint, Tim explained, were the twenty–twenty-five-foot day boats, the shallower ones that were too small to accommodate anyone sleeping on board. People always kept a spare key, he said, in the cockpit locker under the fenders. He jumped into the first likely candidate and I kept watch while he fiddled around. He got out disappointed: there were no keys in the boat. He tried another. Same result. And then another fourteen. Then, from the next came the sing-song contented humming of Tim's voice as he dangled a set of keys in front of me; the hum of an engine followed, and Tim punched the air. That was the cue for me to cast us off from the mooring. I climbed aboard, shaking my head in disbelief.

It was only when the boat was bobbing and the lights of the shore were blinking far away in the distance that we could celebrate our magnificent coup. Its magnificence did, however, dim after twenty minutes on the water when the engine futt-futt-futted to a stop.

'Ah,' said Tim, matter-of-factly. 'It appears we've run out of petrol.' And after a hunt around, we agreed that there wasn't a spare gallon on board.

This might have perturbed some, but not Tim. Fifteen minutes later, he had rigged the mainsail and our boat was being carried by the light night breeze back to harbour. He steered us into the same mooring, timing precisely the dropping of the sail so that we glided slowly to a perfect stop.

Now, on my flight from Bermuda to New York, I am replaying that whole Chaguaramas Bay episode in my mind, rewinding and reviewing it, searching for a glimpse of the Tim I am coming increasingly to know. And I can't find it. Which brings me some relief. Because, in his absence, I am more shocked by Tim than I had thought possible. What Marco told me has left me

incredulous. And I have no concept yet of whether I have it in me to fulfil my promise to keep it from Lucy.

Did I really get him so completely wrong? That night in Trinidad, he was audacity, brilliance, fearlessness, the man for whom no challenge was too much. And in that respect, he was, of course, miles away from me. But he was close too: he wrapped me tight in the flag of friendship; he told me I belonged with him. We shared togetherness: we were brothers pulling off the great burglary-by-the-sea.

There was a time in our friendship when I played second fiddle and he was the lead. There were occasions when we didn't even belong in the same orchestra. Indeed, I think we always made an unlikely duo. I can recall countless occasions when he dominated conversation and I merely squeezed in now and then with the odd pithy line. I can recall the night I first met Marco, in a West End bar with Tim after work one Thursday evening: we talked banking at first so it was understandable that Marco should direct every word at Tim, but then we broadened to boats and still Marco was one-way with his conversation. When we arrived at birds, booze and probably every other cliché occupying the minds of twentysomething males, I was aware that Marco wasn't even making eye-contact with me. Because, regardless of what he had said about investment, Borough flats and superior business practices, he was dazzled by Tim too.

But over the years the balance between Tim and me changed. Occasionally I even got talked to. And that night in Chaguaramas Bay was about as close as we got, not just for the shared experience and the satisfaction of the successful misdemeanour, but because there was depth to the friendship. At least, that was how it seemed. Had he not wrapped an arm round my shoulders and told me over and over again how delighted he was that I was at his side?

And this is the other reason why I am sending the replay of that night in Trinidad on a loop in my mind. Because, otherwise, what is left of us? We're a busted flush. Tim was a man

who kept his true self hidden from me and ours was a false friendship built upon the sand, fortified with deception and rotten to the core.

These are not fleeting thoughts that pass between the arrival of the drinks trolley and the delivery of my lunch tray. They stay with me all the way to JFK and they don't leave thereafter.

MANHATTAN

Nadia, my other titanic misjudgement of character, is head to toe in Madison Avenue labels, an entire new wardrobe that turns male heads as she approaches.

'You look great,' is the understatement with which I greet her.

'I know. It's amazing what separation can do for you,' she replies, basking in the certainty of how good she looks. She bats her eyelids and the corners of her mouth turn up. This is Nadia in her role of confident, teasing, Italian moll, the role in which she's the dominatrix and pins me to the floor with a stiletto. I used to like it; it was one of the last of which I grew weary. But now, it has a different inflection. Now I am not allowed to touch.

We are in the Lounge: a bar in Chelsea, chic, modern, shiny and typically Nadia, swarming with celebutantes and models, the sort of company among whom Nadia has the ability of moving with ease. This bar is her choice, a pointed one. Because every couple has their own directory of venues – the bar where they first got drunk together, the restaurant where they first ate, the place in the park where they lay on the grass and watched cherubic children playing in the sun and first imagined coming back one day with their own – and this is one of ours. We had known the bar staff and they had known us and our drinks of choice: Sam Adams for me, Grey Goose and tonic for the lady, with an ashtray and the small square nibbles plate with the ingenious collection of pickled vegetables. I took her there in the fleeting months when we were happy and when it felt that we were under a spell that would never lift. And I got such a kick

out of it: me, Gregory reincarnate, a virgin at nineteen, in the bar where the beautiful people went, drinking with the best-looking of them all.

And Nadia would play up to it; she dressed up, draped herself over me, sat coquettishly on my lap and hand-fed me the pickled cauliflower. Flirt, tease, play the role. Then she took me home and played the role to its conclusion. Did anyone else ever feel so unbeatable, so much the king of the hill, top of the heap, as if all those little-town blues were melting away forever? Did anyone else ever feel it so strongly that they wanted to burst into song?

'How have you been?' I ask.

'You mean, am I a broken, battered shell still struggling to recover from being fucked over by some self-obsessed London ad-man?' Ouch. She makes a display of flicking back her hair, then looks me in the eye. 'What do you think, sweetie?'

'I think we should order you a drink,' I reply, locating a nearby waiter. 'Your usual?'

'No, I've upgraded. I'm a Belvedere and tonic girl now.'

I order, and contemplate the preening display before me.

'So what's this all about, then?' she asks. 'Why d'you want to see me?'

'I brought you the papers.'

'My divorce papers? Ooh, lucky me! Show me where to sign.'

'You might want to find a lawyer to look through them first.'

'Oh, Dominic! Don't be so boring.' She stands up and unbuttons her leather coat, revealing copious cleavage and a pinstripe, wide-collared shirt thrown in for decorative effect.

'You're in a bit of a rush, are you?'

'Oh, I am. You might find this hard to believe, Dom, but I've landed firmly on my feet.'

'So it would seem.'

'His name's Mike, if you want to know.'

'I'd rather know whether he's been hit yet by the flying barbecue tongs.'

'Too good-looking. I wouldn't want to spoil those strong features of his.'

'Well, tell him from me to practise his body-swerve and his duck for the day you change your mind.'

'I won't change my mind. He makes me happy.'

'Eternally happy?'

'I think so.'

'He hasn't met your mother, then, has he?'

'You fucker.'

And that's round one to me.

'He's better than you,' she says eventually, looking up from her drink as if struck by inspiration.

'What do you mean?'

'You know what I mean.' She lets her words settle and work their way into me. 'He satisfies me, Dominic. That's what I mean.'

And that's round two to her.

And it's lucky that I'm a well-rounded bloke with a reasonable sense of self-esteem and a contentedly buoyant self-perception because otherwise it might bother me. Imagine filing for divorce and jettisoning an intensely physical marriage to the best-looking girl in the beautiful people's bar in favour of a nocturnally nervous, almost completely sexless relationship, and then feeling miffed at the choice you'd made. Lordy, Lordy, that really would be a sad state of affairs.

I have four full days ahead of me in New York and I'm longing to leave already.

I move into Jerry's apartment in East Village where there is a spare room and no Jerry because he is away on business for the day. And maybe I was filling time, maybe I was feeling unfulfilled in my cranny at Duffy's in London, maybe I was trying to buy myself a little breathing space from the intensity of the nervous nocturnals when I arranged this trip, but four days is more than enough. My mission: to hand over the divorce papers

to Nadia, to remove the last remaining items from the apartment we had rented together, to see old friends, to avoid the
Duffy's New York office and, most importantly, to buy a Spider-
Man outfit complete with the crucial mask. That doesn't take
four days, no matter how important the search for the mask. So
I have too much time – time to think about Archdeacon Avenue,
to contemplate Lucy and my foolhardy promise to Marco. I
know I'll soon want to be away from here.

Only Jerry, on his return, can persuade me that I might
possibly want any further part of it.

'Hey! It's Daihatsu Hijet man!' is his welcome. We meet in a
bar below the apartment in St Marks Place, a throbbing,
Bohemian neighbourhood where the prosperous live side by side
with the punks, where hippies and the homeless coexist – a
'melting pot' is how the city guides would describe it, the sort
of place in which Nadia would never be seen dead. Jerry is sitting
at the bar drinking champagne. He looks contented, at home.
As ever, his designer stubble is well judged, and the tiredness in
his face is a fraud. 'You're looking good,' he says. 'Is that because
you've bought the Daihatsu and proved your virility?'

'Am I allowed a drink before the cross-examination begins?'

'Hardly. I've got news. Here,' he says, presenting me with a
glass of champagne and looking me up and down. 'But come
on, how's the campaign going? Is the product selling well in
Richmond?'

'I don't think the target market's completely won over.'

'So you're not driving the Hijet yet?'

'No. I've barely got the key in the ignition.'

'Ah.' Jerry pauses. 'Good to see you anyway.'

'You must miss me terribly.'

'What? With a fucking major account with a medical insurance company to keep the adrenaline pumping?'

'Well, why the champagne?'

'I've got news, haven't I? Serious cross-pollination at Duffy's.
Significant Americans are moving the other way.'

'What do you mean?'

'Kathy? The tequila girl? Don't look at me like that. You know perfectly well who I'm talking about. The one who pulled up her shirt at that bar on Spring Street? Need I say more?' His expression indicates that he knows the answer.

'Strangely enough, the memory hasn't quite faded.'

'She's being transferred to the London office.'

'So?'

'I thought I'd better warn you.'

'Why would an almost-contented, sort-of-settled man like me require warning?'

'Because, my dear friend, the last time you were presented with her navel, your sense of contentment didn't prove sufficient.'

'And you bought champagne just to tell me that?'

'No. The bubbles are for something else altogether: to celebrate our future working together again.'

'You what? You're moving to London too?'

'No. You'll have to move back here.'

He is watching his words sink in. But they don't. 'What are you talking about?'

'Sweet Lord, that's what I'm talking about.'

'I'm not with you.'

'Sweet Jesus, Dom, Sweet Lord. We've got our chance.' He's watching my face again for a reaction. 'Our agency. It's happening. I've been approached. Account handlers and accountants, madmen all of them, but they're men with money, the real thing, lots of it, and ambition. They want to do stuff, be big, be better, you know, the usual spiel, the stuff we used to believe in. But they mean it and the funny thing is they want us, you and me, they want Sweet Lord. And, yes, I know it's ridiculous and there must be far better people out there, far more ambitious people, people who really care about putting on sales for the sodding medical insurance company, but what the fuck? These people want us. They want Sweet Lord and I think we should drink to it.'

For a man prone to cynicism, possessed of a sense of humour

of the most tinder-dry variety and wary of emotional excess, Jerry is breaking his own rules. Usually, when excitement levels rise, he rubs the top of his head, making his thick, greying hair stick up. Now his eyes are wide, his hair is aloft, and his arms are gesticulating broadly, the champagne in his left hand cascading out of the glass. 'Well? Well?' he questions me, triumphantly, as if he has just worked out the meaning of life and wants to be commended for it. 'Come on, Dom. Eh? Eh? Well? Drink to it?'

'Why would I want to do that?'

'Why drink to it?'

'Why come to New York when Lucy's in London?'

'Because you've already said that you're only sort-of-settled, that you're not driving the Daihatsu and that the target market's not convinced. That's why.'

'You're asking me to give up sweet Lucy for Sweet fucking Lord?'

'I'm only asking.' He changes his tone, enthusiasm now on hold. 'It's just a friendly sales pitch.'

And now I have the old Jerry back again. We finish the champagne, he returns to the whisky and I return to the beer. Later we go three doors down where the drinks order is the same; and then the same again.

The topic of debate for tonight: Sweet Lord versus sweet Lucy, woman versus the workplace, a theme that runs through history, taking in Henry VIII, Edward VIII, going back to square one with Adam (as in Eve) and ending in another bar in SoHo with Don Juan, James Bond, Batman and Roger Rabbit. There is, of course, only one conclusion, to which Jerry admits he had resigned himself before he began his champagne sales pitch. The woman wins. Why else would daft Scots set off hitch-hiking to Caracas if they could be content in the workplace?

But the debate doesn't end there. It returns to occupy my mind for long spells the next day when I go in search of Spider-Man outfits, and particularly when I'm plugged into my laptop,

sending Lucy a forty-five-pound bunch of birthday flowers – the 'Lavish Lily Bouquet' – with the message that I'm missing her and will be returning home twenty-four hours earlier than planned. It doesn't help to receive a text message from Jerry when I am sitting in the departure lounge at JFK: 'Spoke to the backers today. Stalled them. You've now got three months to get the Daihatsu into gear. Good luck. And great to see you. J.'

But as relationships go, the current evidence – me and Nadia, me and Tim – is that I'm not too hot with them. I didn't choose well there, did I? Indeed, the emotional edifice of my life would have collapsed if I didn't still have Lucy and Jerry, my two remaining pillars, holding it up. And now I've elected to meddle with Lucy, so first prize for stability goes to Jerry. And Jerry wants me back.

20

It's ten o'clock so Josh will be at school. And I know Lucy is at home because the front door isn't double-locked.

'Hi!' I shout. Silence. 'Lucy?' Still no reply. So, in a sarcastic, mock-Yankee accent: 'I'm home, honey.' Silence again.

The winter chill and the sense of apprehension that accompanied me in my taxi to Archdeacon Avenue were not misplaced. I find Lucy slouched in the deep blue sofa in the sitting room. Her face is pale, the T-shirt and tracksuit bottoms she is wearing suggest that she hasn't got up properly. A cigarette is burning is the ashtray next to her and she doesn't jump up to greet me. She doesn't even leave the sofa. Most significantly, in front of her is a box of yellow tissues, a number of used ones scattered on the carpet and, on her lap, the manuscript of *Book of the Month*. She doesn't look up to acknowledge me: her eyes remain fixed on a sheet of the manuscript as she reads on – or pretends to read on – refusing to acknowledge that after a week away I am back in the same room as her.

I expected this. Or something like it. It would, I suspected, be the price of honesty. On the countless occasions during the last week when I imagined this moment, Lucy's reactions were one of two extremes. Either the make-me-feel-good option: the hyper, kid-at-Christmas type effusiveness as she threw herself into my arms and glued herself to me with the most passionate embrace, or this.

Eventually, rather theatrically, Lucy turns her face in my direction.

'So, you didn't like the birthday present?' is my way of breaking

159

the silence from the safety of the other side of the room.

'I don't think it's quite as simple as "like", is it?' Her voice is deadpan, as if she's building up to something.

'Were you surprised by it?'

'Surprised? If you were on the hunt for a gob-smacking understatement, Grey, then yes, I think you've located one pretty successfully.'

'Do you want a cup of tea?'

'No, I do not want a sodding cup of tea!' She almost spat the words out. 'Grey, I want you to come and sit here and tell me what the fuck you think I'm supposed to make of this book and, more importantly, how much of it you mean.' The deadpan cool is gone now. 'Because you want to know what I thought of the book, Grey? At the start I thought it was amusing. I was touched even. I thought it was pretty sweet to open with a scene that was so autobiographical, where Greg and Kate, your gorgeous, misunderstood hero and his unknowing heroine, make a pact that if they're not married by the age of thirty, they'll marry each other. Goodness me, I thought, isn't that funny? Just like me and Grey. But the story didn't change much after that, did it? Chapter two was kind of like me and Grey too, wasn't it? And so was chapter three.

'And you know, Grey, it's a good book. You write well, you really do. It was so good that there were moments – fleeting ones – when I couldn't put it down, when I started losing myself in the story, when I almost got carried away with it. Especially that bit where Greg is so weighed down by his unspoken feelings that he spends the whole night walking the streets of London, trying to work out what the fuck to do. And it's a pretty long walk, by the way, from his house in Crouch End to her front door in Brook Green. You might want to go back on that and put him in a taxi for the last leg. But I wasn't sure if that was really what you wanted from me. I don't know if I was supposed to be borne along with Greg and all that tension where you're worrying that he might not get to Kate's front door before she leaves for work.

I don't think you gave me this,' she stops and brandishes a handful of sheets of the manuscript, 'to entertain me with some great work of *fiction*, did you?'

I am still in the spot in the middle of the room where I was when this conversation started and, with Lucy's glare pinning me to the floor, it would seem that I'm here to stay.

'I just—'

'I didn't know what to make of it.' Her interruption is immediate. 'I was teetering on being flattered. But I didn't want this sort of flattery. And then I didn't even know if I was allowed to be flattered.' Her tone has softened and her left hand has tightened round a ball of yellow tissue. 'Because there's one crucial difference between Greg and Kate and you and me, Grey, isn't there? You and I are best mates, sharing the closest of equal friendships either of us has ever had, aren't we? Isn't that the premise? The platonic thing – isn't that the foundation of everything we're about? But Greg was different, wasn't he? Because he *pretended* that this sort of thing was the case for him and Kate, but he was lying. He spent most of his adult life lying about it, because he's always been in love with her and he's never had the balls to do anything about it.

'So I've got two questions for you, Grey.' She falters and stops, dabbing under her long eyelashes with the ball of tissue. 'One, am I supposed to admire Greg for being one of literature's great unrequited romantics, or is he just a wimp? And two, just tell me, is Greg a work of fiction or is he you?'

She pulls her legs under her and starts crying, repeating my name over and over, and flapping her hands in a way that conveys uncertainty and despair. Behind her Tim is still resplendent in his seven-photo shrine. Still no photographic acknowledgement of me.

I sit on the coffee-table in front of the sofa and lean forward so that I can caress her hair. After a little resistance she lets me take her hand.

'OK.' I breathe in audibly. 'Question one, you're supposed to

sympathise with Greg. If you think he's a wimp the book doesn't work. Maybe that's why the publishers haven't exactly been fighting over it. And question two, you're right, Lucy, and I'm truly sorry to have shocked or upset you because the last thing I want is to cause you pain. Greg isn't entirely fictional. I do feel the way he feels.' Lucy's eyes squeeze tight as if she is wincing. 'I've been in love with you, Lucy, since long before I even realised it, and this was my way of letting you know.'

She doesn't respond and we are framed in silence with Tim smiling at me from his shrine. From outside on the road comes the growl of a car engine starting. The only other sound is of Lucy shifting in the sofa so that she is now sitting forward, our faces inches apart.

'Come here,' she says. She puts her arms round my neck and pulls me into her so that I can feel the wetness of her eyes on my shoulder through the cotton of my shirt. 'You silly, foolish, extraordinary man!' Her voice is so soft it's almost a whisper. 'You silly, silly man!' She sighs. 'You had to write a book just to tell me that?'

'How can you be surprised?' I pull away from her, only an inch or two. 'The best story I could ever tell was the one I'd been living for the majority of my adult life.'

Lucy shakes her head, gazing longingly away from me and out of the window, and I continue: 'Do you remember that day at Durham when we had that argument with Tim about *Gregory's Girl*? About how the play would work because it was about us and the stuff that we were going through and that we could relate to? Well, I still believe in that. I believe that a book can be more acute, more valuable, better, if it's something the author has experienced. That's why I've grown weary of advertising, because it's the complete opposite. That's why I wanted to write this book, because it's something real.'

'For fuck's sake, Grey!' The soft tone has vanished; she throws herself back into the sofa. 'And don't look at me in that fucking puppy-dog sympathetic way. This isn't a conversation about

artistic integrity! This is a conversation about you and me, about who we are, what we're all about, what for the last month 'together' has been all about. Because I thought I knew the answers to all that. I thought I knew you as well as I've ever known anyone – as well as I knew Tim, even. And, God, did I like what I saw! I liked it so much that I entertained the idea of you, us, a relationship. And now – oh, God! – now you just sling me a book for my birthday that breezily informs me I didn't know the bloody foundations on which we were based! I knew diddly-bloody-squat. What am I supposed to make of that? I don't know what to feel. Flattered? Foolish? Blind? Duped? Or as if one of the dearest people in my life has spent almost the entire time I've known him lying to me?'

She is crying again, her sweet face distorted into a picture of distress.

'But, Lucy, deep down, did it really surprise you? Did you have no idea at all?'

'Of course I didn't!' She throws out her hands, fingers stretched, as if she's about to pull her hair out or, at least, a handful of mine. And then she stops herself, and she rubs her temples. 'But, Grey, the real point for me is this.' She is suddenly composed. 'We, *we* of all people, have a closeness based on understanding, talking, openness. Isn't *that* what we've always been about? You unlocking my soul, me unlocking yours? You know, ultimate honesty, everything on the table, weaknesses exposed, confronted, knowing each other naked, nothing left hidden, complete understanding, tell all, bare all and love each other because of it. That's why I felt I could sleep with you, because it was a physical extension of where we were before. Isn't *that* what our coming together was all about? But here I find that you've kept back from me one of the biggest secrets of your life.'

'But what could I do, Lucy? You got married, I got married. Tim. Nadia. Maybe I've known this for years and years, but only deep down. I didn't confront it. How could I? It wouldn't have

been healthy. Er, oh, sorry, Tim, but you know that nice wife of yours that I like to take out for pizza? Well, actually I'm in love with her. Just thought you might like to know. No, I couldn't quite pull off that conversation.' I stand up and walk over to the double doors that lead out into the garden. 'Lucy, it was only when I realised that I'd got it so wrong with Nadia that I let myself address my feelings for you. Please, please, don't think I've been conniving or dishonest. I've always been as honest as I could allow myself to be. It's really important you understand that.'

'OK.' Lucy spreads her hands as if to show that the rage inside her has died away. 'OK. I see your point.' She lights a cigarette. 'I do see your point.' She exhales with a long, exhausted sigh. 'So what do we do now, Grey? Come on, you tell me. You're the one who's got it all figured out.'

'What do you want to do now?'

She shrugs. 'The only thing I know I've got to do is go to Sainsbury's.'

'OK.' For want of a better plan. 'Let's go to Sainsbury's.'

It makes for a somewhat unreal circuit of the aisles of a supermarket to do it with someone to whom you have just confessed hidden love. On those occasions in Bermuda and New York when I found myself imagining my confrontation with Lucy, it never finished in Sainsbury's. Sometimes we'd end up in bed. Sometimes we went to Hatton Garden to buy her an engagement ring. Once we ended up booking ourselves in for a course of relationship counselling. Mostly, though, we'd end up on a walk, hands entwined, ambling down the Thames towpath on a fresh winter's day when you could see our breath in the cold air. Lucy would wear her woolly sweater with the strawberry, and the 'us' subject would be meticulously covered until no questions remained unanswered. And this walk had a happy ending: by the time we'd gone from Richmond to Kew, we'd have reached mutual happiness and peace of mind. We'd understand. Then

we'd go into one of those nice riverside pubs, order two glasses of champagne and toast our future. So much for wishful thinking.

The idea of reconvening in Sainsbury's had never crossed my mind. It has its advantages: people to distract you, a trolley to push, foodstuffs to discuss. Do we go for cherry tomatoes on the vine or the organic ones? Posh ice-cream or cheap? Bin-liners with handles or ties? And is Josh still banned from the cereal with Michael Owen's face on the pack? In fact, it's something of a relationship fun-park: there's so much to do that you could almost forget you might have just blown your chance of eternal happiness.

Almost, but not quite. By the time we're in aisle three, I can contain it no longer. Lucy says we need margarine and I'm standing in front of an acre of oil-based spreading products, wondering if she's a straightforward Flora girl or more of a Flora Light and asking myself if I really knew what I was doing by declaring my love for someone whose margarine preference I don't know.

And then I do it, because I know the answer to my question. Do I know what I'm doing? Yes. Absolutely I do.

'Tell me, Lucy, tell me about that time at Durham.'

She looks up from the cream-cheese shelf.

'What time?'

'The night you first kissed Tim. That party at Sophie's digs.'

'Yeah?'

'You nearly kissed me first. You were about an inch away from it. We were sitting on a grotty green chair thing and we were about to kiss. We were so bloody close and we nearly bloody did it. Then Tim waltzed along, stopped us in our tracks, whisked you off and married you.'

'Yeah?' There is measured uncertainty in her voice. She puts the cream cheese down and turns to me.

'Tell me. Are your feelings for me really, honestly completely based on this intellectual, soul-baring ultimate mutual-friendship thing? Or isn't there something else? Isn't there a flicker of basic,

everyday, physical magnetism? Because, correct me if I'm wrong, that night in Durham it seemed that there was.'

'Oh, Grey!' Her face falls into an expression of pity. 'Was this what you were holding out for? Some hope that, because I might have nearly kissed you on a green bench at a pissed student party, I'd therefore be ready to take up where I apparently left off sixteen years ago? Oh, Grey! You haven't really been holding out for that all this time, have you?'

'Flora Light or Flora normal?'

'Flora Light. Answer my question.'

'What about Lurpak Lighter? It says it's very spreadable and slightly salted.'

'Flora Light. Answer my question.'

'No. You answer mine. What does that night mean to you? Why were you about to kiss me? And have you ever wondered whether maybe, just maybe, if I'd been a bit quicker that night, say thirty seconds quicker, and you'd kissed me and not Tim, maybe our lives would have been different and you'd have ended up with me?'

'Christmas, Grey! No, I've never wondered that! Not once in my life! Not for the briefest of split seconds has it ever crossed my mind.'

'OK. But were you or were you not about to kiss me?' A bespectacled lady stretches round me to the margarine shelf, oblivious of the conversation she has walked into. 'Look, she's chosen Lurpak Lighter,' I say to Lucy. 'I think it might be worth a try.'

'Flora Light, Grey!' Lucy is smiling. Sainsbury's is definitely the place for these conversations.

'Well? What were you thinking?'

'I was drunk.'

'Sorry, that's not good enough. And I hate this question, but is there or is there not, somewhere deep down within you, a sense of basic, innate physical attraction to me?'

'I've slept with you, haven't I? What does that tell you? But,

Grey, it's not as simple as that. It's not just a case of body and soul, physical and spiritual. The one plus the other equals love in capital letters, the big jackpot and wedding bells. Feelings are more complicated than that, aren't they? I loved Tim. Truly, madly, deeply. You know that, and there's no getting away from it. And yes, I do love you, Grey. I've worked that much out. But in a different way. You and me, we'd reached somewhere, we'd got so close it seemed that maybe we shouldn't be parted. But that's why I found your book so upsetting. Not because of the love you'd hidden from me but because I was under the impression that we were level-pegging, that we were in the same place, that the way I felt about you was mirrored in the way you felt about me, and that because of all that we could work it out together, go as far as we wanted, maybe even go all the way – I don't know – but not get hurt or cause harm to each other. And now I know that's not the bloody case.'

'You mean you saw me as a safe option.'

'Not safe, just different. Now, come on,' she puts her arm round me, 'there must be better places to discuss this.'

'Aisle four or five?'

'Shut up!' She rubs her head on my shoulder and together we manoeuvre our trolley down the aisle.

'Fresh pasta or dried?'

'Dried,' she replies.

'Penne or fusilli?'

'Always penne. Josh finds them easier to spear on his fork.'

Big bag or little? Sainsbury's own brand or fancy Italian? Fresh pasta sauce or bottled? And which brand? Which type? Thus do we continue sharing the load of the trolley and making some of life's great decisions on our way.

'Tell me about Greg, then,' she says. We are in aisle six, the cosmetics area, and no one is near us. 'It's not just some randomly selected name, is it?'

'Correct.'

'Anything to do with *Gregory's Girl*, by any chance?'

'Of course it is. I was Gregory, right? And you were Gregory's girl.'

She shakes her head in dismay. 'You sad old romantic!'

And we move on. We sort out some more issues. Chicken nuggets: dinosaur shapes or smiley faces? Always dinosaurs. Frozen peas or *petits pois*? Always *petits pois*. Together for ever or destined to fail? This is Lucy's issue, aired beside the fruit squash with our trolley nearly full, and – again – no one is near us.

'Because this is what gets me,' she says. 'Your couple in the book, Greg and Kate, there's no happy ending for them, is there? They don't end up together. They try to go through with the planned marriage and they fail.'

'Yup.'

'Well, given that no storyline in your book is wasted, that every bloody page carries some significance for you and me, I want to know what I'm supposed to make of the ending.'

I shrug my shoulders.

'C'mon, Grey, don't duck the question. Why doesn't it work for Greg and Kate?'

'Can't we talk lemon cordial instead?'

'No!'

'Right. OK. I guess it's me being a combination of pessimistic and realistic. What are the chances of you and me working out, Lucy, going the whole way and getting married? Do I really think it's going to happen? It's bloody hard to do what we're trying to do. I don't know if we're actually trying to do it any more, or even if we ever were, but I don't think a bespoke marriage is easy. I don't think it's just a case of two mates sitting down with a piece of paper and drawing up a together-forever relationship plan. I mean, there's quite a lot of feelings out there waiting to get hurt. We've seen enough evidence of that this morning. So, do I think we're going to work out? I think there's a chance, but only a slim one. The bookies would have us at around five to one, maybe four, but no better than that. And the odds have lengthened considerably today.'

'I think those odds are a bit harsh. I'd have a punt at four to one. If you're sure you want it to happen, that is.'

'Sure? I want it desperately – there can't be any secret about that. Not now.' And suddenly – and this is instinct, idiocy, adrenaline, jetlag, in fact probably all the above all kicking in simultaneously. I find myself down on one knee. 'Look, Lucy, if I didn't make myself clear at the Greenwich Observatory a month ago, then maybe I should now. You know how I feel now, Lucy. There's nothing hidden at all. So please, Lucy, will you marry me?'

Lucy's response is a glare of utter disbelief. And, I may be mistaken, but it then seems to be softened by a smile. 'Did you plan this?'

'What? To propose to you next to the Robinson's lemon barley water? Of course not!'

21

To be the proposer sitting on a marriage proposal is not my idea of fun. In advertising we like suspense, but only in short bursts. We might, for instance, like to leave viewers wondering whether a Brut-user is going to get his girl, but sure enough, after a milli-second's nail-biting tension, we are reassured that he is, indeed, the essence of man. Likewise, viewers might have wondered whether my two houseboat honeys were ever going to cut the foreplay and take their Peachey's ice-cream to bed with them, and although we didn't give the answer straight away, we always gave a clue, advanced a little closer to the endgame. At Duffy's, we congratulated ourselves on our smart use of suspense. Very clever.

But suspense doesn't work as well in the way Lucy decides to employ it. I feel like sitting her down and explaining the rules to her. You can't just lock away your thoughts like this: to engage the emotions of your audience you have to open up a little. It's one thing to say that you're not sure if you want to marry me, that you want some time to think — as a dramatic device, that works quite well: it hooks you into the story — but just to say you don't know what to do and that you can't think about it, can't discuss it, can't even think about how you're going to go about thinking about it, well, that's bad use of suspense. It would just about work if she gave me a date. If she'd said, wait till Sunday, or Valentine's Day, or the moment when the light dies in the next solar eclipse, and we'll discuss it then, at least I'd have something to work towards. But with no information and no timetable for the release of all this embargoed information, it's bad for the market audience, especially when the market audience is me.

The check-out process in Sainsbury's was awkward. I'm not given to gender stereotypes – that was more Tim's thing – but at a supermarket check-out, I'm the bloke all the way. The female unloads the trolley, the male bags up. I'm sure all successful marriages are based on such foundations. After my proposal, Lucy appeared shocked into silence. The tension wasn't relieved at the check-out when she discovered a bottle of Robinson's lemon barley water in our trolley and held it up with an expression that suggested it might be Semtex. Here I blame myself. If I hadn't been so bloke-ish and gone for the bagging, we might have avoided this. If Lucy had been bagging – shovelling stuff into bags at breakneck speed, as baggers do – she might not have noticed the lemon barley water. But she did.

'What's this doing here?' she asked.

'I put it in as a memento.'

'Pardon?' she replied, in a tone that implied she was talking to a moron.

'Well, one day when we're married,' I explained jauntily, 'we'll have this bottle of barley water as the witness to remind us of where it all started.'

The check-out girl and Lucy both looked at me with expressions that matched Lucy's earlier tone. Then they set about their business, unloading and checking-out, as if I hadn't spoken. It was only when Lucy had nearly emptied the trolley that she looked at me with a smile, indicating that I had now gone from being simply a moron to a lovable moron. Ah, happy days.

But what next? Two crucial moments prove less crucial than I'd hoped.

One: Josh comes back from school. He launches himself into me with delight, leaping so high that he clears my knee and ends up hugging my thigh and abdomen. And that's before the Spider-Man suit and mask have been produced from a plastic bag in my suitcase. On goes the outfit, on goes the mask. 'Here comes the king of the superheroes,' he announces. 'C'mon, Dom, time to fight.'

'Am I superhero Dominic Lord again?' I enquire, uncertain of the rules.

'No way, butthead,' he replies (a new addition to his vocabulary made in my absence and, judging by the way he delivers it, one in which he takes considerable pride). 'He wasn't very good, was he?'

Confidence dented, I resume the losing battle. Josh squeals with delight. Mess is made. Fun is had. Josh clambers all over me. He pins me down in a special imaginary web. Cleverly, I tear a hole in it and crawl out, but he soon has me pinned down into a 'mega-web'. Lucy comes into his bedroom to see what all the noise is about and I catch her eye with what I hope is a significant expression that says: Your boy is so happy, so very happy. Look, we have formed this incredibly tight bond – isn't he just crying out to have me anointed as his new father? And maybe Lucy interprets it perfectly: her response suggests as much. Even though it's not the one I want. She shakes her head with a smile that bears the message: Yes, this is, indeed, extremely sweet, but one Spider-Man suit and a game of rough-and-tumble don't make a marriage.

Two: bed-time. Lucy's and mine, that is. The first bed-time since my return. A crucial one, and I wouldn't be surprised if she's been thinking about it throughout the ten o'clock news too – because by the time we are in the Corridor of Uncertainty, she has it all worked out. She stops outside her door and hugs me – a consolation hug that says: Sorry, mate, this is as far as you come.

'Grey,' she whispers, 'you've said some amazing and lovely things to me today and don't think my head isn't spinning. But I don't know what to do. And I don't think my mind will become any clearer by sleeping with you. Sorry. I do love you, you know that, don't you?' I nod obediently. 'But my love and your love suddenly seem so far apart.'

And that's it. Subject closed. Thereafter the days pass and I am left dangling in some purgatorial joke, denied romantic

contact, left to stew in a pit of my own awkwardness, wondering every time we meet, every time we part, when I leave for work and when I return, whether she'll surprise me with an answer: 'Sorry, Grey, you're like a brother to me. Let's keep it that way.' 'Let's not ruin what we've got, let's just be friends.' 'Let's find another cliché to bring your hopes crashing round your ankles.' 'You're such a good guy, you're too nice for me.' What? You'll only marry someone who isn't nice? 'I'm not ready for all this yet, you're not the Adonis Tim was and you don't satisfy me in bed. Here's a one-way ticket to Caracas.' One of or all of the above: they all come to mind. As does the pleasant alternative: 'Yes, Grey, I've thought about your offer and, after due consideration, I have decided to accept it.'

A man could be broken and beaten by the policy of silence that I am up against. He could shrivel, lose his confidence, become self-conscious around the object of his desire. I know this because I was like that with Daisy, the Roman-nosed biology student. When she decided that she and I were no longer to be bedmates, I took the news badly. I imploded; I couldn't look Tim in the eye. I knew that nothing like that had happened to him and felt desperately uncool that it had happened to me. I could barely speak to Daisy. Even though she had done me the most enormous favour by hauling me into bed with her and relieving me of the burdensome Big V, I was lost for words.

But that was then. This is the Dominic Lord of the new millennium, fortified by an ice-cream ad and a below-average number of half-decent sexual conquests. So, self-confidence is mine now, albeit a little frail. I've learned enough to know that were I to crumple into a heap my cause would not be advanced. I've got my product properties and brand personality to protect. Now, more than ever, I am being tested. I've got to remain the bright, cheery, ever-reliable Daihatsu Dom; maintain brand recognition, increase brand value. Or something like that.

There is, of course, the other option, which involves breaking my promise to Marco. That would certainly produce an emotional shift in Archdeacon Avenue, and although I turn it over in my mind every day, I remain loath to use it. My intention is to make Lucy happy and, for all the lugubrious temptation, I feel sure that breaking my promise is not the way.

So here we are, day three post-proposal and my vow to Marco still intact. Lucy and I are in the kitchen together, preparing supper and getting in each other's way. I need the chopping knife to cut up the cherry tomatoes for the salad, she needs it to chop some parsley for her chicken dish, and our hands land on it at the same time. 'Oi, you!' says Lucy, in an unconvincing impression of a thug.

'It won't be like this when we're married,' I reply, smiling. 'I want you to know that when we're married, I'm going to be the boss around here.'

And Lucy laughs. It's not an easy laughter, more an embarrassed chortle, but any kind of laughter is better than monastic silence.

And that may not be a comedy moment of Pythonesque quality, but it is a landmark. Thereafter I am in a position to make light of my place in Purgatory.

More weak jokes on the marriage theme: 'I'm sorry, but smoking's going to be banned when you're Mrs Lord.' She does seem to be smoking quite a lot. 'Are you going to bring me breakfast in bed when we're married?' 'Are we going to share a bed again when we're married?' 'Would it help the decision-making process if I said that I'd bring *you* breakfast in bed?' 'I'm going to Savile Row today for a wedding tie. Will you come too and help me choose?' 'If I did bring you breakfast in bed, how would you like your eggs done?' 'But please remember there'll be no breakfast in bed without a wedding.'

It's not a campaign to force her into submission, and it has to be played out with sensitivity. If I'm too pushy I'll lose her;

I have to avoid being assertive and obsessive. But by being bright, amusing and sensitive – making light of an awkward situation might just help.

Then, on day nine post-proposal, another breakthrough suggests that my approach is right. It comes in the same light-humour wrapping at shortly before midnight when I arrive back at Archdeacon Avenue having had a liquid dinner and at least three vodkas more than was wise. 'You'll have to sharpen up your act, Mr Lord, if you think you're ever going to make a decent husband – to anyone, that is. Coming home late,' she thwacks me over the head with a rolled-up copy of the *Guardian*, 'stinking of booze. It'll never do, you know. Not so much as a phone call to tell us you're OK. And here we were, all two of us, sitting up, worrying about you.'

And from thereafter Lucy is able to refer to 'the situation' too. I leave for work one day and return twenty seconds later having realised I've no money on me for my train fare. And when I ask to borrow some, Lucy's quick-as-a-flash reply is: 'I think you could call that a case of bad husbandry. I'm afraid I'll have to take note.' Again, not exactly John Cleese, but it's the attempt that counts. Word-play on the marriage theme – it's got to be a breakthrough.

We are at breakfast the next morning when Lucy swoons at the sight of a council-tax bill. 'More bills.' She sighs. 'Tim used to pay the bills round here, you know. That's the deal for husbands in my life.' And the boundaries were pushed back even further.

No news, of course, about when she might give me an answer – the suspense thing is still misplayed there – but at least there is banter: two people who like to believe that they have a most extraordinary closeness are now able to joke about the extraordinary situation that has come between them.

But at last my patience cracks. Day fourteen post-proposal, I come home from work. I am happy: I have been the recipient of good news. I have bought champagne, I want to celebrate. I want

Lucy to celebrate with me. There is no one in the world with whom I would rather celebrate.

'Hi, Lula,' I greet her. Kiss on both cheeks.

'What's the bottle for?' she asks.

'Good news.'

'Can't be that good.'

'Why?'

'Because you've bought Moët & Chandon. Big mistake.' She is joking. Half joking. But it grates.

'What's the mistake?'

'Cristal!'

'What?'

'Louis Roederer Cristal. It's my favourite champagne. Come on, Grey. Smarten up your act.' Still teasing, but the joke's lost on me. 'Tim only ever bought me Cristal, and if you want to be meticulous, stick wherever possible to the 1993 vintage.' She moves to squeeze me under the ribs, where she knows I'm vulnerable, but I move away.

I put the Moët on the kitchen table with a bang. Lucy looks at me, brow furrowed. 'I'm sorry,' I answer. 'I'll go back and get the Cristal.'

'No, no, no!' She skips round the table, barring my way to the front door. She knows she has overstepped the mark. 'I was joking, Grey. And it was Tim who was the champagne snob. You know me, I like any bloody bubbles. You weren't supposed to take me seriously.'

'I know. But I just want you to take *me* seriously *some time*. Please! I can't be Tim. Stop comparing me to him.'

She responds with awkward silence. 'You know,' she says eventually, 'you're mistaken there, Grey. I'm not perpetually comparing you to Tim. *You* are.'

Another silence. Lucy and her perceptive observations. 'When Tim proposed to you,' I ask, 'how long did it take you to answer?'

'Er, it was pretty quick. I don't know – two seconds, perhaps?'

'And how much longer am I going to be left stranded?'

'You want an answer?'

My shrug indicates the affirmative.

'Come on,' she says earnestly. 'Let's go next door and sort this out. And bring that splendid champagne with you.'

22

So the pressure's on, the tension high. But, first, four short stories that helped it get that way.

STORY ONE

The day after the proposal, around midday, I went back into work at Duffy's, less sure than ever about my future. Thoughts of Sweet Lord flittered by, but Lucy, love and lemon barley water were omnipresent. I knew I should go and report to Ray first thing, it would have been rude not to, but I couldn't bring myself to discuss my future commitment to the agency when I was no closer to knowing if I wanted one. I sat down, read my email, wrote some replies, looked at my watch and wondered if Lucy would give me an answer that evening. Then Kathy walked in.

'Excuse me, sir,' she said, in the familiar New England twang, a forefinger pressed to her chin. 'I'm the new girl here. I don't know my way around yet and I'm a bit lost. You couldn't help me out, could you?'

'Kathy! What a pleasure.' I meant it. She looked good, in a short-skirted, female power-suit sort of way. New haircut, blonder than when I'd last seen her six weeks ago; young, vibrant and pleased with herself. 'I was told you were coming, but I didn't realise how soon.'

'Yup. Happened pretty fast, didn't it? This is day two. I didn't get lost on my way in this morning, got your Toob sussed, no problemo. And, I can tell you, my office is a damn sight nicer than yours, mate.'

'I think "cosy" is the word for my cubbyhole. They keep trying to upgrade me, but I'm holding out.'

'Well, you need to click out of this identity-crisis thing. You're too good for this shit-hole.'

'Ah, if only I could be a going-places character like you, Kathy, but we're diametric opposites now, aren't we?'

'Yeah, right! You're back up the top of the ladder in one bound, and don't you know it!'

Which was indeed a pleasure to hear, from someone of my more recent past, someone who still held me in 'big fish' regard rather than the other going-places graduates here, who had now ceased to treat me like a person they might meet one day at the top. I guess it was a gentle ego-massage. Either way, it was sufficient to persuade me that we should go out for dinner the following week.

And so to our 'date', as Kathy insisted on calling it.

It was on day nine post-proposal, the day I got home drunk having failed to eat and having consumed three-too-many vodkas and plenty more. In retrospect, I blame it on Kathy. She finished work later than planned, then said she didn't want to go to the Three Feathers because it would be nice to get away from the other Duffy's drinkers and, anyway, this was 'our date' not a company night out. We walked into Soho and found a wine bar where Kathy insisted we'd be able to eat. After we'd shared a bottle of wine we asked for the menu and were informed that there wasn't one. So we ordered another bottle of wine, and when we'd finished it, I agreed that it was too late to find a restaurant, so drank on instead.

And this was the crux of it. Kathy: inebriated, good fun, witty, self-deprecating and teasing, asking questions about my failed marriage to Nadia. How was it? Was I OK? It was never going to work, was it? Being single wasn't all that bad, was it? Me: inebriated too, enjoying the company of someone who was making me feel good about myself and aware that the way we were sitting – on two high stools at a round chrome table in the corner of the bar – meant there was body contact, nothing overt,

just knees brushing and elbows touching. And telling her that everything was OK, that although nothing had really happened yet, I'd found someone else I liked.

Kathy: 'Let's have another vodka.'

Me: 'Fine, why not?'

Kathy: 'The first time I ever had a drink with you, you licked the salt for a tequila shot off my tummy.'

Me: 'I know, bit naughty.'

Kathy: 'You don't regret it, do you?'

Me: 'I didn't feel very proud of myself. Nice tummy, though.'

Kathy: 'Yeah, right!'

Me: 'Honestly. Super-top tummy.'

Kathy: 'Want a tequila shot now?'

Me, looking into her eyes, trying to ensure that she really means what I think she means: 'I shouldn't.'

Kathy, left eyebrow raised: 'But you could.'

Me, looking into her eyes, sorely tempted, because it's a damn fine offer and I'm under no contract elsewhere. Indeed, it's exactly the sort of offer that I'm *not* getting elsewhere.

Kathy, doing a funny thing with her eyebrows. The left goes down and the right goes up simultaneously. The 'come on' of eyebrow body language.

Me, right hand brushing her face in a light sweep from forehead to chin: 'Sorry. I'd love to. Don't get me wrong. It's just not right for me right now.'

Kathy: 'OK. But think about it, tequila man. It'd be fun.'

STORY TWO

This was bad. Four days post-proposal. It was a Saturday, Josh had been round at Sam's house, he had stayed overnight after school the day before, which was apparently quite a grown-up new development for him. Playdays were old hat, overnighters were the big thing and this, I gathered, was his first. On the Saturday morning, Lucy wanted time-out to do

some shopping and I was delighted to be dispatched to pick him up, thrilled with the new responsibility and the chance to show that picking up Josh was a paternal duty I could perform well.

I rang the doorbell and was greeted by Alice, who was frowning. And no kiss. She bustled me into the sitting room and positioned herself in front of the fireplace, holding her chin in a vice-like thumb-and-forefinger grip.

'Is Bill in?' I asked, but got no response, just more chin holding. 'Where are the kids?' Weighty silence.

'What do you think you're doing?' she asked, as if I was supposed to know what she was talking about.

'I've come to pick up Josh,' I replied, in the knowledge that this wasn't the reply she was looking for.

'Little Joshie,' he doesn't like being called Joshie, 'is proud of his Spider-Man outfit, isn't he?'

'I bloody hope so. It took the best part of a morning in New York to track it down.'

'Joshie told me that it was his reward from you for not sleeping in his mummy's bed. I said I thought that that was a funny thing to be rewarded for. And he replied that it was because you wanted to sleep in his mummy's bed instead.'

Her schoolmistress tone made it clear that this wasn't a laughing matter. I stood on the spot, feeling awkward, saying nothing, shrugging my shoulders.

'Dominic, tell me,' her tone was condescending now, 'do you think it's right to bribe a four-and-a-half-year-old so you can sleep with his mother?'

I tried to reply but she cut me off mid-sentence. 'And tell me, Dominic, do you think it'll be good for Lucy who, let's face it, hasn't had a particularly good run of it and has fought to get her life back together? Do you think it'll help her to have her supposed "best friend" bouncing back from a failed marriage and straight into her bed? Talk about destabilising her! Got any other tricks up your sleeve?'

'I get the impression that you disapprove, Alice.' Not the most conciliatory comment I could have come up with.

'Aren't you the sharp one today?'

'Listen,' I had had enough, 'I don't see how Lucy and I can have anything to do with you, Alice, but if you really think I'd muck Lucy about, then you have no idea of the sort of person I am.'

'It can't work.'

'You don't know what you're talking about.'

'I know she still loves Tim.'

'You may not have noticed this but Tim's not much use to her any more.'

'Does she know that you bribe her son so you can sleep with her?'

'Not exactly.'

'I think it's fair to say that I know what I'm talking about, then,' she shrilled triumphantly.

'Alice, please, leave us alone,' I said, attempting to sound unruffled.

'Sorry.' She looked more pleased with herself than ever.

'You'd do well to work on your own marriage instead,' I countered, which was ill-considered and below-the-belt, and as I waited outside afterwards – Alice made me wait on the pavement while she got Josh – I reflected that it would probably have been better to have Lucy's best friend on my side than set firmly against me. And, to a certain extent, Alice might have been right: cohabitation by bribery doesn't sound that good, does it?

STORY THREE

Emails. From Jerry. Lots of them. A one-track, one-way email monologue that started on day six post-proposal as a mere trickle but soon threatened to wash me away.

From: Jerry Sweet
Subject: Sweet Lord

Dom,

Any news? You know I want you to be happy in your lovelife, you know that's my prime concern, don't you? But I'm just wondering if I could enquire as to how the long-term future's looking romance-wise? Because interest in Sweet Lord is gathering.

From: Jerry Sweet
Subject: Sweet Lord

Dom,

Have you seen that new Peachey's ad? Doesn't it really piss you off? I mean, no one can do it like us. Is ours a lost art? Don't you feel like getting together again and reminding the world what a good ad looks like?

From: Jerry Sweet
Subject: Sweet Lord

Dom,

How's Kathy? Have you bumped into her yet? Has she made her move yet? You must be tempted to run off to somewhere far away like New York.

From: Jerry Sweet
Subject: Sweet Lord

Dom,

Have you been getting any of my emails? Because I haven't had a single reply. Maybe your server's gone down. Investigate.

From: Jerry Sweet
Subject: Sweet Lord

Dom,

There's nothing that pisses me off more than a one-way conversation. The backers of Sweet Lord rang me again today. I think they may be getting wind of the fact that you're lukewarm on the whole operation. I'm getting to the stage where I need to say something to them. Please email me back. If I don't hear from you, I'll start phoning you. And there's no escape then.

And so finally:

From: Dominic Lord
Subject: Sweet Lord

Jerry,

How lovely to receive so much cheerful correspondence from you. Is it just me, or is there a theme running through these emails? But how strange of you to be referring so much to Sweet Lord when you know I'm 'busy' over here.

From: Jerry Sweet
Subject: Sweet Lord

Dom,

Nice to know you're still alive. Listen, seriously, please: this Sweet Lord thing is serious. I understand your predicament and you must understand mine. I want Sweet Lord to work, I think it could be brilliant. And I understand that, for you, Lucy comes first. Fair enough. But it would be a shame if we ended up losing both. So please keep me informed. I'm hoping to come to London in the next few

weeks anyway. But think of us as having a three-month deadline on this. That's all I'll say.

STORY FOUR

Day ten post-proposal, sitting in my cubbyhole, my head throbbing from the three-too-many vodkas the night before, hoping that Kathy didn't wander in 'lost' to see me again. The phone rang. It was my mother.

'Darling?'

'Mother?'

'I know I'm breaking all the rules about parental contact during work hours, darling, but there's a not inconsiderable streak of rebellion pulsing through me today.'

'And why's that, Mother?'

'I think you're about to become a published author, my darling.'

'You're joking!'

'Comedy couldn't be further from my mind.'

'How? Why? How much?'

'No figure yet.'

'What's happened, then?'

'Not a lot.'

'Sounds like you're making a mountain out of a molehill.'

'Darling, you know me and my garden better than to suggest the possibility of molehills.'

'And you, Mother, know perfectly well that you have me exactly where you want me, in the palm of your hand, so please explain what you are talking about.'

'OK. I spoke to my person today at Moses Press – they're an up-and-coming publishing house, just the right sort of place to nurture a first-time author with a glorious future like you. And he's keen. He's passed it round his colleagues and they all love the way you write, they think the book's got potential and that it would sell.'

'Brilliant!'

'But there's a catch.'

'Go on.'

'They want you to change the ending.'

'How?'

'How do you think?'

'They want a happy ending, do they?'

'Are you surprised?'

'Not hugely. But you know how important the ending is to me.'

'I also know how important getting the book published is to you.'

'I hope you didn't say I'd do it.'

'Of course not.'

'So do you think I should sacrifice my artistic integrity?'

'You went into advertising, didn't you? It's too late for an integrity debate.'

'Thanks, Mother. Do *you* think I should change the ending?'

'You know how much I'd like to see you and Lucy happy together.'

'Mother, we're talking about Greg and Kate.'

'I don't think the names matter, darling. This is autobiography, you and I both know that – there's no point in pretending otherwise. And, look, I'm emotionally involved in your life, just as your readers will be emotionally involved in Greg's, and I desperately want you and Lucy to work out. And I don't think that's a ludicrous outcome. I think it's believable. And if it's believable in real life, you can make it work on the page.'

'Thank you, Mother, for the benefit of your opinion.'

'Don't sound like that,' she replied, taking offence at my sarcasm. 'We're about to make you a star.'

23

'Come on.' Lucy takes my ill-thought-through, second-rate bottle of champagne in one hand and me in the other and leads us into the sitting room. Tim smiles seven times from his card-table shrine.

'What's the champagne for?' she asks.

'I think I've got a deal for the book.'

'Fantastic.' She drapes herself over me and I find my thighs tensing at the informality. 'So . . . I don't understand. You've had this brilliant news . . . Hang on a sec, I'll get some champagne flutes.' She jumps to her feet.

'Don't!' My response is too loud and fast. Tetchy.

'As I was saying,' she sits down, ignoring my reaction, 'you've had this brilliant news . . . so what's the problem?'

'The publishers want a happy ending. They think we should end up together.'

'Well, unless I'm horribly mistaken, you do too, don't you?'

'But you don't.'

'Pardon?'

'You don't.'

She doesn't contradict me. She breaks the silence with a long sigh. Still no contradiction. I get up. There's a piece of music I want to play. It might make the moment. It's not the 1812 Overture. It's not fireworks. Our heads aren't spinning, the earth hasn't moved for Lucy or me. Erik Satie's *Gymnopédie* No. 1 gives us symmetry. It gives us calm. It is what we are about. No explosions. And at the sound of the first piano chords, she smiles with recognition and understanding.

'OK.' Her voice is gentle. 'Time for answers? You want

answers? This is the way I see it. And don't think I haven't been looking at it over and over again in search of a better answer. The fact is, Grey, I want you, but I can't give you what you want. Would I marry you? Yes, I would, but only if I could be the Mrs Lord you wanted. And I don't think I can.'

'You can.'

'I can't be in another relationship the way I was with the handsome old bugger behind us.' She flicks her head at the shrine. 'I've worked that much out.'

'What about the same sort of relationship, but better?'

'Sorry, that's not an option.'

'Is that what it's come down to, Lula? Tim versus me?'

'I know that's what you think.'

'But is it what *you* think?'

Silence again. I know which way I want this conversation to go but for the moment I resist temptation.

'Come on,' Lucy is agitated, on her feet again, 'let's have that champagne.'

'Why?'

'I don't fucking know. Something to represent closeness, happiness, us, I suppose. And to break all this tension, which is so *un*-us.'

She returns with glasses and I watch as she eases the cork from the throat of the bottle. Neither of us knows what to say. Erik Satie isn't working his magic.

'I've got a toast.' I get to my feet; Lucy frowns at me. 'I could toast my new life at this new New York ad agency, which is being planned as we speak in my name. I am being courted to be one of the two named partners. I haven't told you about that because it's irrelevant. Exciting? Yes. Flattering? Hugely. But irrelevant because I want to stay here. I don't want my own glamorous, highly successful, big-earning agency in New York. I want to be here with you. Alternatively I could toast my new life as an author, but I won't because I don't believe in the book I've been asked to write. I won't write our true romance unless I believe in it, and it's none

too credible right now. Finally, if it was sex and carnal communion that I wanted to toast, I could raise a glass instead to Kathy, this delightful new Boston babe who's just arrived in Duffy's London office, who happens to be something of a slapper and would appear to believe that I am the essence of man. But I won't drink to her because I'm not interested in anyone, Lula, except you. I can't drink to anything apart from you and me. It's the only toast that makes sense. And if it's a case of Tim versus me, I want to pick you up and shake you because I think I win every time. I piss on Tim. I don't think he's a patch on me. He's not even close. It's a no-contest. We don't even belong in the same sentence. So here we go.' I clink my champagne flute against hers. 'To you and me.'

I sip long from my glass, aware that Lucy isn't touching hers. Her deep brown eyes seem deeper and browner than ever as they stare up at me in amazement, the long eyelashes barely flickering. I didn't know where I was going with that toast: it came out unprepared, but I know where I'm heading now. Straight for the hi-fi. Erik Satie isn't right at all. I know the record I'm looking for, not a CD – Tim never completed the move over to CDs, he loved his vinyl collection too much – and I've known its position in the rack from the first day I moved in here. Squeezed in between *Country Road* and Tim's first ever album, *John Denver and the Muppets*, was *Greatest Hits*. Thus the silence is broken next by John Denver and me in a rendition of a song that has been packed away and kept under the dust sheets ever since the day when we were all gathered to sing it at the songmaster's funeral some two years ago.

And this might be about as cruel a thing as I've done in my life, but here I am belting out 'Leaving On A Jetplane'.

'*Au revoir*', we thought the words were saying until that day in the church when they meant 'goodbye'. But tonight the interpretation is something else altogether and I'm blasting it out so loudly that I might wake the little prince upstairs.

''Cos I'm leaving, on a jetplane,' mine is a shout more than a song, 'don't know when I'll be back—'

'Stop it! Stop it, Dominic,' Lucy interrupts, a note of hysteria in her voice. 'Stop it! Please!' I am now right in her face, taunting her with my singing, and she wails, 'Stop it! Stop it, Dominic, please! You're not Tim. *This* is Tim! *It isn't you.* It's Tim. It's Tim! It's Tim!'

'But listen to it, Lucy please!' I've stopped singing and I'm on the sofa, my arm round her, trying to prevent her shrinking away from me and I have to shout to be heard above the John Denver chorus. 'Lucy, listen to it!' We are now almost through the chorus and on the verge of the second verse. 'Lucy, have you ever really listened to these lyrics? This song might sound to you as though it's about a lover saying goodbye, but it's more than that. It's a confession that's straight from Tim's heart.

'Come on. Sing the next two lines with me,' I urge, 'two of the lines in Tim's favourite song.' And I sing them and Lucy sobs, blinking at me through her tears, agog with horror.

> '"So many times I've let you down,
> So many times I've played around . . ."'

And then I sing them again. The song moves on but I sing the lines again and again.

> '"So many times I've let you down,
> So many times I've played around . . ."'

'This is Tim's signature tune, Lucy,' I say, more quietly now, 'and in it he's crowing about being an adulterer. Don't you get it? So many times he's played around. That's what he's saying. How can you let him still tower over you, Lucy? So many times he let you down. You deserve better. For God's sake, I am *so* much better.'

'Tim loved me.' Lucy's reply comes back fiercely, punctuating her sobs. 'He did.' She draws deep breath. 'Of course he wasn't as perfect as everyone seemed to think he was. But never once –' she breaks off again, John Denver still going '– never once, when we were married, was he unfaithful. I was the only one he loved.'

'You were the only one he loved? I'm sorry, Lucy,' my voice is hard and direct now because I am delivering the line I hoped never to inflict on her, 'you weren't even the only one to mother his children.'

Silence. Tim's signature tune and Lucy's crying stop simultaneously. And 'Jetplane' is the last song on side one of *Greatest Hits* so there is nothing to fill the void. Just Lucy looking up at me with the sort of astonishment you see in characters in war movies when they have been shot. A kind of incomprehension. Likewise Lucy. Shot in the back by the man who professes to love her.

Lucy, the colour bleached from her face, slowly shakes her head. 'Why did you say that?' Her voice is uncertain.

'I'm sorry, but you had to find out eventually.'

'Find out?' She is louder and harder. 'What are you saying? Tell me what I *had* to find out.'

'Tim, Lucy.' I am forced to spell it out. 'Tim had another child.'

'No, he didn't!'

'I'm afraid he did, Lucy.'

'Why are you saying this? You're lying, Grey!' She is screaming hysterically now. 'It's not true! It's a fucking horrible lie, Grey, and you know it! How could you possibly say this to me?'

'Come here, Lula! I'm sorry.' I try to hug her to me.

'Get off me, you lying bastard!'

'I'm not lying, Lucy.' I try again to pull her towards me, to suppress her anger in the physical warmth of my embrace, but she pushes me away so fiercely she almost loses her footing.

'Get away from me! How could you say that horrible thing?'

And with that she is gone, one swish of her left hand collecting her cigarettes, running for the back door and slamming it behind her.

You never envisage causing hurt like this. At least, I don't. I sometimes wonder if Tim ever considered the pain he was

capable of inflicting on Lucy – or did he just march blinkered onwards? There are people, some of them exceedingly intelligent people, who are born with no rear-view mirror; Tim was one and, with his charisma and temperament, would probably have been their captain. The irony of this situation is that Tim only loaded the gun: I'm the one who picked it up and fired it. We were never perceived as a likely pair of mates, but here we are in perfect tandem at last.

Lucy is like a wounded animal. And she didn't need to shout or scream or door-slam for me to harbour a sudden deep regret for my histrionics, my champagne toast and the merciless rendition of 'Jetplane'. I suppose I had to get myself worked up to deliver the blow, but a stronger personality might have found a more clinical way of doing it. Either that or stayed true to the promise they made to Marco.

The result, suddenly, is that Archdeacon Avenue is a lonely place. I want to go after Lucy but I don't want to make things worse so I sit on the sofa and wait. I don't know if the situation is retrievable. I guess I've just played my joker and, right now, it doesn't look a very smart card. If I was Tim, what would I do? Break into song? Charge off on a cricket tour and come back when the storm had blown over?

I'd like to switch on the television, but that might suggest lack of feeling. Instead, I pick up the bottle of Moët and the two champagne flutes, one still full. I tread softly into the kitchen and flick on the kettle. Just as it boils I hear the door closing, heralding Lucy's return.

She stands in the kitchen, her face pale and tired, her arms wrapped round herself; she looks broken and vulnerable. 'I ran out.' She shakes an empty cigarette packet. 'And it's bloody cold outside too.' She pauses. 'So I figured I better come in and hear what you have to tell me.'

'Do you want one of these?' I gesture at the coffee jar.

'Yes, please. And I need a blanket, a box of tissues and something to smoke.'

We are soon ensconced in the sofa. Lucy looks smaller than ever, her feet tucked under her, a picnic blanket round her shoulders. When she has lit a cigarette, she nods at me. 'Come on, then, Grey. Break my heart.'

To have it put like that doesn't encourage the beanspilling process, but I embark on it nevertheless. I start as far back as the story goes and explain how my original, altruistic intention to discover the whereabouts of Tim's missing fortune had led me to Marco's doorstep in Bermuda. And then I tell it pretty much as Marco told it to me.

'Remember Marco's New Year's Day party? Remember the girl who sent you into such a rage?'

'Of course I do. Vicky.'

'Whom Tim had a fling with when they were at BZH together.' She is silent. 'Well, it wasn't a fling, Lucy. It didn't end when he left the bank.' Lucy's gaze won't leave mine, but it is as though she is staring into an abyss. 'Vicky is a single mother,' I continue uneasily. 'She has a son called Ben and Tim was Ben's father.'

'Oh, God!' There is fear in her voice. 'Oh, God! Oh, God! Oh, God!' Then, quiet and wavering: 'Was he still seeing her after we got married?'

'I'm afraid so.'

'Oh, God.' Her eyes are filled with tears now. She pauses to collect herself. 'And do you know how old the other boy is?'

'Six months younger than Josh.'

'Oh, fuck.' Her head drops and she puts a tissue to her eyes. 'So I was six months pregnant at the time . . . Some husband.'

'I'm sorry, Lucy.' Which is pathetic, because sympathy doesn't count for much right now. I reach over to her and guide her into my shoulder.

'How could he do that?'

'I don't know.'

'So the man I loved spent the four years of our marriage living a lie.'

We are quiet for a minute, the only sound is of Lucy's distress. 'And I suppose you're going to tell me,' her voice is barely audible, 'that the mystery trust fund isn't Josh's, after all.'

''Fraid so.'

'So he didn't even put little Josh first? Oh, my God! How could he?'

'All I can do, Lucy, is tell it the way Marco told me.' And I do. 'Whatever his faults, Tim was a proud man and he wanted to do right by everyone. That, at least, is the way Marco puts it.' I explain about Tim's finances and how he'd lost a lot of money from some bad investments, but how he assumed that everything would come up trumps for him in the end. He had set up the trust fund for Ben and his intention was to do the same for Josh as soon as the money became available. He had never considered that his life would be cut off before he could.

When I am done, Lucy is stubbing out another cigarette and a patchwork of wet tissue is scattered around her. The vacant look on her face suggests that she is punch-drunk from the blows. There is another long silence before her small voice pipes up again: 'Do you know whether he kept his affair going with Vicky beyond the birth of her child or did it stop there?'

'I don't know.'

'Do you know where she lives?'

'Nope, but I could find out.'

'Could you, please?'

'Sure.'

Lucy lights another cigarette. By the time she is half-way through it, she is ready to talk again. 'Grey, forgive me for shouting at you earlier. I hope you understand – it wasn't easy to hear all that.' She stubs out the cigarette and gets to her feet. 'Now I think I've got to go and cry long and hard on my own. Goodnight, Grey. I'll see you in the morning. Will you be around or are you going to work early?'

'No, I'll stay around.'

'Good. 'Cause I'm not quite sure how completely my life's

just fallen apart. I might need someone to help me hold it
together.'

'No problem.'

'G'night, my darling.'

I move to hug her but she recoils. 'Sorry, Grey, not now. I'm
too confused to be close to anyone.'

'Sure.'

'And that might remain the case for some time.'

24

Wednesday midday, thirty-six hours later, we're getting into Lucy's car. I had tried to persuade her that this was counter-productive, but she wouldn't listen. In fact, from first thing yesterday morning, she was set firm, jaw jutting, her 'on-a-mission' expression, as I called it. No smile, just determination. Find out where Vicky lives, she told me, so I did. And we're setting off for Vicky's house.

We don't even know if she's going to be at home. In fact, we're resigned to the idea that she probably won't be. That's why Josh was booked in to go to Sam's for the afternoon after school, which was Lucy's share of the organisation (I had no great desire to phone Alice). My share was to find out where Vicky lived and that was easier than I'd expected. I had about three plans of which the first involved ringing the Roof Gardens, speaking to the manager, persuading him that I had fallen in love with a guest called Vicky at the New Year's Day party and could he help me get in touch? He had explained that he wasn't supposed to divulge such information, but here was her address anyway. 'Good luck, Romeo,' were his parting words. Fantastic.

The address: Fairways, Old Road, Little Buckenham, Buckinghamshire. I check it in the road atlas. Not far from Marlow. Lucy drives and we set out on the M4. After about half an hour we turn off the motorway and I start map-reading us along the smaller roads. The journey is a little surreal. I try to engage Lucy in small-talk, but the ground rules for conversation are a little blurred when one of you is off to doorstep the mother of your dead husband's bastard son.

'Do you know what you're going to say to her?' I'd asked the same question three or four times the day before.

The answer remains the same: 'No, it'll come. I'll think of something.'

'Are you going to ask for the money back?'

'No. Wouldn't touch it.'

'How horrible are you going to be?'

'Dunno.'

'Is it going to be the lead-piping in the kitchen or the candle-stick in the dining room?'

'I haven't worked that out either.'

Question, answer, question, answer. Nervous banter. Lucy's only leading contribution comes about ten miles away from our destination when she puts her left hand on my knee and asks if I'll come in with her.

'Of course I will.'

'Really, Grey, I need you more than ever right now, you know.'

'Sure, no problem,' I reply. But with that reality check, the opportunity for banter is closed. Now is not the time to point out that if it wasn't Tim's long-standing bit-on-the-side that we were going to see, this journey would be rather uplifting, dramatic in an English-countryside-bleak-late-winter way. Under a pale grey sky, the trees are bare and bowed by the steady breeze, the road is wet, winding and hemmed in by hedgerows, and the landscape is an undulating patchwork of agricultural colour. In the car, we are warm and protected, and Lucy is noticeably quieter.

'You all right?' I ask.

'Yup. Think so. I just seem to recognise this. How far away are we?'

'Dunno. Five minutes. The last sign to Little Buckenham said three miles.'

'Oh, God.'

'What is it?'

'Not sure. Nothing. Nerves.'

The road trundles downhill to Little Buckenham, which is

nothing but a crossroads in the centre of a collection of old stone cottages, a Red Lion selling Young's, a shop and an out-of-use garage forecourt. Quaint. Just the sort of picturesque rural seat where Tim would have liked to keep a mistress. Walk in the countryside, lunch in the Red Lion, charm the locals, beat them at darts, then home for adultery, tea and toast.

'We're looking for Old Road.' We are stopped at the foot of the crossroads. 'See it anywhere?' Lucy says nothing. I lean out of the window, looking for a road name, but Lucy sits still at the wheel.

'Grey,' she sounds impatient, 'I can't see that road sign ahead. What does it say?'

'Right to Hamming Green, left to Lower Upchurch and Farleygate, straight on to Wittingsfold, Denham and Scaresbrook.'

'How far to Wittingsfold?'

'Mile and a half.'

'Oh, shit.'

'What?'

'Nothing. Let's try that.'

With that, she puts the car into gear and we head on. Over the crossroads, we see the road name. Old Road.

'How did you know?'

'I'm not sure I can do this,' she replies. But we drive on slowly.

'The house is called Fairways. I'll look left, you look right, OK?' But Lucy's face is set grimly forward. I try to scan both sides of the road, which is easier as the terraced houses become semi-detached, then stand alone and thin out. The road climbs uphill, small driveways breaking the hedgerows with neat square houses adorned with ivy. Lucy is driving so slowly that I can read almost every house name. A thicket of oak trees hangs darkly over the road as it flattens out, then bends right.

'You OK?' I ask.

No answer.

I read out the house names. 'Barn Cottage, Hill Ash Cottage, Cobbles, Oak Cottage, Dunsdale House, Saxonwood House.

Blimey, er, can't read that one. Calenick, Milestones, Fairways. Fuck. Fairways. There it is. Lucy, we've gone past it. Are you going to turn round? Lucy?'

Lucy has barely raised an eyebrow. She drove past Fairways without braking. She hasn't even registered it. The road curls left and we are now on the top of a ridge.

'Do you just not want to do this any more?' I ask sympathetically. 'Is it too much?'

No answer.

The road dips towards a stream. Lucy lets the car take in the speed of the slope towards the humpback bridge at its foot. Over the bridge, a bend right and I am thrown forward as Lucy pulls over, slamming on the brakes, bringing us to a sudden standstill next to another overhanging oak. She collapses forward and buries her face in her arms. She is whimpering at first, then sobbing loudly. She raises her head as if to address me, then sinks back into her arms.

I put my arm over her. Suddenly she sweeps it away, unclips her seat-belt, opens the car door and swings herself out, panting hard.

'Here, Grey!'

'What is it, Lucy?' I am out of the car now too.

'Here! It was right here!' She is sobbing hysterically. 'Right fucking here. Look, someone's still putting flowers down.' There are indeed some cut flowers – a delicate white swathe of snowdrops – placed carefully at the foot of the tree. 'This is where he died, Grey. He came down the same hill, over the same fucking bridge and right into this tree. Right here. Oh, Grey! The bastard! He died a few hundred yards from her fucking house!'

Lucy is screaming now, arms outstretched. 'Wittingsfold! We always knew it as Wittingsfold! Not Little sodding Buckenham! Wittingsfold is where he died, Grey, not Little Buckenham! No one ever mentioned Little Buckenham. Half a stone's throw down that road is Wittingsfold! I'd never heard of Little Buckenham. He died between Wittingsfold and Little Buckenham! I thought

we were coming to see her. I didn't know, Grey, I didn't know! I didn't know that she lived just up the hill from his deathbed, that she sent him spinning down the hill in his sodding BMW to his death. She sent him here! She did! She did! Oh, Tim! Oh, Tim! Oh, Tim!'

Lucy sinks back on to the bonnet of the car. When I wrap her in my arms, she clings tightly to me and I feel the convulsions of grief sweeping through her.

'I didn't realise, Grey.'

'I know. Lucy, I know.'

'You see,' and suddenly she is talking clearly, quietly, as if she is in shock, 'when we came after it had happened – and I always insisted I would only come once – it was from the other direction.'

'You don't have to explain, Lucy.'

'I had to come, you see. Alice came with me and we cried together and put down flowers. But we came from Wittingsfold. I didn't know about Little Buckenham. Or what brought him here. He said it was business. And I believed him, the bastard.'

I insist on driving. I turn the car round and, at the top of the hill, I need to apply only a touch to the brakes for Lucy to shake her head, confirming that the Fairways visit has been abandoned.

Thereafter she stares listlessly out of the window, head resting on her hand. Flecks of rain appear on the windscreen, the sky darkens moodily and we share a strange silence.

'Grey,' we are half-way home when she speaks, 'just tell me one thing, will you?'

'What's that?'

'I shouldn't ask but I need to know. It's very important.'

'Go on.'

'You didn't know that Vicky lived there, where Tim crashed, did you? You didn't set out on this trip knowing how it would unfold?'

'Oh, Lucy, no. I knew Tim had been taken to Wycombe

General. I don't think I ever knew where the accident happened. Good God, no – Lucy, you don't think I'd do that to you on purpose, do you?'

'No.' She looks at me reassuringly. 'Not at all. But I'm not, all of a sudden, feeling too good at assessing people. Not surprising, is it, really? Forget I mentioned it.'

She resumes her silent contemplation out of the window and doesn't speak again until we are coming into London.

'Come on.' There is an upbeat note in her voice. 'I've got an idea.'

'What's that?'

'Let's go to Greenwich.'

'Greenwich?'

'Yup. Come on.'

'What about Josh?'

'He's fine. I'll ring Alice. He can sleep over. He'd love that.'

We continue through West London and along the South Circular. Lucy puts on the radio and tunes it to Heart FM, good old cheerful chart music. I'm not sure what to say so I just listen to good old cheerful chart music all the way to Greenwich.

We park. I still can't place Lucy's mood so I just go with it.

'Come on,' she says, as if the adulterous-dead-Tim storyline has been wiped from the storyboard of her mind, and sets off towards the park, winding her pale blue scarf round her neck. It is seven weeks since we were last here together, on the first day of the new millennium with hangovers and hope all rolled into one and with Japanese tourists, the occasional dog-walker and General Wolfe all bearing witness to Lucy's and my nervous statement of God-knows-what. Now I chase after her, and when I am close, she runs on ahead, laughing, inviting me to continue the pursuit. She continues her game all through the slow incline of the park until we are at the foot of the steep, winding path up to the Observatory. Here she grabs my hand, smiles and leads me uphill, urging me to go faster: 'Come on – do I have to drag you all the way to the top?'

We resume our old spot on the bench at the foot of General Wolfe, the afternoon light fading, the street-lights sustaining a glow over the city spread before us.

'Right.' Lucy sits forward, looking back at me. She takes my right hand. 'I thought we should go back again, try to rewind to our own little start of time.'

'Nice concept. We could probably do a guided tour of the Observatory too.'

'Shut up, smartarse! Listen, this is us, you and me, another new beginning. Ask me anything you want.'

'OK. Do you think I'll ever get to beat Josh at either dinosaurs, superheroes or rough-and-tumble?'

'Not a chance. Bad question. Keep asking. More personal.'

'OK. How are you feeling after the events of the afternoon?'

'Umm . . . Better than I'd have expected. Deflated, abused, duped, utterly foolish, homicidal, but strangely positive.'

'Why positive?'

'You'll have to keep asking.'

I pause. 'I suppose it's too early to ask how you feel about us, isn't it?'

'No, not at all. Go on, ask.'

'OK. How do you feel about us?'

'You'll have to be more specific, sweetheart.'

'Sweetheart?'

'Is that what I said? Anyway, you'll have to be more specific. Generally my answer is 'positive', but the question needs to be better thought through.' She raises her eyebrows as if I'm missing something obvious. 'Oh, Lordy, Lordy.' Lucy's enjoying this.

I don't know what to say but I'm saved by my mobile. 'Sorry, Lucy, hang on a sec . . . Hello? Christmas, what a surprise . . . Hello, Kathy . . .' I get to my feet and slink off behind General Wolfe. No, Kathy, not a good time to call. Will call back. Yes, must go out again some time soon. Yes. See ya. 'Bye.

'Sorry about that.' I return to our bench.

'Slapper Kathy, was it?'

'Yup. She's not a slapper. That was a bit harsh of me.'

'Is that why you took her off behind General Wolfe, then, for a bit of privacy?'

'No. Not at all. Stop teasing. Now, where were we?'

'Talking about Kathy.'

'No, before that. Annoying person.' I put my arm round Lucy and she burrows into my shoulder. This is as intimate as we've been for two days.

'You're supposed to be asking me the most deep and personal question that you can think of, the one you've been toying with for months, years, maybe.'

'Oh, yes. Thanks.' I plump for the easy option, the lighthearted one. 'Do you believe in the transmigration of souls?'

'No. Idiot. Next.'

'Do you believe in New Labour?'

'No. Come on!'

'But it was you who advocated the Labour policy of making everything up as we go along.'

'Next question.'

'Right. D'you believe in Father Christmas?'

'No.' She squeezes me affectionately under my ribs.

'Marriage?'

'Better question. Yes.'

'Second marriages?'

'Yes. Very hot. Try shifting your arse off this bench for the next one and locating one of your knees.'

'Blimey.' This is going faster than I'd imagined, but I'm not complaining. 'OK.' I steady myself. I'm on one knee and my heart is beating fast. 'Lucy, if I get my jeans dirty from the down-on-one-knee position, will you wash them for me?'

'I will.'

'Will you love them and cherish them, in sickness and in health?'

'I will.'

'Will you also love and cherish a very dear bottle of Robinson's lemon barley water?'

'I will.'

'Blimey, I'm getting cramp down here.' I make as if to get up but Lucy's hand on my shoulder stops me.

'You're not going anywhere, mate!'

'OK. OK. One last thing, then.'

'Actually, no. Not yet. Stop.' She gets up and so I do too. 'No, not you, Grey,' she says. 'You stay down there. I've got something to say first.' She walks slowly round the bench, lost in contemplation, leaving me glued to the ground.

'Right.' She returns to her seat. 'Listen. You're wondering what the hell's going on, aren't you? You're wondering if I'm in a stable frame of mind to do what I'm doing. You're wondering if I really mean it or if I'm deluded. You're thinking: two and a half hours ago, this girl was at an emotional nadir and now this? This must be the worst, most obvious case of rebound of all time. Go on – that's what you're thinking, isn't it?'

'Pretty much.'

'Good. Right.' She tucks her legs under her. 'It's like this. It came to me with complete clarity in the car on the way back from Little Buckenham and it makes sense, more sense than I've known maybe all my life. Before today, I saw Tim as representing the big thing, the real all-singing, all-dancing true love, and because I'd known it so completely with him – or thought I had – I couldn't see how anyone could replicate it. I *could* see myself with you, Grey, but not in that way. I saw a life with you as an extension of friendship, you know, ultimate closeness, real depth, more intellectual – no, that's not the word – cognitive? I don't know. The ultimate in Platonic, a meeting of minds, the union of souls, blah-blah, all that stuff we talked about. But you didn't want that. You wanted the Tim thing.'

She pauses and then, in an animated burst, continues: 'But today, Grey, I realised that I never had it with Tim. I was suckered from the start. I was the victim of the most fraudulent

romance known to man. I invested my heart and soul in Tim and he gambled it away. Grey, I haven't a clue how long it will take me to come to terms with what I now know about my late bloody husband. I suspect it will take years and, if I allowed it to, I'm sure it could fuck me up completely. I could check into the Priory and spend the next six months pulling myself together, or I could grasp the chance I have now.'

She leans forward and shakes me gently by the shoulders. 'And that's you, you lovely man. You're the chance I have. How stupid would I be if I ignored the love of the best person I've ever known? You're offering me a love that I now know I never had, Grey. I want it, I deserve it – I need it, for goodness' sake.'

I sigh. Good moments. Overwhelming moments. Uncertainty. 'But love, Lucy . . .' How do you say this? 'You know . . . it's got to be a two-way thing. What about all that Plato shit?'

'Sod Plato. I'm all Tennyson.'

And that is good enough for me. We are staring into each other's eyes, acknowledging the enormity of our pending destination. My knee is aching but I have to ignore the pain because this is too big, too momentous. It seems as if the world is slowing, and I wouldn't be at all surprised if, at this very millisecond, a minor tremor is being recorded in Dorking, with bedside lamps, water glasses and clock radios tumbling groundwards.

'Come on, then,' Lucy says softly. 'Over to you. And make it good.'

'Lucy,' I take her hand in mine, 'I hate to sound like a broken-down record, but will you marry me?'

It is a while before she gives her answer, but her body language – she hands me off the ground, then clasps me to her in a long, passionate kiss – already suggests it will be of the affirmative variety.

'I will,' she whispers breathily. 'I will, I will, I will.' Then she pulls back. 'And you can bribe Josh all you want to stay out of my bed.' Chuckling, she presses her mouth to mine again.

And I suppose that this is my taste of ultimate fulfilment.

Sitting here on Greenwich Hill, officially cementing the start of the life I'd always wanted with my mouth locked to that of the girl I'd always wanted to be locked to. And I might be wrong, but this kissing is different from all those nervous darts in the Corridor of Uncertainty back at Archdeacon Avenue. It's more, it's bigger, it's straight out of the no-holds-barred, I'm-all-yours, no-ifs, no-buts, let's-sail-away-into-the-sunset school of embraces. I've got terrible pins and needles in my knee and, for all I know, Dorking has just disappeared into a hole in the ground, but this is good. Bloody hell, is it good.

25

Some reaction to our news.

> **From: Jerry Sweet**
> **Subject: Sweet surrender**
> OK, OK. I give up. Sweet Lord RIP. Dom, you have fucked up my dreams of world domination and advertising will be the poorer for it. However, while there's nothing in all this nuptial nonsense that remotely benefits me, I realise that it would perhaps be poor form to look at it from an egocentric point of view. So a begrudging hoorah. I might be brimful with selfish old gittishness, but I am nevertheless exceedingly happy for you. You chivalrous old knight, you deserve it. Good luck to you both and love to Lucy, my rival, who has so thoughtlessly taken you away from me.

Some sweetly chosen words from Kathy in my cubbyhole at Duffy's. 'You silly arse. And there was me thinking I had a half-decent chance of seducing you again. Why is it that whenever I get anywhere near you you run off to a wife? She'd better be good, this second one, Dom, because if you ask me, you've messed up big-time.'

Card from Alice to Lucy:

My dearest Lucy,
I don't write these words easily, but take them as the well-considered thoughts of a dear friend who has your best interests at heart.

I just wanted to ask you to reconsider your engagement to Dom. I'm not asking you to give him up, I'm just asking you to slow down. Don't throw yourself into this or you might find out in twelve months' time that you've made a monumental error. God knows what you've been through recently, Lucy. I just worry that you're being bounced around on some cruel emotional rollercoaster and sometimes I wonder what sort of shape you're going to be in when it stops.

Honestly, honestly, honestly, Luce, it pains me to be doing this, really it does, but you know I've got your happiness first and foremost in my mind and I just think it's time a friend took you aside. I know that Dom seems to make an ideal father figure for dear little Joshie and I know you and Dom have had your funny, long-standing millennium day love pact. But, come on, that's not sufficient. That doesn't make a marriage. And with the problems that Bill and I have had recently, I feel I understand better than ever what *does* make a marriage.

Marriage isn't easy, my love. Marriage is bloody hard. You can't just skip down the aisle because you think you've ticked all the boxes.

So there, I'll leave you with those thoughts. Just one other thing: your engagement dinner. I don't think I should come. Please don't be offended but I mean what I say about your engagement to Dom, and I feel it would be hypocritical to pitch up and celebrate something that I don't believe in.

Sorry.
Alice

Postcard from my mother in response to the one I sent her, with a stylised picture of a female hand wearing a massive, sparkling engagement ring and, on the other side, two words: 'Lucy. Really.' My mother's reply has a picture of a champagne bottle:

My darling
Do I keep this on ice? Or do you mean what I think you do? You infuriating boy. Please ring. If I'm about to become a step-grandmother, then I have a right to know. An unforthcoming fiancé? You complete oxymoron.

Your ever-loving Mother

Letter from Nadia to me:

You bastard,
I always said it was her you were in love with and now I know I was right. If only you'd told me that it was flat-chested British college girls who took your fancy we could have saved ourselves all that grief. Bastard, bastard, bastard.

Anyway, I hope she's a better shot with the wedding-present crockery than I was. Please, God, assist her in the throwing of expensive projectiles, and may they all locate you between the eyes because that was the bullseye target I always fucking missed. These sentiments, by the way, come fully endorsed by my lovely mother, as I'm sure you would expect.

But I don't mean to sound bitter. Of course not. You know how important your happiness is to me. Otherwise I wouldn't be sending you your signed divorce papers with such pleasure and alacrity. Please deal with the whole dirty deed as fast as you can.

And finally some news, because I know how much you enjoy my small-talk. Here in SoHo, Mike and I have now moved in together and we've decided to avoid leaping into marriage with the worrying haste espoused by yourself and your paper-thin bride-to-be. We've decided to enjoy the other more romantic

pleasures of cohabitation instead. He satisfies me in every way that you can imagine. Did I ever tell you that you didn't?

All my love, naturally,

Nadia

Postcard from my mother to Lucy, not a real postcard but a blank card with a photograph of me, a cherubic, gap-toothed eight-year-old with a pudding-bowl haircut, sellotaped to the front:

Lucy,

Will this splendid boy always remain so infantile? We have this relationship where he starves me of information. And it gives him such pleasure. There is something very Nazi about him. I think he finds it funny but enough is enough. Please encourage him to communicate.

My garden is showing glimpses of colour, sparks of life, revivifying signs of early-spring bloom. Please reassure me that there is something deeply symbolic in all this.

All best,

Dom's mother, Patricia

Monologue from Ray, creative head at Duffy's: 'Dominic, you old dog. Fantastic news. Everyone's thrilled. And you're getting married too? If it took female charm to persuade you to see sense and cement your place here at Duffy's where you belong, Domo, that's fine by me. Heartstrings, sweet music and all that. I'm just delighted you're staying and that we can get down to some really good work again. When are you moving out of this hovel-like office of yours back to something more befitting of your status round here?

'And have you heard about this new account we've got? The National Birth Control Association. It sounds right up your street, mate. Big account. Perfect for you. Have a think about it. It's not been touched yet, we haven't got a team together or anything. Virgin territory. Will get back to you on it, OK?'

From: Bill James
Subject: Bloody Alice

Dom,

So, so sorry about Alice's note. The silly tart. I knew how she felt but I didn't think she'd do anything about it and I certainly didn't know she was going to write a letter until she proudly announced last night that it had been dispatched. Did we have a row or what? If it hadn't been for the fact that I only got her back a few weeks ago, I'd have really let rip. As it was I just told her that she was a meddling, insensitive, shrivelled old bitch and that she should butt out of it. So we're not really talking much today.

Anyway, please apologise to Lucy and make it clear that, whatever Alice said, it is not representative of the pair of us. As for your engagement dinner, I am not joining the boycott. If I'm allowed to come on my own, I'd love to.

Bill

From: Marco Bury
Subject: You fucker

You fucking fucker. So you broke your promise, spilled the beans and walked off with his bride. Tim will be turning in his grave. Some mate of his you've turned out to be. And after all he did for you. I don't give the marriage twelve months. Even if you are faithful.

Another note from my mother to Lucy and me that came with flowers, really unusual exotic ones with a vivid blue tongue and brilliant orange petals:

I wanted to send flowers, of course, and chose you Birds of Paradise. Very special flower, perfectly appropriate, used to be classified in the banana family, but no longer. And nothing to

do with the bird (feathered) of the same name found mainly in New Guinea. But enjoy them. Enjoy your love together. So happy. Well done for phoning me, Dom. Maybe you are a changed man. At least you appear to have got the choice of bride right this time. Can we go with the happy ending now?

More sweetly chosen words from Kathy, delivered while she drapes herself over my desk as I am packing up my cubbyhole and preparing to move somewhere that more befits my status: 'Hello, sweetie. Still doing the getting-married thing? No second thoughts? No time for a quick tequila with an old mate? No? You used to be so much more fun last time you were married . . . Anyway, heard the good news? The National Birth Control Association. Glamorous or what? The boss has just been briefing me. You and me, it seems. Working together. Just like old times. Can't wait.'

Letter from Vicky to Lucy entitled 'From one of Tim's widows to another':

Dear Lucy

How strange to be writing to you now having known you from afar for so long. And I can't believe I'm saying this, but two weeks on, I really feel it was such a pleasure to meet you. I admire your bravery in finding me and I admire you too for coming with such an open mind. You could have been armed with a shotgun.

And I can't believe how well Ben and Josh got on. Josh seems a really spirited little boy – you must have a lot of fun with him! And you should be very proud of him too.

But most of all I can't believe that you have so embraced the possibility of friendship that you have invited me to your engagement party. In the spirit of all the goodwill that you have shown, I would like to accept. It is very kind of you and I look forward to seeing you and Dominic again.

All the best
Vicky

26

It had been Lucy's request that we revisit Vicky and it didn't surprise me. Closure was needed.

She was devoting her life to me: she appeared convinced of that and little things convinced me too. She started phoning me at work, two or three times a day, nothing particular to say, nothing she wanted to discuss, just phoning for a chat. Funny stuff: 'Oh, hello, Grey, that thing you asked me about on top of Greenwich Hill, the marriage thing. You still up for it? Oh, good. Me too. Just checking. 'Bye.' 'Hello, Grey, I'm in the supermarket. Well, now that you're kind of with us on a forever basis, I thought you should have some input into our margarine choice. Flora, Flora Light, Lurpak Lighter? Whatever you want. I think I was a bit unilateral with the decision-making last time. But you were only a non-paying lodger then.'

She let me hold her hand, stroke her hair, stub out her cigarettes if I felt she was smoking too much, change the TV channel with all the unchallenged authority of someone who owned a telly. And I also found that it was not a different margarine that started appearing in the fridge but the butter I had requested. The symbolism might not have been good enough for my mother, but here was a whole new life wrapped up in dairy produce.

There were the big things too: telling Josh about our engagement, getting on the phone to tell Lucy's parents, moving bedrooms (officially), making love in the new marital suite, discovering that the faces in the frames on the antique card table had changed. The day after the proposal, Tim's seven smiling mugshots had been reduced to two and he vanished from Lucy's bedside table. In his stead on the card-table shrine, I made an

appearance, two, in fact, and not much sign of a receding hair-line in either. And to choose two pictures so kind to my obvious flaw – that's a real sign of devotion, isn't it?

The highlight of it all? A self-centred man would probably say the sex. I can't make up my mind how self-centred I am, but that night, the engagement night, it was different. There was no nerv-ousness, no awkwardness and we didn't read a single page of a single book. There was a sense of excitement as if we were doing something different from what we had done before. Lucy set about the task with unprecedented enthusiasm, and when the deed was done, she set about it for a second time. 1812 Overture with the fireworks blasting? Maybe. No cymbals or drums or pyrotech-nics, though, but it was as close as we were ever going to get.

The highlight for a nicer bloke would probably have been the moment we told Josh – and his reaction for the rest of the week. He had spent the night of our engagement having a sleepover *chez* Sam, so Lucy and I picked him up after school the next day together and informed him that there was some exciting news for him at home.

Back in Archdeacon Avenue, we gave him a Diet Coke, sat him down and set about explaining the whole business of man and woman and the marriage sacrament. But Josh didn't give a stuff about explanations, he worked out the conclusion to the speech before it had even got half-way and then went hyperac-tive with delight. 'I can't believe it! I can't believe it! I can't believe it!' he shrieked. 'Does that mean you're going to be my daddy?'

'It certainly does.'

'I can't believe it!' he shrieked, even more loudly than before, jumping up and down on the spot. Then he hugged me hard and peppered me with kisses, did the same to Lucy, then turned to me again. He wasn't quiet for a single moment in the rest of the day, a stream of 'da-da-da-ing' punctuated by repeated rendi-tions of a new song 'I'm going to have a daddy, a daddy, a daddy' delivered, it seemed, to the tune of 'Following The Leader' from Peter Pan, plus particularly vigorous bouts of rough-and-tumble,

further rounds of superheroes and a long game of Red Injuns, which produced a deeply significant conclusion: a first, historic victory for me.

Throughout all this Lucy's face was aglow with joy, but even better for me was what happened three days later. Before he left for school, Josh asked Lucy if he could borrow a photograph of me. 'Of course,' she said. 'Why?' And he explained that it was 'Show and Tell' Friday at school and he wanted to show his classmates what his new daddy looked like.

As this happy week wore on, Lucy made increasing mention of Vicky. It would have been strange had she not: it would have been dishonest to pretend that we hadn't hurtled towards our new-found happiness just after the wound Lucy had sustained, which still lay open and bleeding. The more we discussed Vicky, the more it became clear that Lucy felt a deep-seated need to communicate with her. She didn't want to take the same secretive, aggressive doorstepping approach as before. Instead, on the Sunday night after Josh had gone to bed, she sat down at the kitchen table to make two telephone calls, the first to Directory Inquiries to find Vicky's number, and the second to Vicky.

I sat opposite her, trying to assess the gist of this extraordinary conversation. 'Hello, is that Vicky?' was Lucy's opener. 'I don't want to surprise you or shock you or anything, but it's Lucy Cassidy here, I think you probably know who I am.'

The gist appeared to go from extremely awkward to slightly less awkward and even a notch better than that. Vicky, Lucy recounted to me afterwards, had told her that she always suspected that the day would come when her cover would be blown and the entwined storylines of their two lives would collide. She sounded, Lucy said, remarkably composed and unperturbed. And, no, she hadn't apologised – Lucy seemed surprised that I should suggest it.

The upshot was the return trip to Little Buckenham the following Saturday. Vicky issued an invitation: come for lunch and bring Josh. We had to promise, though – and Vicky had

stressed this heavily – that we would leave the boys in the dark. Ben, she said, didn't even know that Tim was his father and he certainly didn't know that he had a long-lost half-brother.

En route to Little Buckenham, we told Josh we were off to visit some old friends, and soon we were parking in the drive at Fairways. It was at this stage that Lucy drew a deep breath and seemed to freeze. This trip would not be as traumatic as the first, but certainly as memorable, stirring, bizarre and weird.

We spotted our one-man reception committee as we drove in. He was at the side of the house, repeatedly kicking a football against the wall and singing: 'One–nil to the Arsenal, one–nil to the Arsenal, one–nil to the Arsenal, one–nil to the Arsenal.' Great song. Only when we called out an inquisitive 'Hello?' did the thud-thud stop and the sound of feet heralded the arrival of the young man. Ben: dark-haired, taller than Josh, goofy-toothed, but handsome. The significant feature was his eyes and it was inescapable: mini-Tim, Tim incarnate, Tim reborn about three foot tall and with a black-and-white football under his arm. I looked at Lucy and the expression on her face told me she had seen it too. I glanced at Josh, hiding shyly behind Lucy's legs, and wondered whether there would be the faintest click of recognition. Would a four-year-old recognise anything of his dead father on being introduced to his illegitimate half-sibling? The child psychologists would have a field day.

'Hello,' Lucy said, crouching down to his level. 'You must be Ben.'

'Yes, I am,' he replied. 'Do you want me to show you my football tricks? A boy in year two at school taught me a drag-back. It's quite hard for most people but not me.'

Josh was thus persuaded to emerge from behind his mother's legs and the unknowing half-brothers scampered off to play football together. Tim would have loved it.

Almost simultaneously, the front door opened. Vicky was standing there looking nervous. 'Come in,' she said warmly.

'Hi, I'm Dom,' I said.

'No need to introduce yourself,' she replied disarmingly. 'I know who you are. You look the same as you did in all Tim's photographs. Slightly less hair, though. You were always a bit self-conscious about that, apparently.' Lucy and I exchanged a glance. 'You see, you're going to have to remember,' she continued, 'that although you might know little about me, I know you so well, you feel like long-lost family.'

Vicky was good-looking, although that should have come as no surprise given that she had been Tim's mistress. But good-looking as in nice-looking, with an unmade-up, welcoming face. She was short and dark, like Lucy – Tim tended to conform to type – she lacked Lucy's diminutive, boyish appeal but was attractive in a not-too-obvious way. She wore designer jeans and a fitted floral shirt – fashionable, effortlessly eye-catching, just as Tim would have liked.

She led us into a sitting room that, like the hall, had a cosy-cottage feel, low, dark beams against a whitewashed low ceiling. Vicky excused herself to get some drinks and Lucy and I sat next to each other on the cream sofa, a sofa on which Tim had no doubt sat countless times before. It was hard not to think otherwise.

'Right, what do we do now?' Vicky asked, as she rejoined us. 'Do we talk about Tim, or do we make nervous small-talk? It's a bit freaky all this, isn't it?'

We went for the latter option and joined her in nervous laughter. Lucy explained that she and I had recently got engaged and Vicky congratulated us, but then we found ourselves with no small-talk handy, listening instead to the half-brothers playing football outside.

'OK, I'll take the plunge,' was how Vicky opened proceedings, following with a Titanic ice-breaker of a question. 'How much do you hate me?'

'I don't know,' Lucy replied. 'I don't think I do at all. I used to. There's no doubt about that. But that was back in the BZH days when I thought I owned Tim. Which I now realise I never

did. There's a part of me that still says I should despise you, but I've been bringing up Tim's son on my own for almost two years now and you've been doing the same. I lost my man, and you did too. Maybe I feel some sort of kinship. I certainly didn't come for a fight.'

'So why *did* you come?' Vicky smiled as if she sensed that Lucy needed to be put at her ease.

Lucy sipped her mineral water as if assessing her answer. 'I just need to know. I'm moving on in my life and I need to know – I think I have a right to know – exactly what I'm leaving behind.'

She then told the story of our first drive to Little Buckenham and the realisation that Tim's lover's house almost overlooked the scene of his death. Then it was Vicky's turn – to tell the whole story about the man we'd thought we knew so well.

'Right.' She took a deep breath, glancing from Lucy to me and back again. 'Here we go.'

She had met him at BZH, she said. Tim was young, popular and thrusting and had been earmarked by the powers-that-be as one to watch, a future star, perhaps. She was PA to Angus, one of the partners to whom Tim reported. She wasn't sleeping with Tim initially, but with Angus, and it was not long after Tim's arrival that Angus and she were married. But while Angus was clever, smooth and forty-five, Tim was vivacious, compelling and four years younger than her. She soon realised it was a no-contest.

Vicky spared us the gory details – how their affair started, who made the first move, how often they saw each other. All she was keen to impress on us was that it hadn't felt like a normal fling. 'Not that I'd done anything extra-marital like that before,' she said, 'but it did feel special.' She said she had tried to persuade Tim that they should be together, that they were a perfect match, that she didn't care for Angus, that she would run off with Tim into the sunset if he suggested it, but he wouldn't. 'Then there was that time when you caught us together – when I answered his phone?'

'The Radisson, Peterborough.'

'That's right. He was like a wounded animal after that. Said he couldn't go on with our affair. Full of remorse, guilt. Or, at least, his own version of it. I didn't see him for quite a while after that. At least, not outside work. You moved in together, didn't you?'

'Yup.'

'He was lovely to me, Lucy, but you were always non-negotiable. I had to accept that you were at the front of the queue, take it or leave it, you were number one.'

Vicky continued. 1993. She and Tim had been seeing each other again, she had stopped working for Angus – 'Working for a husband – impossible! Far too claustrophobic!' – and was PA to another director. 'Angus was doing a lot of work with clients on the continent,' she said, 'and this meant lots of trips abroad, which also made access to Tim easy. But then I messed up. I went and blew the whole thing with a stupid gaff.'

It was in the pre-email days of internal company message systems. Angus was away and she sent Tim a message – again she spared Lucy the gory details, but it was an invitation to sleep with her on the night before Angus got back. However, she sent it to Angus instead of Tim, Angus read it on his return and Tim was fired.

'I'm sorry, Lucy. I suspect this is all rather upsetting for you,' Vicky said.

But Lucy shrugged. 'I remember how he was when he got home the day he was sacked. I understand that now at least. But, please, go on.'

'So, chapter two.' Tim left BZH, Vicky left Angus and Tim left Vicky. 'He told me that it had gone on too long and that we were too close and that we had to call it quits.' She made a career change and went to teacher training college. They didn't see each other for almost a year. Then, by chance, early one spring evening, they bumped into each other outside Holborn Tube station. They had a drink together for old times' sake and then, for a bit more old times' sake, went back to Vicky's flat.

'And that was how it continued,' she said. 'On-off, more off than on. I knew where I stood in his pecking order – behind you. But I liked him enough for it not to matter. And I wasn't some sad bunny-boiler plotting to win him at all costs. I knew him too well to cling to any belief that he would make me a decent life-partner. I always thought – hoped – that someone else would come along for me, but they never did. I just saw Tim when he deigned to call. The thing is, Lucy, and it might sound hard to believe, he wanted to be a good husband to you. At least, he thought he did. Cherishing you was important to him. When you and Tim got engaged and then married, I didn't see him for about a year. We'd talk on the phone occasionally, but as friends. I knew the rules and I was kind of happy for him. Jealous of you, I suppose, slightly heart-broken, yes – I wasn't *that* cool.'

'But you carried on seeing each other,' said Lucy, almost aggressively.

'Yes. I'm sorry, but we did. Not regularly, but, yes, we did. We had a nice time together. But then Ben was conceived and the whole thing became this huge mess.' She gestured at Ben and Josh outside in the garden. 'You were pregnant and Tim felt more guilty than ever. And for the first time in years I found myself wanting part of him. Or needing part of him, I suppose. I wanted to keep Ben. So Tim felt guilty about you and then he felt guilty about me. He'd buggered it all up, hadn't he? But, being Tim, he thought he could handle everything.'

Lucy shook her head. 'King-of-the-world Tim, you mean?'

'Yup.'

'Tim who could conquer all and every situation?'

'Yes, we know the one, don't we?' And they laughed together.

'What did you do?' Lucy asked. 'How did you handle it? Tim didn't live a complete double life as Ben's father, did he?'

'No, but it was important to him to do the right thing. He was quite old-fashioned in his own screwed-up way, wasn't he?'

Lucy nodded, chuckling.

'He insisted on being the provider, and while it hadn't been

my intention to squeeze money out of him – I wanted to feel independent – I wasn't going to say no to any offers. But neither was I going to let him play father. I don't think he wanted to, actually. I think he realised that a complete double life was beyond even him. So he accepted my proposal: to be Ben's special friend, a kind of super-charged godparent, to visit as often as he wanted, to be as close to Ben as he wanted, to bath him, feed him, play with him, whatever, but never to acknowledge the relationship.'

'And that explains all his apparent business trips to Oxford, does it?'

'I suppose so. If it means anything to you, and I don't suppose it does, Tim was a brilliant non-father to Ben. He visited – I don't know – once a week? Once a fortnight? He and Ben became real mates. As soon as Ben could talk, he called him 'Naughty Tim', which made me laugh, and Tim'd spend hours kicking balls with him in the garden. That was their special thing. Balls and books.

So Ben, Vicky explained, never knew who his father was. In fact, no one knows who Ben's father was, apart from Vicky, Marco and now Lucy and I.

'Who does he think his father is?'

'Well, it was around the time that Tim died when he started asking me. And that was convenient because it meant I didn't have to lie too blatantly. Ben believes that his father died when he was very young and the person I describe when he asks about him is part Tim, part fiction. I know I'll have to address the situation properly one day but, for now at least, it works all right.'

We were silent for a minute. 'How are we doing?' asked Vicky, brow furrowed. 'I haven't got a clue what it must be like for you to hear all this, Lucy. Are you OK? More water?' She laughed at the banality of the second question.

'Well, we're nearly at the end, I suppose,' Lucy said.

'What else can I tell you?'

Lucy paused. 'OK. Two things I need to know, that I suppose I'm scared of. One, were you together, you know, *together* right up until he died? And two . . .' she screwed her eyes tight shut. 'The night Tim died, what happened? Exactly what happened? Because, until a fortnight ago I thought he was on the way home from meetings with clients. The question,' she waved a hand, indicating that it wasn't easy to ask, 'is whether you and he had slept together that night. What I find myself needing to know is whether or not it was his infidelity sent him to his death.'

Silence. Vicky held Lucy's gaze and then started. Their relationship had changed, she said, when Ben arrived. She and Tim had grown up, found themselves struck down by adulthood. Any excitement in an illicit affair evaporated. 'Yes, we *slept* together, as in *together* together,' was how she put it, but it was rare, once a month, once every other month, perhaps, and 'just out of mutual appreciation'. It didn't mean anything, 'a pleasant habit that we never completely quit'. It didn't feel like an affair any more, she said, more an acknowledgement of a deep friendship.

'And on that last night?'

'No. That last night Tim came round quite late. He *had* been seeing clients and he hadn't seen Ben for two weeks. He rang me, late afternoon, from his car. Could I keep Ben up for him? So I did, just as I'd done a few times before. Tim got to us at around half past eight and had his usual little muck-about with Ben, read him a book and put him to bed. He stayed for supper. He was a bit preoccupied and wanted to chat. Business hadn't been going well, he said. I knew he'd been on a bad run for a little while. But that was it, Lucy, that and nothing but. Supper, a glass of wine and then goodbye. I told him to drive carefully, which I always did, and he gave me this disparaging look as if to say he was immortal, which was what he always did too. That was our familiar goodbye exchange – me badgering him about his driving. And, for some reason, I added, "You're not immortal, you know." And that was it. Sadly I was right.'

Suddenly Lucy jumped up, blurting, 'Sorry,' as she went, her

face clearly about to crumple. I followed her out of the front door to the car, where she was doubled over by the bonnet, breathing deeply to choke back any tears. I put my arm round her to comfort her. 'Please, Grey,' she said, when she could control herself enough to formulate words, 'I need to be on my own. Let me be, just for a minute.'

It was more than a minute, more like ten, but when Lucy came back to Vicky and me, she was smiling. She walked to Vicky and hugged her. And there a friendship began.

We had lunch. Josh talked us through his newly learned drag-back and announced that he was an Arsenal supporter, and he and Ben spent the rest of the meal competing for space in the conversation. Afterwards, Lucy packed me off to play football with them. 'I think Vicky and I need a natter,' she said, and it clearly went well because it was another hour before she announced that it was time for us to go.

As we left, her spirits seemed buoyant again. She and Vicky did another big hug and agreed how 'freaky' and better-than-expected it had been to meet. 'Just one thing I want to leave you with,' said Vicky, taking Lucy out of the boys' earshot. 'Whatever you think of me, please remember this about Tim. He loved you, Lucy, really loved you. I guess maybe it was in a way that isn't quite how a wife would want, and that may or may not be acceptable, but the way he did love, he did it for you. Not me, I was nowhere near. You were the special one for him. You. I truly believe he gave you everything that it was within his power to give.'

27

The last time Lucy hosted an engagement bash it had been the mother of all parties. It was held at the Polish Club in Exhibition Road near Hyde Park. Some two hundred people turned out to celebrate in unrestrainedly bacchanalian fashion; the vodka was copious, at least three guests vomited – one of whom was Marco, who fell asleep in the gents' with his trousers round his ankles and was woken up by the security guards when they were locking up at half past three in the morning. The music was excellent: a live band who could do a cover version of any song requested and who contributed to the highlight of the evening, which was the all-too-predictable Tim Cassidy-accompanied rendition of 'Jetplane'.

Her second engagement party, this evening, is going to cut a contrast. Marco, for one, isn't invited, the 'Jetplane' has long since crashed, there will be neither dancing nor vomiting, and no vodka, not even in the red, star-shaped jelly dessert that Josh insisted he prepare for us this afternoon. Josh has also insisted that he be allowed to stay up late in his pyjamas and dressing-gown to take our guests' coats at the front door, to pass round the crisps and be in charge of the music for Musical Bumps. Indeed, he appears to have invested more excitement in the evening than either Lucy or I. Not even the news that there will be no Musical Bumps could dent his enthusiasm: he decided we'd be playing Sleeping Lions instead.

Ours has been a great engagement for Josh, his delight only waning when I have allowed myself to grow weary of my role as permanent playmate. I'd thought I was doing a good job at being a friend to him, but since my identity changed from

naughty-godfather-who-missed-the-christening to daddy-to-be, I've discovered levels of attention-giving that I never knew existed. Thus the new vow I suggested to Josh: to have and to hold, to love and to cherish, and now 'to play endless rough-and-tumble, superheroes and Red Injuns till death us do part'. Josh and I may be the best of mates but occasionally he doesn't appreciate my sense of humour.

With today being our engagement-party day, given Lucy's precedent in this department, I've taken to calling it 'engagement-small-social-gathering day' instead. She didn't find that funny either. I've taken the afternoon off work and I've got jobs: collect Josh from school, buy wine and cheese, take old newspapers and bottles to the recycling bins, change lightbulbs, keep Josh out of Lucy's hair while she cooks and – importantly – keep my mother's Birds of Paradise alive for another twelve hours so that she can see them in all their wilting glory. It doesn't help that Josh, who I am supposed to be keeping away from the kitchen, insists on making his own culinary contribution to the evening – the red jelly in his favourite star-shaped jelly mould. And neither does it make it any easier that when Josh is about to pour the jelly mix into the mould, when assistance is crucial, Kathy rings from work, wanting to talk about the focus groups for the National Birth Control Association campaign.

'I'm sorry, sweetie,' she says, rather too informally for my liking, 'but I'm conducting these first thing Monday and I need you to sign it all off.'

'Kathy,' I reply, one hand on the phone, the other trying to keep Josh from the jelly, while Lucy frowns at me from the sink, 'there's no need to consult on this. I trust you implicitly.'

'I could pop round to your house if that would be quicker and easier.'

'No, you bloody couldn't. We're entertaining.'

'What? Not even a glass of champers for little old me?'

'Kathy!' I'm trying to be lighthearted. 'Stop that and bugger off.' I put down the receiver.

'So that was the Boston slapper, was it?' came the follow-up from the sink.

''Fraid so.'

'Ringing you at home.'

''Fraid so.'

'Hmm. And I'm not too keen on the B-U-G-G-E-R word in present company either.'

'Right, Josh.' I wince. 'Let's get on with this sodding jelly.'

I remember the Polish Club party particularly because Lucy had asked me to turn up early. While Tim was making jokes and winning approval, she wanted me to be her pillar of moral support. I remember the vibe, the people arriving, eager and ready to indulge. And Tim and Lucy – who was in no need of a pillar – flying high on adrenaline and lemon vodka.

Tonight in Archdeacon Road there will be just eight of us; we could have gone up to ten with Lucy's parents but she insisted that inviting them down from Scotland would build the evening into a bigger show than we had intended. We could have gone all the way up to nine but for Alice's determined belligerence. 'Sod Alice,' we said. And we repeated it a number of times. 'Self-righteous cow,' was Lucy's breezy elaboration, which failed to disguise how much her friend had hurt her. 'What right has she to judge?' I mentioned something about taking the plank out of your own eye first, and Lucy went to telephone Vicky. Since our visit to Little Buckenham, she had taken to calling her and had asked her to come early tonight. Big night, Dom's scary mother coming, she explained, moral support needed.

So this is the line-up: the happy couple, my mother, Bill un-accompanied, Vicky for moral support, Jerry, who happened to be in town on business and will be good on light relief but will arrive late from a meeting, and Rhys and Emily, who I hope will do a good job on light relief too.

Vicky, as appointed, is first to arrive and Josh has her coat off her back before she has even got inside the house and runs upstairs with it in triumph. 'Da-da-da-diddly-da,' he sings as he goes.

Lucy hugs her and I get an air-kiss.

Soon our small social gathering is under way in an intimate circle in the sitting room.

'Lucy, for the last bloody time,' Bill says apologetically, 'I'm damned sorry about Alice tonight.' Except his apology is too loud.

'Oh, yes?' Emily says, picking up the scent. 'Where is she?'

Struggling for an answer, Lucy buys time by lighting a cigarette and Rhys butts into the conversation to rescue her: 'Tell us, Lucy, what was it that made you accept the old dog's hand in marriage?'

'Erm . . .' All eyes are on Lucy and she doesn't find this line of conversation any easier. The real answer – 'Because he proved to me that my last husband had spent his life cheating on me' – isn't what anyone wants to hear. Finally she smiles and replies: 'I thought I should do it quickly before his hair fell out altogether.' Very good: chuckles all round. I put my arm round her shoulders. And only very slightly does she stiffen.

But this gathering is fraught with difficulty. 'How do you know Lucy and Dom?' my mother asks Vicky. Unhelpfully.

'Through an old friend,' she replies, rejecting the obvious alternative: 'Because I spent ten years sleeping with Lucy's husband and am mother to his secret love-child.'

'Oh, really? And what friend is that?'

Vicky pauses. 'It's Tim,' says Lucy, helping her out. 'My old Tim.'

'He'll be looking down on all this with pleasure, I've no doubt,' says Rhys, failing to inject the intended light relief. 'I'm sure nothing would give him more pleasure than to see his old mate looking after Lucy.'

Vicky is blushing and sipping her drink nervously, Emily is looking at her feet and Bill has turned away from the throng as if to study the photos on Tim's old shrine. Half an hour into our engagement party, the conversation has dried up. Thank God for Josh. He doesn't just take coats and pass crisps, he tells our

guests what nice coats they have, informs them what flavour crisps they are being offered and asks if they wouldn't prefer a Diet Coke to 'that funny stuff Dom keeps going on to me about'. And when the conversation is becalmed, he fetches a ball to show Vicky, my mother and Bill the drag-back he has been practising.

'Come on, Josh, you know football's forbidden in the sitting room,' says Lucy gently.

'Even on special occasions, Mum?' he responds, looking innocent and wronged. He is rewarded with a cooing, smiling audience, heads all tilted to one side in awe of a sweet boy who clearly has his father's ability to entertain a crowd.

He also delivers word-perfectly the line I have been practising with him. 'Mum, that champagne's a very superior vintage, don't you think? It's probably even better than Cristal.'

Laughter all round. Almost. Lucy smiles at me, ruffling Josh's hair. 'What champagne is it, Grey?' she asks.

'Veuve Clicquot – La Grande Dame 1990 – not quite as expensive as a Cristal but probably better.'

Lucy raises her eyebrows. 'Are you trying to make a statement?'

'No. Just . . .' I shrug '. . . just wanted, you know, something special.'

'Is Cristal not special?' she says, through clenched teeth.

'Yes. I guess I meant something *different*.'

'Well, if it's so bloody good, it's wasted on me,' says Rhys, finally locating the light relief – or a Luddite version of it. 'All we need now is to wash it down with a good square meal.'

'Oh, let's not do a square meal today,' my mother interjects. 'I've never seen the point in a square one, and when did you last eat square anyway? In my experience, meals have best been served up round, rarely square. I'd have been happy to help out if I'd known there was a crockery problem – it is, after all, a special occasion.'

The silence that results is broken by the doorbell, another burst of enthusiasm from Josh and the welcome arrival of Jerry. With the party now complete, we sit down to eat. And it is soon clear that Jerry is at his convivial best.

'I hope I haven't missed the toast,' he says, turning first to Vicky on his right, then Lucy on his left. On discovering that he hasn't, he gets to his feet: 'Let us all drink to this revoltingly happy couple and their revoltingly happy life together.' He raises his glass. 'To Dom and Lucy.'

'Dom and Lucy,' comes the pleasantly cheery response. I turn to Lucy to share the moment but get no eye-contact. She looks self-consciously at her plate. Caramelised Brie or me, and she chooses the cheese.

'Right, Lucy,' says Jerry, turning to Lucy, 'I need information.' Jerry is performing his party act for the evening and it makes me nervous. 'Now that we're allowed to know that Dom has been in love with you for most of his life . . .' I'd been right to feel nervous '. . . tell me, what did he do? Which one of his limited supply of charms did my dear friend manage to impress you with? How much ale did he ply you with? What on earth was going through your mind? I want to know exactly what persuaded you to look him deep in the eyes in a way that you had never done before and say in your sweet still-ever-so Scottish tones "I will."'

I look at Lucy, who is again eyeballing her cheese. So I get to my feet. 'More wine, anyone?'

'Sit down, Dom,' Jerry orders. 'I'm trying to understand about love. This is important.'

'Well,' Lucy clears her throat and smiles unconvincingly, 'as I said to Rhys earlier, before we had the benefit of your company, Jerry, in the years I've known Dom, I've been watching his hair get thinner and I concluded that marriage was the only thing that could possibly halt the decline.'

'Come on, Lucy!' roars Jerry jovially, rubbing the top of his head so that his grey hair sticks up. 'You know that's not good enough for me. I want to understand! I want information! I'm a middle-aged soak who's never experienced love and I want to go away from here this evening quivering with envy of this all-enveloping kaleidoscope of emotions that you two are sharing,

this feeling that's so strong it's about to burst out of you. I want to feel your love, baby! I want to understand every single one of those clichés that I hear on the radio a hundred times a day and that I've used over and over again to advertise everything from ice-cream to life insurance to bloody birth control. C'mon, Lucy, give me your love!' Jerry thumps the table with his fist as he delivers the last line, which diverts Lucy's eyes from the cheese in the direction of help.

'The point about that feeling, Jerry,' I say, filling glasses with wine as I go, 'is that it is indescribable. And I know that's the cliché of clichés, but it's only become so because it's true. It doesn't sit in a neat little sentence. It doesn't work as a sound-bite with a bit of background music. It's more than an essay subject. Isn't that why it's the most written-about subject since man first learned to write? No words are ever enough.'

'That's a bloody cop-out, Lord,' Jerry responds, smiling, 'and you know it.'

I shrug him off.

'Lucy,' he continues, tenaciously determined, 'just a little morsel for me to go home with. Just a tiny one for poor old Jerry. What was it? What happened? What made you go from thinking this man's the best thing since Peachey's ice-cream to wanting to be his wife?'

'Jerry!' I say chidingly. I know that the only way to treat him in this frame of mind is as a child. 'Enough!'

'OK, OK,' he says, hands raised in a gesture of defeat. 'Calm down.' And he turns theatrically to Vicky. 'Tell me, Vicky, how did you come to have the pleasure of the acquaintance of this beastly happy couple?'

Vicky, well-acquainted now with the complications of the evening, bluffs her way unobtrusively round the question, and Jerry retreats from centre stage and allows a kind of standard(ish) dinner party to come fleetingly to life. We even find a marriage topic that we can discuss without anyone having to stare too hard at their starter. Where and when are we going to get married?

'Bermuda, four weeks' time. As soon as the school holidays start.'

'Fantastic,' says Jerry. 'I'll dig out the suncream. You'll need a best man.'

'Very kind of you, Jerry,' I reply, 'but Josh is already lined up for the job. We wanted a really good speech.'

'Bermuda? Fantastic. That's a whole new kettle of fish,' says Rhys.

'Really?' says my mother, next to him. 'How fascinating! They make fish kettles differently in Bermuda, do they? I can't wait to see them.'

'Mother!' I admonish her. 'I see the language police have come out tonight. They're very welcome to go off-duty if they like.'

Somehow Lucy charms her way round my mother's intention to be as conversationally awkward as possible and her presumption that our wedding plans involve a trip to Bermuda for her too. It will be just the three of us flying to Bermuda and somehow my mother is persuaded to agree that this is, of course, the best course of action. So we sail through the starter and are still going strong through the fish ('No, Mother, it wasn't cooked in a fish kettle'), when the phone rings. Lucy stretches behind her to answer it, then passes it to me. 'Kathy from work,' she says, eyebrows raised.

'Why the fuck are you ringing now?' I ask angrily, the moment I have left the kitchen and am out of earshot. 'It's half past nine and we're entertaining. You know that.'

'Sorry, darling!' she replies, as if surprised by my tone. 'Some of us are still working.'

'Well, you shouldn't be. What do you want?'

'Just to check you're having a nice time while I'm hard at it in the office.'

'Fucking hell, Kathy!' The expletives explode through gritted teeth. 'You're bunny-boiling mad!'

'No, I'm not,' she says, laughing. 'I'm joking. I've rung up about the NBCA campaign. The focus groups. The client really

231

wants to know what you think of the proposed discussion points.'

'Kathy! We talked about this earlier. I couldn't give a monkey's about focus-group discussion points. It's your job. I trust you to do it. You don't need my input. Now, leave me alone.'

I can feel Lucy's eyes on me as I make an apologetic return to the party.

'That girl,' she says, 'doesn't want to leave you alone, does she?'

I shake my head but find Jerry chimes in with the wrong answer: 'She never has done, Lucy. Chased him all round New York, you know.'

'No, I didn't, actually.'

'Caught up with him once or twice too, didn't she, Dom? I bet you didn't know that either.'

'No, I didn't,' replies Lucy, her voice suddenly so frosty that not even Jerry could fail to spot it. Jerry looks at me for support but gets none. I am already thinking ahead.

It is another two hours before everyone has left and they aren't too painful. Either that or I'm numb to it. No one mentions Tim or asks whether he had any illegitimate children or whether anyone else at the party had committed long-term habitual adultery with him. We talk Bermuda, *Book of the Month* and babies, and I am delighted to hear Lucy committing me to an intensive search for a sibling or two for Josh. My mother relaxes, becomes less self-satisfied and annoying, and, even better, is the first to go home. She is followed by Vicky ('Must relieve the babysitter'), then a little later by Bill, Rhys and Emily.

This leaves Jerry, customarily the last guest at a party. As Lucy begins the washing-up he whispers, 'I haven't fucked things up, have I?'

'You've had a pretty good go at it.'

'Sorry, old mate. Just wandered blindly into it. Didn't see it coming.'

'Don't worry. We'll be strong,' I reply unconvincingly.

'I really am sorry, mate. I hadn't thought for a moment that she didn't know. You always said you told each other everything, no secrets, all that crap. I thought that was what was so special about you two. I thought that was your USP.'

'Well . . . yes . . .'

'Do you want me to leave?'

'It wouldn't be a bad idea.'

'OK, Domo, I'm off.'

Two minutes later I'm closing the door behind him, and by the time I have returned to the sitting room Lucy has ensconced herself on the sofa, a cigarette smoking between her fingers. I sit down next to her and try to read her mood.

'I'm sorry,' I say gently, eventually breaking the silence.

'You cheated on Nadia, didn't you?' Her voice is quiet but hard.

'Yes.'

'And you lied to me about it?'

'I'm afraid I did.'

Silence again.

'Oh, Grey!' Cold disapproval fills her voice. 'What . . . I mean, Christ! Please, please, tell me you're not like Tim. You're supposed to be different, for Christ's sake. You swore to me that you were.'

'I am, Lula.' I try to put my arm round her but she recoils.

'Then how can you have done this? You're supposed to be the real thing, Grey, the good guy, my rock, everything Tim wasn't. God! I don't want another unfaithful husband!'

'You won't have one, Lucy, I swear.'

'But you've just admitted I have.'

'Look, Lucy. Yes, I was unfaithful to Nadia. Twice. And that's all. But it doesn't count. It doesn't reflect on me as a husband. That's not the husband I am. I wasn't in love with Nadia, you knew that all along. I didn't cherish her because I didn't love her. So, not honouring my marriage vow didn't seem to matter.

But I'm in love with you, Lucy, and so deeply that I would never do anything to jeopardise our marriage.'

'Oh, Grey!' She sounds as if she has been beaten into submission. 'I can remember Tim saying almost the same thing.'

'But I'm not Tim, Lucy!' I try again to put my arm around her, but she pushes me away.

'No, Grey! You can't just give me a cuddle and tell me it'll be different this time. I'm sorry. You, the person you are, your fidelity – that's the foundation of everything this marriage is supposed to be about.'

'Not *supposed*, Lucy, *is* about.'

'How do I know?'

'Well, all I can say is that you'll just have to carry on believing in me, Lucy. I *am* the real thing, I promise. You have to trust me.'

'And that's another thing Tim used to say.'

28

The Sexual Life of Dominic L. Or, Another Long Day's Journey into Night.

THE NIGHT OF THE ENGAGEMENT PARTY

Not a great night for the sharing of bodily warmth although, frankly, this isn't a shock. What we have here is a lifelong cuckold coming to terms with the fact that her second husband-to-be is another adulterer. So when I drape an arm nervously over her in bed – no come-on intended, purely in the spirit of friendship, indeed, more as a testing of the water – it is tetchily swatted away.

What would Tim have done in such circumstances? Because, as Lucy says, I am now saying the same things he said, doing the same things he did. I've become Tim, but without the charm, the *je ne sais quoi*, the *chansons* and the shagging. Tim would probably have rolled out of bed and recalled a last-minute business engagement near Oxford. And he'd probably have got away with it. But I've got no long-haired lover from Lower Basildon, couldn't get one if I tried, and Tim is bringing me down with him.

THE NIGHT AFTER THE ENGAGEMENT PARTY

Not my proudest moment. I don't think this is an exclusively male trait but I know it's one we're especially good at: avoid the issue, duck the question, pretend there's no problem, stick your head in the sand, go about life pretending everything is tickety-boo when tickety-boo it ain't. For me, the male in the Dominic-Lucy special relationship, this is a heinous crime: not avoiding

issues and not ducking questions is what is supposed to make our relationship so special. As Jerry said: that's our USP. 'No secrets, all that crap' – or maybe it was crap, after all. Maybe every couple is under the illusion that that's their USP too, until they realise it's become necessary to lie to each other.

It being Saturday, I suck up to Lucy by proving what a good father I'm going to be and construct an entire day's programme around Josh: drag-backs in the garden in the morning, then Richmond Park, out for a cosy lunch-for-two and a spot of shopping (buying their love is supposed to be a last resort, but I've got to do everything to ensure that he's firmly on my side and, in that respect, £6.99 for a Spider-Man T-shirt seems a bargain). We get home for Josh's tea ('Don't worry, Lucy, I'm perfectly happy to do it.' 'OK, but can you make sure it's not all freezer food this time, and no going soft on the Diet Coke') and I'm just about to take him up for his bath when Lucy intervenes: 'You're doing a great job, Grey, but I've hardly seen my son today. I'll put him to bed, if you don't mind.'

Of course I don't mind. It works either way: if I'm doing Josh and Lucy isn't, or if Lucy's doing Josh and I'm not, the end product is still the same: I have constructed a way to avoid intimacy with my fiancée. Indeed, when Lucy's putting Josh to bed and I'm sitting in front of the TV, with a glass of red and *Stars In Their Eyes* about to start, my mobile rings and it's Bill, suggesting a drink in the pub and thus the possibility of completing the intimacy-free day. I grab it. And I don't waste it. Indeed, I make the most of it. By suggesting a post-pub curry, I can ensure that Lucy will be tucked up for the night long before I return home.

SECOND NIGHT AFTER THE ENGAGEMENT PARTY

Bill has reappraised his sex life. He's decided to come clean with me. He was lying, he told me last night, his face reddening. When he'd told me that he and Alice had sex about once a week, well,

it wasn't strictly true. They don't have sex once a week, it's more like once every two or three. At least, it was before he joined Tim and me in the ranks of adulterers, but now that he's a fully paid-up, self-confessed adulterer, the signs are there, he thinks, to suggest that his strike rate is likely to dip and he's not sure now whether he'll even be a once-a-monther. It doesn't help, he says, that he and Alice are split on the Dominic-Lucy issue. His thought was that maybe he should give up with this month and go back into battle in March. And this is by no means his worst-ever run, he says. That was after Sam's birth, a hundred days in solitude. More, actually: four and a half months. But that doesn't count, he says. A post-natal low is to be expected. But it's different now. It's crisis time. What did I think?

These are my thoughts as I put away my toothbrush and prepare to go back into battle: there was I thinking that Lucy and I had problems. Admittedly we haven't celebrated our ten-year anniversary yet or reproduced in quadruplicate, and it would be understandable if some of the varnish on any relationship were to dull a bit after such an ordeal. But once a month? Once every two weeks (at best) pre-adultery?

I find this strangely encouraging. If once a fortnight has sustained the Bill-Alice relationship – and they had been perceived, until adultery, as one of the strongest couples around – that surely augurs well for Lucy and me. Because while we're not going to be rewriting the *Kama Sutra*, we're still – and I'm fairly confident of this – going to be at least as regular as, say, the rubbish-men or the Sunday papers. And so, even given all our unusual circumstances, maybe we'll be one of the strongest couples out there too.

With this in mind I skip into bed and cuddle up to Lucy, a manoeuvre she fails to register beyond the turning of a page. Three pages later she is at the end of the chapter and my presence has still gone unacknowledged. And I know, or at least it's the sort of thing that a *Daily Mail* survey will inform us of at least once a year, that Jeremy Paxman is attractive to women and one of the

most desirable unmarried men out there and I know, or at least its back cover tells me, that his book (her book) *The English* is intelligent and witty, but I'm not prepared to take this lying down. So to speak. Paxman is dominating her. I am not getting so much as a look-in. I take a deep breath and slide my hand slowly and sensually up her left leg, lightly massaging her inner thigh.

'Not tonight, Grey,' she says, not looking away from the page. 'Sorry.'

Which is a shame, but this is a minor blot, barely a smudge, on an altogether promising landscape. I'm still seeing sunny brush-strokes. Indeed, I've got an idea for the Birth Control campaign.

THIRD NIGHT AFTER THE ENGAGEMENT PARTY

Paxman is in good form again. If it hadn't been for revelations of my own indiscretions I would complain about him slipping so unscrupulously into bed with my fiancée while my back is turned. But instead I try to take him on. Fool that I am. As Lucy snuggles up with Paxman, I flick through holiday brochures of Bermuda, murmuring enthusiastically, folding over the corners of pages in a brave attempt to hook her attention. Paxman and *The English* versus me and a perfect strip of Bermudan sand.

But Lucy reads on, immersed in her book. She chuckles to herself and turns a page. She chuckles again and shakes her head. She chuckles a third time, so amused that momentarily she puts down the book. God, he's so droll she can't take it any more. In less than five minutes, I'm defeated. Bereft of ideas, I try the left-inner-thigh massage again.

'Paxman says here that Englishmen are obsessed with having their arses beaten,' she says, as a distraction.

The massage is terminated. 'Literally or in the international sporting arena?'

'Literally. I just think you should declare yourself here and now, Grey, if this is the case with you. Because I'm suddenly extremely Scottish.'

So, no flagellation, then. No sex. Just the man from *Newsnight*.

FOURTH NIGHT AFTER THE ENGAGEMENT PARTY

Nothing to report from the bedroom. Only that I've accepted my place sub-Paxman in the pecking order and that Lucy has nearly finished with him. Only two chapters to go.

Lunch with Rhys is more encouraging. I take him to a West End restaurant favoured by B-list celebrities and posers, exactly the kind he'd love, and explain that my hospitality is in return for a frank conversation on the state of his sex life.

'Having problems, are you, mate?' he asks.

Of course not, I explain. Me? As if! No, it's all in the name of research, you know, for an ad.

Rhys accepts this, and when the second bottle of wine arrives, he gets to the point. Emily, he says, laughing, might as well be sleeping with a shotgun next to her. 'If I came within a foot of her, she'd shoot me. Sex? Ha! Oh, yes, I do have some vague recollections!' But he seems at ease with it, not at all concerned. 'I can't believe it's particularly unusual,' he says. 'When you've just had a baby, it's bound to take a while.'

So these are Rhys's stats. Last time he and Emily had sex: fifty-three days ago, three weeks before the arrival of their first baby and another month added on after. Regularity of sex in non-natal times: varied, quite often two or three times a week, but sometimes not for a fortnight and never at all when England are playing Test cricket in Australia and Emily is displaced by the television as his night-time priority.

FIFTH NIGHT AFTER THE ENGAGEMENT PARTY

Self-doubt is creeping in. On the home front, it seems that all the holiday brochures and leg massages in the world would not

make the required impact. And at Duffy's, they don't seem to find it funny either.

With some excitement, I unveil my Birth Control campaign proposal to Kathy in the office and Jerry in New York via a conference call. My argument is that we should stop using sex to sell – it's *passé*, a cliché, and we're better than that. Sex may be the biggest single influence on the history of advertising, but let's move on, I say. Let's get past the era of the phallic Flake ad, Peachey's horny houseboaters and the Daihatsu Hijet. Let's do the opposite, I say, let's change perceptions. Let's not sell people pills or caps or condoms or coils, because couples out there aren't *actually* having much sex. Let's use *that* as our way in. Let's tell our market that if you're not having multiply-orgasmic sex in a variety of different positions at least seventeen times a night, and every one of those lasting a good twenty minutes, then actually it's OK. In fact, contrary to almost everything our industry has been saying for the last century, it's normal. And let's make light of it: it's not embarrassing. There's nothing wrong with the fact that many couples hardly have sex at all. And people will buy into the campaign because they will recognise what we're saying, they'll feel liberated, at home with it, they'll laugh and say to themselves, 'Yes, that's me.' At least, that's my preamble.

So this is the ad. Its simplicity is its strength, I explain, and it works in print and on TV: 'The proposal is to have a couple – two couples, three, four, five couples – cuddled up in bed like a series of talking heads. The man will say to the woman "Not tonight, darling." And she'll smile warmly as if she's delighted by the news. She'll reply "Fine," or "No problem," or "Maybe next month," or "Maybe in two weeks' time," and the picture is of a couple at ease and happy with the fact that they're not having sex. The next couple will do the same, then the next and so on. It'll be like a mini-series of five-second flashes, but every one of them using the line "Not tonight, darling." Because "Not tonight, darling" is a cliché brush-off line. The common perception is that when you get "Not tonight, darling", it's bad news.

But we would make "Not tonight, darling" look acceptable, cool, even. And the ad would close with the punchline: "Abstinence makes the heart grow fonder."'

I deliver the last line with a flourish.

Squeals of approval are not forthcoming.

Kathy looks mystified. 'Well, yeah, right. It's certainly left-of-field.'

'Exactly!' I crow triumphantly. 'That's the whole point.'

'I understand you're using an extreme to make it,' she says ponderously, now frowning, 'but I just feel, c'mon! Once a month is an insult, isn't it? I mean, who are these sad, frigid worshippers of abstinence? Do they really exist? I mean, I know you English are supposed to be a bit restrained, but I'd assumed that was a national stereotype – not the truth, the whole truth and nothing but. God! Times can't be that bad for you guys, can they?'

'I'm afraid I agree, Dom,' says Jerry. 'I've never been married, but it can't be *that* bad. Christ, you must be terrified.'

'I'm not talking about me.' I laugh nervously. 'It's the population out there I'm referring to. Sex is out of fashion. No-sex is hip. It's the new black.'

'How do you know?' asks Kathy, annoyingly. 'Have you researched it?'

'Kind of, informally.'

'I think we should do more,' says Jerry, with an air of finality. 'Kathy? That's a job for you.'

'No problemo.'

'God, Dom! Have we really been getting it wrong all this time?' He laughs.

'No, but maybe it's time to do it a little differently.'

'OK, I hear you. But you want to know my immediate concern? I'm not sure it fits our target market. We're not pitching to the married classes who are maybe happier watching the ten o'clock news in bed, then switching the light off. We're talking the late teens, the guys who are just so exploding with hormones that they can barely control themselves and are desperate to do something about it, no matter whether we tell them it's cool or not.'

'We could have teens as our talking heads.'

'Hmm. We'll see. Look, must go. This is a plan very much in its infancy. But it *is* revolutionary.'

SIXTH NIGHT AFTER THE ENGAGEMENT PARTY

I'm now a man of split loyalties. There's a limit to how many of Lucy's 'not-tonight-darlings' I can take by reassuring myself that my hunch with the NBCA ad is correct. If there is indeed a population of frigid abstainers out there (and I'm already doubting it), I had no intention of becoming a fully paid-up member, and this is a point that, very gently, I attempt to impress on Lucy.

'Oh, Grey!' She puts down her book (which isn't Paxman – she has finished, thank God, with Paxman) and studies me, her face a mesh of worry lines. 'It's not purely sex you want me for, is it? Please tell me we're better than that.'

'Of course we are,' I reply, and I mean it. 'I loathe the fact that you should even have to ask me that. I don't see sex as some kind of reward for a good day at the marriage bank. I think of it as an expression of physical intimacy.'

'Grey!' she says it with concern, the worry lines tightening. 'This is becoming our *Groundhog Day* conversation, isn't it? But I'll say what I feel – what I've always felt. Our intimacy has always been emotional rather than physical.'

'Yes, but it's still quite a lot more than that. Yes, mentally we're close, but it goes a bit deeper, surely, than being a pair of people who enjoy doing the crossword together.'

'We don't do the crossword together.'

'You know what I mean.'

NINTH MORNING AFTER THE ENGAGEMENT PARTY

Sunday morning has become a cosy family affair in Archdeacon Avenue. Josh hops into bed with us. Sometimes we say, 'Hop into bed, Josh,' and he'll do his hop-into-bed joke by taking us

literally and jumping in one-footed. Oh, how we laugh, such merry times are these!

Today Josh plays a blinder. He's not done the hopping joke: he seems quiet and preoccupied.

'What is it, Josh?' asks Lucy.

'I was just wondering, Mummy,' he replies, 'when do you think my baby brother's going to arrive?'

This is a stroke of genius from the boy. Here am I reading holiday brochures, massaging inner thighs and doing bedroom battle with *Newsnight* presenters, but a four-and-a-half-year-old gets to the nub of it. When are we going to reproduce?

I study Lucy's face for the answer. But she's cleverer than the pair of us. 'It might be a sister, you know,' she says, unflustered, and renders Josh silent. She plays him brilliantly. She watches him digest the information, and in the very millisecond that he's about to come back with another family-planning question, she cuts him off with a question of her own: 'Would you prefer a brother or a sister?'

'Er, brother.'

'Would you mind if it's a sister?'

And so on and so on. Thus is Josh led away from the topic of enquiry. What he – and I – wanted to know was *when*? But she has circumvented the pair of us.

If you look hard, though, good news is buried deep in there somewhere. Because somewhere, most probably over the rainbow – as I'm sure I recall Tim singing from time to time – there is reproduction to be had.

THAT NIGHT

'Lucy?'

She puts the book down. 'Yes, Grey.'

'Well,' I'm talking in romantic but corny, sarcastic *sotto voce* and, without having planned it, I find myself delving nervously

in search of an inner thigh, 'it's that issue of a sibling for Josh. When, um, well . . .' my left hand has found the thigh and is describing a soft-tipped circular motion just above the knee '. . . well, was there a particular time when you thought we might explore that possibility?'

Lucy laughs, which is good. Laughter was my desired intention. Because laughter – rather than sex – was what we used to specialise in.

'I don't know, darling.' She runs her hands through my hair in a matching *faux*-romantic way. 'Definitely some time this millennium!'

More laughter. Albeit one-sided.

THE FOLLOWING NIGHT

Another Paxman book has appeared on Lucy's bedside table. *Fish, Fishing and the Meaning of Life*. You don't have to be a rocket scientist to spot the subtext. I suppose I might be reading too much into this, but it's hard not to when all the signs point to the fact that your sex life is taking second place to an anthology of angling literature. And Paxman's only contribution is as the anthologist, plus a handful of introductory paragraphs. It's one thing to come between a man and his fiancée because of the calibre and wit of your prose, but it's another fish kettle altogether if you're simply putting your name to the *bons mots* of others. Shall I fight it head on? Or should I concede defeat to the great angling anthologist without going into battle?

BACK AT WORK THE NEXT DAY

A small paperclipped file of A4 sheets is sitting on my desk, with a yellow Post-it on the front. 'Dom, here's the research on the NBCA campaign that Jerry asked for. I've emailed it to him. Kathy XX.'

The research is a 'sex survey' conducted by Durex, the

prophylactics company, which claims that married people have sex ninety-eight times a year on average. Slightly more than I'd bargained for. Americans, astonishingly, come out top at 132 times per annum, followed by the Russians at 122 and the French in third place on 121. We British come in above the global average on 109; the Japanese are bottom on thirty-seven. Maybe, without knowing it, Lucy and I are Japanese.

THE DAY AFTER

'Well, what do you think?'

Kathy has walked into my office without knocking and sat down on my desk. She looks good today, as almost any girl would do if they were well shaped, short of skirt, nice of legs and had their pelvis perched inches away from where my hands are resting on my keyboard.

'Of what?' I reply, feigning ignorance. 'Of the fact that I've got some really tasteful office furniture in here and you appear not to have noticed it?'

'Nope. The stats I dug out yesterday. You know, the Durex shagathon.'

'Hmmm. Yeah, thanks for doing that. They certainly make a point, don't they? I was sort of going off my idea anyway.' Liar that I am. Kathy studies me, unconvinced. 'Honestly, wrong concept and, as Jerry said, wrong target market.'

'Too wrapped up in wedding plans, are we?' She uncrosses her legs. Her left buttock is now nestling against my keyboard. The shift and cap-lock keys are under threat.

'No. It's always about turning over ideas, isn't it? Out of twenty ideas, nineteen are normally shit and one's a gem.'

'Well, I'm relieved we agree. I mean, that whole no-sex concept – did it scare you a bit too?'

'Just put it down to a bad day at the office.' I sink into my chair, push myself away from the danger zone and put my feet on the desk.

'Wanna better day today?'

'Wouldn't mind.'

'Good. It's just that I've been fretting about your wedding present.'

'Oh, you don't have to give us one.'

'Well, I've come up with something, but it's really more for you.'

'Oh, yeah?' I'm trying to sound unconcerned. I'm failing.

Kathy looks at me, smiling, saying nothing. She's waiting for a reaction.

'Oh, yeah?' She wins. I've repeated myself.

'Yeah. I was stuck for ideas initially,' she eases herself off my desk and moves two spaces towards me so that I'm looking up at her, 'but I eventually realised that the best idea was to give you anything you wanted.' As she says this, in one splendidly threatening movement she cups a hand over each of her breasts, then thrusts them down the curves of her body, inwards to her crotch and slowly down the inside of her thighs. 'Honestly anything.'

And for some reason that I cannot quite fathom, a thought comes into my head. Lucy doesn't fish, she has never shown any interest in fishing, she has never to my knowledge ever been fishing or even mentioned it.

THAT NIGHT

Lucy seems surprised and impressed. I had booked the babysitter and a table at Isabella's pizzeria without telling her and she sits in front of me, smiling quizzically at the menu.

'What was the deal here last time, Grey? I can't remember.'

'I pay for your extra pepperoni topping and you give me your body in return.'

'And I agreed to that?'

'Certainly did.'

'And that's why we're back, is it?' She laughs.

'How can you suggest such a thing?'

'Have you forgotten? I know you quite well.'

'You underestimate me.'

'Do I?' Her eyes dance with delight, and she turns to the waiter, who has come to take our order. 'Hello. Can we order? Good. Now, tell me, you know your Pepperoni Feast?'

'Yes, madam?'

'Can I have that, please . . . but with the pepperoni taken out?'

'Of course you can, madam, but it would be a bit strange.'

'I know, but it's what I feel like today.'

'Very good.'

She turns back to me, squealing with pleasure. Indeed, so pleased is she with herself that she sticks to her guns and finishes her pepperoni-free Pepperoni Feast as if it's the commonest order on the menu.

We walk home arm in arm, sharing a contented silence until she pipes up: 'So, two and a half weeks till we get hitched. Nervous? Excited? Terrified? Overwhelmed with second thoughts?'

'Can't wait,' I reply.

'You can be honest if you like.' That flummoxes me and I say nothing. 'This isn't the easiest of things we're attempting to pull off, Grey.'

'I know.'

'And occasionally I do find myself wondering what happened to that blissfully uncomplicated friendship we had two months ago.'

'Yup. Know the feeling.'

'Really?' She squeezes me. 'So tell me about it.'

So I do. And when we get home, I put my arm round her, she spins into me and in one movement locates my mouth with hers. At which point it happens. It. Garments are unbuttoned and discarded with above-average haste, teeth remain unbrushed, books and holiday brochures untouched. Bodies are entwined and love is made. It seems natural, unforced, and it's good. It

seems good. At least, Lucy doesn't give the impression that she thinks otherwise.

Afterwards I lie awake while Lucy sleeps, her tiny frame curled into me in a way that it does all too rarely. So, what's changed? There are times, long periods, whole days, even, when I wonder about Lucy and Tim: he might have receded in the photograph stakes and he's very much in her bad books, but he's still hanging in there, isn't he? And she clearly *wants* to be over him, she's convinced herself that she *has* to be over him, but has she *really* got there? But after a night like tonight, it seems that she has. And I've done nothing different: I've not been working out in the gym, changed my aftershave or my thigh-massage technique. All we've done is go out for a pizza and operate as we used to before we set foot on Greenwich Hill and, once again, I am the essence of man.

THE DAY AFTER

Letter to Kathy, deposited on her desk at a moment mid-morning when I know she is out of the building seeing clients.

Dear Kathy

Thank you so much for putting all that kind thought into your wedding present. And what a splendid idea. You may be surprised to hear that I've not had another like it. I didn't the last time I got married either. It really is the most generous offer and I feel quite sure that you will understand how much I'd like to accept it. Unfortunately, however, I am unable to. It doesn't fit in with the way Lucy and I have planned our future. I haven't discussed it with Lucy, but I feel that it is unlikely that she'd want me to accept.

So, again, many thanks from the pair of us, but you know . . .

Love

Dominic

FIFTEEN DAYS LATER

The eve of our trip to Bermuda. Lucy and I are in bed. It happens again. It. That's three times in a month. We are, as I suspected, Japanese.

29

'I can't believe we're really going to do this!' exclaims Lucy, her face pressed against the window as our plane descends towards the late afternoon at Bermuda International Airport. Josh is asleep, but Lucy and I are gasping at the colours of the beaches and the direction our lives are about to take.

'Come on, Grey! Can we really be about to come good on a marriage pact we made at half five in the morning thirteen years ago when you were so drunk you could barely talk?' she asks, disbelief in her voice.

'You weren't exactly sober yourself.'

'OK, question: what if we hadn't made that pact? What if we'd never got drunk that night? Or if we'd gone to bed early and never sat around having that conversation? Would we be here?'

'I'm sure you'd have found a way to reel me in eventually.'

She rolls her eyes and kisses my lips. 'OK, another question: how spoiled are we going to be at this hotel of yours?'

'I think you'll be sufficiently impressed.'

'Will we have to behave like grown-ups?'

'No.'

'Can we lie around in bed watching old films?'

'If that's what you want to do in bed, yes.'

'Brilliant. That's exactly what I want.' She squeezes me under the ribs, giggles, and we turn back to the window and the sunny island ahead.

Bermuda remains sunny during the late afternoon. It is warmer than when I was here two months ago. I have a wife-to-be and a stepson-to-be, and we are soon in our hire car retracing the route I took to the Reefs.

To no great surprise, I find that Lucy is sufficiently impressed with the standard of the accommodation. We are in one of the cottage suites, a carefully thought-through arrangement that gives Josh his own bedroom next to ours, though any such attention to detail is lost on him.

'C'mon, Dom,' he says, within minutes of our arrival. 'Let's go to the beach.'

'You wouldn't rather go to the pool, or play tennis, or maybe have a few cocktails on the veranda?'

'No, you great wally!' (When did 'wally' reappear in the English language?) 'C'mon, let's go.'

So we enjoy the last of the sun on the beach. Josh is hell bent on completing the perfect handstand but after I've watched him flop around on the sand like a beached salmon for five minutes, I'm forced to lie: 'Josh, that was perfect,' I tell him, and his face fills with pride. 'And now it's time for me to get you.'

So I chase him up and down the sand at the water's edge, finally slinging him into the sea, a foolhardy piece of bravado that nearly ends in tears, although as soon as he's convinced it's a laughing matter after all, the tables are turned and he starts chasing me. Lucy watches us, laughing. When we are exhausted and the sun has lost its heat, Josh and I sit down to catch our breath on the edge of Lucy's sun-lounger, and she drapes her arms round the pair of us.

'Aah, my men!' she says. 'My two lovely men.'

'Dadadadadiddlydiddlyda,' Josh sings, tracing a circle in the sand.

'My two gorgeous men.'

The plan is this. We have less than forty-eight hours of Bermudan bliss before we are man and wife. The Bermuda bit will continue for the rest of the week. And the bliss will continue for the rest of our lives.

We are to be wed in the middle of the day in a tiny jewel of a sandy cove just a few hundred yards up the coast, appropriately called Chaplin Bay. We will be barefoot, I shall wear a linen

suit and Hawaiian shirt, Lucy's outfit is to remain a secret and Josh, my best man, has been granted his wish to wear his Spider-Man outfit. As yet, he's undecided on the mask but I suspect it may not make the cut. Everything has been arranged by Dinny, our personal wedding-planner, including a set of posts for Josh and me to play beach football and an extremely comprehensive picnic, including three bottles of Veuve Clicquot La Grande Dame to help us all get splendidly drunk. 'Us all' is a tidy group: the only other guests are Sophie, who is to be Lucy's bridesmaid, and Andrew, our Chaplin Bay chaplain. Marco has gone away on 'hugely important business', which was the deal I struck with him: Marco to be away from Bermuda for the week of our stay in exchange for Lucy and me promising not to tell Sophie about his role in siphoning off more than half of the remains of Tim's estate and giving it to Tim's illegitimate son.

Bermuda seems pretty much perfect as a Marco-free zone. Josh – in turns both overexcited, jet-lagged and run off his feet – goes to sleep, and Lucy and I are soon settled in at the Sand bar where Lucy takes a strong liking to Dark and Stormy, the island's signature rum punch. Indeed, we are both just ordering our second when Sophie arrives.

'How are you two enjoying Paradise?' she asks, hugging Lucy. 'I can't believe you're really here, Lucy. I thought you'd never come.'

'You didn't think I'd be true to my word?'

'Nope. And I certainly didn't think you'd come all this way so that I could be at your wedding. You're very thoughtful.' She then hugs me, exclaiming: 'And you are an extremely lucky man. I hope you realise that.'

'I've just about managed to work it out,' I reply.

Sophie is tanned, happy and beautiful as ever in her increasingly statuesque way, and Lucy is thrilled to see her. We order bar food, because that's all that Lucy and I feel like after our day's travelling. Then I order a bottle of champagne, and the three of us make tentative plans for the week ahead.

'The only real problem you're going to have is working out which beach to go to,' says Sophie, sarcastically.

'Or where you're going to take us on your boat, Soph,' says Lucy.

'Or when you're going to take Josh for the day so that you can give the newly-weds some time to get to know each other.'

'Good idea,' says Lucy, her hand on my thigh.

'You're very welcome,' Sophie replies. 'Anything else? Baby-sitting? Boat trips? You name it. Which reminds we, I've sorted your other outstanding issue, Dom.'

'What's that?'

'Oh!' Lucy giggles. 'That was something I meant to discuss with you, Grey. I, er, never got round to it.'

'What is it?' I put my glass to my lips, attempting to look unfazed.

'Have I put my foot in it, Lucy?' Sophie asks.

'Not at all!' Lucy swivels in her chair and bats her eyelids at me. 'Now, Grey. A thought. The day after tomorrow, I'm supposed to be marrying you.'

'That's the general idea.'

'And it's kind of traditional that the night before the wedding, bride and groom should be apart.'

'Aha. So you're moving out?'

'Um . . . no. You are. Soph?'

'Yup.' Sophie clears her throat, as if to address me formally. 'I've been asked to mastermind your one night apart and I think I've cracked it. I've had Marco's boat decked up for you: clean linen, beer in the fridge, a video of *Gregory's Girl*. Nice touch that, I thought. We're all going to have dinner at the Mid-Ocean Golf Club, which is five minutes' walk from the boat, so you can roll back there afterwards. A taxi's booked to take you to Chaplin Bay the following morning. I think you'll be happy.'

'So, I'm being evicted from the hotel I'm paying for, am I?' The girls find the idea amusing. 'How are you going to survive without me?' I ask Lucy.

'Well, it'll be tough. But we both have to be brave – for tradition's sake.'

The Bermudan rum and the arrival of the champagne render my forthcoming eviction vaguely acceptable. We toast Marco's boat and tradition, then the soon-to-be-married couple and, afterwards, their babysitter. Eventually I see that Lucy is looking as tired as I feel. 'Come on, my bride,' I say. We bid Sophie goodnight and wander arm in arm, in a contented, tipsy silence, under a sparkling night sky, past a hedgerow exploding with pink and white hibiscus, and back to our cottage. This is the ambience I brought Lucy here for. Together we check on Josh and find him sleeping peacefully. Lucy puts her arm round my waist and we watch him for a few seconds. She rests her head against my shoulder and it feels as though we have found mutual peace.

I press a kiss into her cheek and we go through to our bedroom where I turn to her and kiss her again, below her ear, moving on a path down into her neck. She melts into me and I continue to her nape. Her head rolls back as I move round her, kissing above her collarbone, below it and down towards her breasts.

'Dom.' Her whisper halts my progress. 'Come on, let's get into bed.'

So we do. Or, at least, I do. Lucy undresses, hangs up her clothes, unpacks her washbag, applies moisturiser and brushes her teeth extensively and, though I don't say so, it seems a funny evening to choose to floss. I was never aware of her ever flossing before. Maybe I should be more appreciative of the effort she's making: this is, after all, our last pre-nuptial night together.

But when she joins me, I'm still at the ready. I roll into her, put my right arm round her and pull her towards me, pressing my mouth to hers. And then it begins. I am leading the way, there's no doubt about that, but Lucy comes with me. I resume where I left off, smothering her with kisses, slowly working my way down her body. She gasps and runs her hands through my hair and her body starts to move. I slide a hand past her navel

and down. Her legs begin to part and I ease them further but find resistance. No matter. Let's start again.

I swivel round so that we are face to face, softly kissing. Again I am leading the way, but again she comes tentatively too. I caress her back, long, firm, slow strokes up and down, up and down. Then down lower, significantly lower, to the sort of depth that fiancés two days from marriage might feel free to go. The resistance again. The muscles in her back are tense. Her bony shoulders are suddenly hard and square. I remove my hand and look into her face for a message. There is none. Just the kissing, still the kissing, albeit not notably enthusiastic, albeit that it's me who's kissing her and not much the other way round.

Maybe I'm going too fast. Maybe I'm like a novice fisherman, expecting a bite the moment the bait goes into the water, too impetuous and naïve to know how to hook the big fish and frustrated that I've hauled in nothing. What would Tim have done? He'd have landed a whopper every time.

But again, no matter, no panic. It's back to the battlefront. Just be more relaxed, play your hand a bit more intelligently, take your time. So I do. I start with a simple cuddle, nothing dangerous, hands conspicuously placed far from the problem areas. The response is good. The kissing starts again. Me leading, no threatening hand-movement, Lucy's face serene. God, she almost looks as if she's enjoying it. Time to mix things up a bit – but nothing aggressive. I run my left hand through her hair. Good. Good move. Well received. What next? Right hand. Something for the right hand. I unpeel the hand from her back where it was sustaining the cuddle, round and upwards to her face. It brushes her left breast. Clumsy, very clumsy, but Lucy's fine: nothing registers – it's as though she may even have liked it. Maybe that's a come-on for more. So I slide the hand back down in a cupping/massaging type movement around her breast. Suddenly she freezes, then swings up and away from me so that she is sitting on the far side of the bed, her hands clenched over her ears.

'What's the matter, sweetheart?' I ask, moving over to her. 'What on earth's the matter?'

I put my arm round her, but the moment I touch her, she pushes me off violently and stands up, her arms crossed protectively over her body. She leans against the wall facing me, with tears in her eyes.

'Why did you have to keep on doing it?' she sobs, tears tumbling fast.

'What's the matter?'

'Not today.' She breaks off in tears. 'Not today of all days.'

'What do you mean, "today of all days"? Today is one of the best days. It's our last night together before we get married. What's "today" got to do with it?'

'Oh, God!' She is shaking her head, hardly able to talk. 'Don't you know?'

'No, I haven't a clue what you're talking about.'

'You know how much it meant to him!'

'What?'

'He was so bloody boyish about it. You must know!'

'Know what, Lucy?'

'It's Tim's bloody birthday, isn't it?'

Silence. I stare at Lucy and she stares back, the crying suddenly over. She doesn't move, a strange crumpled creature, her arms still hanging across herself.

My head drops into my hands. I can't look at her now. The silence is broken only by the whirring of the extractor fan in the bathroom. Lucy tilts her head, trying to lock into eye-contact with me, but I won't let her. I won't let her get close. She sits on the edge of the bed and still I won't look her in the eyes.

'Grey?' Her voice, when at last she speaks, wavers. 'Grey? Didn't you know?'

'No, I didn't. More to the point, I didn't think it mattered any more.' Lucy says nothing. I raise my head and watch her, waiting for her to say something. The silence speaks volumes. So I try to edge her towards the answer. 'It does matter, doesn't it?'

Strange to think that thirty-six hours before we even get there, she has the opportunity to save our marriage. There is no problem with eye-contact now. The silence between us is intense, the whir of the air-conditioning unit the only sound. I study her face in a desperate search for salvation. Just a hint, a glimmer, anything. But she doesn't soften, she doesn't melt into a smile that tells me everything's all right. She looks hard, still attractive in her boyish way, but her face is unforgiving in its honesty. And she says nothing. This is another Dominic-Lucy conversation that is exchanged without words. And in saying nothing she says it all.

'Well, thank you for being honest with me.' My voice is unemotional. Lucy pulls her feet under her on the bed and closes her eyes, as if shutting out the situation. I pull a towel round my waist and still she doesn't reply. 'I thought we were going to be the closest couple in the world, Lucy, yet we barely share the same orbit.'

Lucy purses her lips as if to stop herself crying. 'Grey,' her voice is shaky, 'I'm so sorry. Just, please,' she pauses, gasping for a breath, 'please remember that I do, honestly, love you.'

'Come on, Lucy! We've been tossing that word around for too long.'

Again, Lucy has no reply. I pull out my suitcase and start to pack.

30

The next morning Lucy offered me the easy opt-out. She said I could just vanish if I liked and leave her to deal with Josh. But despite the atmosphere of cold, efficient awkwardness that was suddenly all-pervasive between us, I refused politely. While we were resigned to a life apart, we were together on one thing: that Josh would be as big a casualty as either of us. He had set his heart on our marriage, he had gone perhaps to the ultimate extreme he knew by giving a 'Show and Tell' presentation on the subject at school.

This was a failure on our part that he would bear for a long time. We had built up his hopes but, Lucy repeated masochistically, it was her job to catch the fragile young soul, not mine. She berated herself for having allowed him to be caught between us. But there was a strong hint of Tennyson in all this. We had tried and failed, but at least we had tried. Where we had gone wrong was in trying too hard.

We were thoroughly decent to each other too. I booked myself on the flight out before midday, organised a taxi for a quarter to ten and reserved Josh for a romp on the beach at nine o'clock. They could keep the holiday, I was firm about that, I didn't want any dispute, thanks, or money back. All I wanted was for Josh to have as good a time as possible, for me to get off the island as soon as I could and to say a proper goodbye to him.

It is a warm, clear morning and the sea looks gorgeous; a great place to spend the first week of married life, no doubt. Josh and I descend the steps cut into the cliffs that slope gently to the bay. He grabs my hand as we go and I realise he has never done this before.

'Dom?'

'Yup.'

'If I beat you in a race up the beach, will you stay with us and not go home?'

'Sorry, matey. I don't think it would be right.'

'What if I beat you in a race up the beach and then throw you into the sea? Then would you stay with us and not go?'

'I'm really sorry, Josh. I'd love to, but it just wouldn't be right.'

'OK. If I beat you in a race up the beach, throw you in the sea, and then every time when we play Red Injuns at home, you can have both T. Rexs and two of the three knights and you never have to have the wonder-hen with super-rooster powers again, what about that?'

'It's a generous offer, but I don't think even the wonder-hen can change the situation.'

We sit down on the sand, just out of reach of the water. We have the beach entirely to ourselves.

Josh doodles a picture in the sand. 'You and Mummy are stupid,' he says.

'You're right. We are a bit stupid. But you mustn't be angry with your mum. It's not her fault.'

'Whose fault is it?'

'No one's. It's just one of those things.'

'Another one of those things! Why are there so many of *those things*? I hate *those things*! Why can't we just not have them?'

'I'm so sorry, Josh.' I put an arm round him and he leans in to me. 'It's sad for everyone. I'm very sad too. But it's just one of those times when you have to be brave.'

'C'mon, then. I'll race you.'

So we race. Josh wins. He's come on well in the time he's had me as a coach. And, amazingly enough, he wins the sea-side wrestling competition too. Another race, another wrestle, and he is four–nil up. Then it's handstand time. I give the Dominic Lord demonstration, which clearly wasn't as good as a Tim Cassidy version would have been – he'd have done it on one hand

and given a juggling display with the other – but I can stop thinking that way now. Then Josh resumes his impression of a salmon flipping in frustration on the sand. He's not quite ready for handstands yet; that's my conclusion anyway. And it's time for me to go.

'Just one more race, Dom?' Josh pleads. 'Please. Just one.'

Three races later, we agree that it's time to call it quits, and I tell him there's something I want to say. We sit cross-legged opposite each other, he doodles again in the sand and, hesitantly, I begin: 'I want you to promise me something, Josh.'

'What?'

'Your mummy is probably the best person in the whole wide world, and I want you to promise me, once I'm gone, that you'll be a big boy and look after her. Will you promise me that?'

'OK, Dom. But only if you promise never to miss my christening again.'

'OK, matey.' I'm trying to laugh but my voice is faltering and my eyes are wet. I attempt to compose myself, then press on: 'But there's something else I want you to promise, Josh.'

'What's that?'

'That you'll always be my friend. Because I'll think about you every day. And I'll come and visit you whenever I'm in London. Will you promise me that? Always to be friends?'

'OK, Dom.' His voice is crisp – he's unaware of the emotional overload opposite him.

I engulf him in an enormous hug to prevent him seeing the evidence about to burst from my eyes. 'You lovely boy,' I whisper, holding on to him too long.

Finally, simulating a version of cheery normality, I put him on my shoulders and carry him back to the hotel where a taxi is waiting, with Lucy and my suitcase alongside it.

'Just a moment,' I say to the taxi driver. Lucy, Josh and I sit together on a wooden bench overlooking the ocean, me in the middle, an arm round each of them. Lucy has tears in her eyes. Beneath the surface, I am shedding floods.

'Do you mind if I rest my head against your shoulder for a minute?' she asks quietly.

'No, I'd like you to.'

A sad silence falls between us.

'I'm sorry,' she says.

'Me too.'

'Thank you for loving me.'

'It was an infuriatingly limited pleasure.'

More silence.

'So you're just going to go home, are you?'

'No. I'm off to Caracas.'

31

FIVE MONTHS LATER

The rather impressive-looking New York office of Sweet Lord.

I return from a meeting to find a large brown square package on a work surface by the wall in my office. This is a kind of cinematic moment because the shafts of sunlight have pinpointed the package as if to make it glow. The light plays this curious trick every day because even though my office is next to Jerry's and is furnished with the same trappings of seniority and privilege, I was too slow to realise that the morning sun would penetrate his full-length glass outside wall a couple of hours before it did mine. It is at half past ten, on clearish days, that it drills a spotlight on to the work surface by the wall, then flows in slowly until the whole room is filled. It is now ten thirty-five and the sun is shining on my package.

I know what it contains. I tear it open with boyish excitement and three copies of *Book of the Month* tumble out. These are the first three printed copies I have seen and they have a certain beauty that I suspect will only appeal to me. But it looks good, really good. I put one of the shiny copies against my cheek to feel its newness, then run my thumb through the pages. Mine. The artwork is nice: a clever sepia treatment of the cliché bride-and-groom picture outside a church, engulfed in confetti. The title is embossed in a heavy arty font – I chose it myself – and underneath is a subtitle in the same font but

smaller: 'Thirty-one days and then a friend for wife'.

I run my thumb through the pages again and leaf inside to the dedication: 'For Lucy, my inspiration'.

I take a copy to my desk, sit down with a biro, write the address on an A4 envelope, then turn to the inside page. I know what I'm going to write because I've envisaged it a million times.

'My darling Lucy. My friend for wife. Here we are in a happy ending. I don't think it sounds too bad . . .'